Praise for Lynne Connolly's
Eyton

"This is a book filled with romantic love, well done, and a murder mystery. ...Richard and Rose have great chemistry, and I thoroughly enjoyed reading about them. ...I recommend this book to others who love historical fiction and am likely to pick up the other books in the series."

~ *Long and Short Reviews*

"I say well done Ms. Connolly, and I am hoping to read a little more in regards to a few of the secondary characters soon. Hint. Hint."

~ *Literary Nymphs Reviews*

Look for these titles by *Lynne Connolly*

Now Available:

Triple Countess Trilogy
Last Chance, My Love
A Chance to Dream
Met by Chance

Secrets Trilogy
Seductive Secrets
Alluring Secrets
Tantalizing Secrets

Richard and Rose Series
Yorkshire
Devonshire
Venice
Harley Street
Eyton
Hareton Hall

Eyton

Lynne Connolly

A Samhain Publishing, Ltd. publication.

Samhain Publishing, Ltd.
577 Mulberry Street, Suite 1520
Macon, GA 31201
www.samhainpublishing.com

Eyton
Copyright © 2010 by Lynne Connolly
Print ISBN: 978-1-60504-910-6
Digital ISBN: 978-1-60504-691-4

Editing by Sasha Knight
Cover by Mandy M. Roth

First Samhain Publishing, Ltd. electronic publication: January 2010
First Samhain Publishing, Ltd. print publication: November 2010

Dedication

To you, dear reader. You've waited so long for this book—it's my privilege to bring it to you.

Chapter One

My birth pangs came in the night. I lay awake and counted them, making sure this was the real thing before I woke Richard. He stirred, raised his head and smiled sleepily, his short blond hair tousled and boyish. When he saw me tense, he snapped awake, sitting up to study me closely. "Is this it?"

I nodded. "Yes, without a doubt."

Another man would have slept elsewhere, particularly in recent months when I'd slept so restlessly, but not Richard. He slipped an arm over my bulk and kissed me, one for the baby and one for me, as he'd taken to putting it. He got out of bed and fetched his robe, and I sighed when I looked at his well-muscled, lithe form. I might never get my figure back after this.

He sat on the bed and took my hands in his, blue eyes blazing into mine. "Every time you breathe, remember I love you. Even if they deny me your presence, I'll be here in spirit, and if you need me, nothing will keep me away. I'll come, and damn the conventions."

A sharp pain cut off my answering smile.

"That's it," said Martha. "You can lie back now, Rose. You're done."

I sank against the banked-up pillows with gratitude as Martha helped the midwife to smooth the bedclothes over me. The process had exhausted me more than I thought possible, even though the midwife had assured me I'd had an easy birth.

I listened to the lusty cries of my newborn infant and wondered if Richard could hear them too. They'd sent him away as soon as the midwife arrived and I hadn't seen him since, but the room was full with my midwife Mrs. Rooke, my *accoucheur* Mr. Simpson and my sister-in-law Martha, Lady Hareton.

My newly born, newly washed child was put into my arms, and for the second time in my life, I felt the rush of sudden love. I gasped with astonishment and joy. I had expected to care for my child but not like this. We gazed at each other for what seemed like an aeon. "Welcome, sweet baby," I said.

The baby mewed a little. A physical tug came from somewhere deep inside me.

"Can I feed—?" I stopped. This child, this miracle. I hadn't thought to ask.

Mr. Simpson's wide face shone with pleasure. "A fine girl, my lady. Perfect in every way. Lie still, and we'll make you comfortable now. Yes, you may suckle her, but it will only be foremilk, and she'll need a proper feed afterwards."

"Bring the wet-nurse in here," I ordered. "Let me watch."

I loosened my night rail and let the baby reach my breast. She seemed to know what to do better than I did, which was just as well because I felt clumsy, a giantess next to this tiny scrap. I took one of her hands in mine and watched her curl her fingers over my thumb. I lost my heart all over again.

Martha got to her feet. "I'll go and tell him, shall I?"

I nodded. "But don't let him in just yet. I don't want him to see me like this." Hot, tousled, still recovering.

"I'll give you some time." She kissed me and left.

I watched the wet-nurse, Anne Potter, a respectable woman who had a six-month-old child of her own, and milk to spare. Unlike me, she knew exactly what to do and handled the baby with sure confidence. I could only hope I would feel the same way soon.

While I watched the babe feed, they made me comfortable. They washed me, dressed me in clean garments and changed the sheets.

The baby had fallen off the nipple asleep, completely sated, before the nurse put her in the crib brought forward to the side of the bed.

My attendants left the room, and I gazed at my child, filled with love for her. I heard the door open, but I didn't look up immediately.

It was only when the bed sank next to me that I turned my head. His eyes were riveted on the baby. "My God." He turned to me and smiled before he kissed me very softly on my forehead and on my mouth. "Clever girl."

"I'm sorry," I said.

He leaned back and stared at me, startled. "What on earth for?"

"It's a girl."

"So?" He took my hand. "She's healthy and perfect. My parents are downstairs. They're thrilled."

"Truly?"

"Truly. My father has already planned the ball at Eyton, and the next addition to the family." He gave a light laugh. "But there's no chance of that just yet, if I can help it."

Something had dropped away from him, the anxiety he fondly thought I hadn't noticed. He took my hand to his mouth, kissed it, and kept hold of it afterwards. "Gervase sends his love."

"It must be crowded downstairs. Do they want to see me?"

"I've forbidden it. Simpson says you need to sleep, so Nichols will sit with you while you get some rest."

"What time is it?"

"About eight. You can receive people tomorrow, if you're up to it." He took a deep breath and let it out again slowly. His gaze never left my face. "You know how relieved I am to see you again, dearest love. Say the word and you need never go through this again."

It was the last thing I expected him to say. "But the title, the estate. It's why they let you marry me."

He smiled tenderly. "Let me? Nothing could have stopped me. None of it matters. That's not what I married you for, you know that. I love you."

"I know. And I love you too." I glanced at the sleeping baby. "I can do this. I can give you sons if you want them." I couldn't believe I was saying this after what I had just gone through, but I knew it was true.

His reply was to kiss me. "I'm very proud of you."

"Do you want to hold your daughter?" My heart ached when I remembered his other children. He'd only discovered their existence last year, and it had caused him great pain. I let the thought pass. Now was not the time.

He got up and walked around the bed to the crib. He looked down at our child for a long time. "She doesn't seem to look like anyone I know except perhaps the Duke of Newcastle."

I laughed. "Oh dear, I hope not."

He glanced back at me, and his attention turned to the baby again. He didn't move to pick her up.

I wanted him to. "Will you pass her to me?"

He bent down and gently lifted her.

Richard seemed to know how to hold babies, or perhaps it was instinct. She slumbered in his arms as he stared at her, and he touched her hand, which was outside the shawl she was wrapped in. I refused to allow her to be swaddled. The minuscule fingers clutched his thumb, and at that moment he was lost. I watched my husband fall in love with his daughter as I had done, and I thought I would burst with joy.

When he tore his gaze away from her, he must have seen my tears. He laid the baby in my arms, straightening up and studying us. "I don't think I've ever seen anything so beautiful before."

I heard the emotion in his voice, and I smiled. "Fool," I

chided tearfully.

He sat by us and the baby opened her eyes, so blue, heavenly blue, not at all like the deep sapphire of my husband's. He smiled. "Pleased to make your acquaintance. What shall we call you, sweetheart?"

We hadn't really discussed names. If it had been a boy, it would have been Richard, because all the Southwood heirs were called that, but with a girl we were free to call her what we chose. We didn't want to call her anything too unusual, but on the other hand, nothing too common. We knew a lot of Elizabeths, Georgianas and Annes. Pamela and Stella had become popular because of the literary associations, and there were many Sophias, Carolines and Charlottes, called after members of the royal family.

I frowned. "Frances, perhaps." We looked at our daughter and she looked back at us. "Ancilla, Emily."

"Helen." He looked at her, watching the rosebud mouth pucker in sleep. "Or how about Eglantine, or Richenda?"

His seemingly genuine suggestion made me stare at him in amazement before I saw the teasing glint in his eyes. We burst into laughter.

The baby opened her mouth and roared. We both laughed a little more from relief and joy as much as genuine amusement before our daughter drowned out our paltry efforts.

To my surprise, I knew what she wanted. "I should feed her."

She couldn't be truly hungry because she had fed such a short time before, but my breasts ached and I thought it might comfort both of us.

"Shall I go?"

"Only if you want to. You may take her downstairs afterwards to show her off."

He drew up a chair next to the bed while I held her to my breast. She caught hold and reached up one tiny hand to touch me. "This won't satisfy her much, it's only foremilk. If she's still hungry we'll have to call the wet-nurse."

He smiled as he watched. "You could have been born to it."

"I shan't do it for too long, but Mr. Simpson says it's good for me. You can have me back soon."

He touched my shoulder. "You never went away."

What I had to offer did seem enough for the baby, and she fell asleep. She had been working, too, and perhaps she felt as tired as I was. I tucked myself away. "I like Helen. Can we call her that?"

"I like it too," he answered, and he came back to take her up.

He laid her gently in the crib, came back to sit on the bed and took my hand in his. "I'll sleep in my room tonight, but the connecting doors will be open. Or, if you prefer it, I'll sleep in here."

"I don't mind, sleep wherever you're most comfortable. Nichols says she'll sleep in my dressing room so she's within call." I sighed. "I'll miss you."

"And I'll miss you, but you'll need to get better before I can come back." He smiled wryly. "I'll miss not waking up with you in my arms. But it's more important that you get better." He stood, leaned over me and kissed me lovingly. "I'll go now. I'll send for the nurse—what's her name again?"

"The wet-nurse is Potter and the nursemaid is Whitehouse. And could you ask them to get me something to eat, please?"

He smiled, kissed me again and left.

I woke in the early hours at about the time my pains had started the previous day. When I turned over I saw Richard, sitting in the chair by the cold fire, his head back, sound asleep. He looked most uncomfortable. I slid out of bed, wincing with soreness, and went into my dressing room for the necessary, almost tripping over the truckle bed that had been moved in there for Nichols.

I didn't wake her and returned to the bedroom when I had finished. I couldn't bear to see him so uncomfortable so I touched Richard on the shoulder.

He started awake and got immediately to his feet. "You shouldn't be up."

"If you don't tell anyone, I won't," I replied.

Putting one arm under my legs and the other around my back, Richard lifted me and carried me to the bed. "I wouldn't have been able to do this so easily yesterday," he remarked fondly as he set me down.

"I somehow imagined I would spring back into shape, but it will take some time, I'm told."

He laid the bedcovers back over me and sat next to me. "You've performed a miracle. It's bound to take some time to come back down to our level."

"Do you love her?"

"I love her," he answered, in the same level tone. "As I was bound to." He smiled. If his colleagues at Whites' could see him now, open and loving, they wouldn't have recognised him. "Can I get you anything?"

"No, no thank you. You should sleep. Did the family like her?"

"Of course they did." He lifted his legs onto the bed and slipped his arm around my shoulders. "They all sent their best wishes, of course." He kissed my forehead. "And the babe slumbered through it all. I went to see her before I came here. She's not as red as she was, and she's still beautiful."

I felt myself drift. "You should go to your own bed, my love."

"Hmm. Be quiet and go to sleep."

He stayed with me all night.

Chapter Two

When I was well enough to travel, Richard took me to our home in Oxfordshire, a very private, informal house where I rested and recuperated, but we had to go to Eyton in Derbyshire, the Southwood family seat, for a formal christening. I spent the remainder of my confinement surrounded by care and love and getting used to the idea of being a parent.

We travelled to Derbyshire in an impressive entourage of carriages. I was completely well now, rested to total boredom. We finally arrived at about two in the afternoon on a warm, late-summer day. The three carriages rolled gently up the undulating well-kept drive to the great house at the end. It was all such a contrast with the drive at Hareton Abbey, the place where my future had changed forever. That had been unkempt, overgrown and eerie, but I had met Richard there, and James had inherited the earldom. Now the place was abandoned to the mice and crows, after its previous owners had mercilessly run it down.

I had learned to stop questioning my good fortune. After all, the man who had seemed perfection itself on the surface had turned out to be a vulnerable, damaged person who seemed to need me as much as I needed him. Nothing is ever what you expect it to be.

Having seen Helen installed in her bright, pleasant nursery, I dressed for dinner and went down to meet Richard in the drawing room. All heads turned when I entered. Richard introduced me to his extended family, and I took particular interest in his two male Kerre cousins, who had been at our wedding but I hadn't noticed in the crush, other than to murmur that I was pleased to meet them. Perhaps I'd do better this time. We walked in to dinner, to a long dining table gleaming with crystal and candles, processing by rank even at this family occasion.

The eldest Kerre, Giles, was a tall, well-built young man who I recognised as the kind who could well attract my sister Lizzie. The younger son was not as strongly built but had a gentler air and paler appearance. I saw the square shape of a book in the pocket of a coat that seemed well used to accommodating them, and wondered if he would make a friend of my brother Ian. Their parents, Sir Barnett and Lady Sophia Kerre, were charming to me and showed none of the animosity I had half expected. After all, I would put their noses out of joint if I succeeded in bearing Richard an heir.

"We could not be more pleased that Strang has found such a charming bride," Lady Kerre said, flourishing her fan to great effect. She was a large lady, with an expanse of creamy flesh many men would admire. "And to produce a child within a year. Such unexpected fortune!"

Before I met Richard, he'd bedded many women, and his family had doubts about my husband's fertility. At least all but his parents, who knew about the twins Richard had conceived with a maid. He hadn't known before last year, a cruel decision I wouldn't forgive Lord and Lady Southwood for making.

His twin, Gervase, was never likely to produce children, due to his personal preferences, so Richard was the hope of the house and the reason they had not objected too much when he chose to marry me.

"I trust your child suffered no ill health on the journey," Lady Kerre enquired, her face a picture of concern.

"She slept for most of the time," I said. "She only cries when she wants something."

Lady Kerre sighed, a reminiscent smile wreathing her lips. "If only it were always so simple! Now my children want carriages of their own, all the jewels in the world and money to burn." She leaned towards me, revealing an expanse of generous bosom. "This is the best time. Make the most of it."

"Indeed, you're quite right," Richard's mother added from farther down the table. "They become so much more complicated as they grow up. Strang has always been unfathomable to me since he reached his majority, and when he decided to marry, he barely consulted us. I can only be thankful he settled on a thoroughly suitable woman, for he might have settled on—anyone." To translate, she meant I had begun my duties as a breeding machine.

She cast a frosty smile in my direction, but I said nothing. I knew she hadn't approved of Richard's choice. He should have made his choice from the girls presented to him by his parents as suitable partners. It was not for him to go home and announce the fact he had every intention of marrying a stranger. Richard's mother resented me and would never cease to do so, but that made me in the majority amongst Richard's friends.

"A shame your brother could not attend the ceremony," she remarked now, as if his recent attack of measles was entirely James's fault.

"Indeed. He is recovering well." I chose to pretend that she had asked about James's health, instead of complaining about his absence. "The rest of us suffered from the illness when we were children, but James somehow missed out." He'd contracted the measles from his oldest son, the redoubtable Walter. "Martha did not consider the risk of spreading the illness to Helen worth taking."

Lady Southwood sniffed. "She is no doubt right. But you cannot protect your daughter from such things forever. Or the other requirements of her station."

"It is best she is pampered when she is so vulnerable,"

Richard's father said. "That is all very well when she is a baby, but when she begins to become more aware, you must take care to introduce proper discipline. I have taken the rod to my sons, and they grew up the better for it."

I couldn't imagine taking a rod to my sweet angel upstairs. I couldn't think it was right, and it hadn't changed Richard one whit. The emotional hurts his parents had delivered to him were worse than a whipping and went far deeper.

Sir Barnett twirled the remains of his wine in the glass, watching the opaque air twist in the stem's design rise as he did so. "Perhaps I should have undertaken the chastisement of my children more often. I assumed that was what tutors and governesses were for. I must have been fortunate in my choice, for I never had to strike my sons in anger."

"I preferred to keep a close eye on my sons' progress," said Lord Southwood.

"So we turned out a credit to you, sir," Richard said. His father turned his attention to him. His voice was tight with tension. "You must be proud of the product of your careful tutelage."

Lord Southwood had deeply disapproved of both sons. The scandals both had caused some time before had rocked an already sceptical society back on its heels. I got some of the credit for reforming him, and Gervase was widely thought to have learned his lesson. In fact, the only lesson he had learned was to be more discreet. I didn't care. I loved Gervase anyway.

His lordship fixed my husband with a steely eye. "I believe you have become more aware of your responsibilities, my son. Now you have a family, you will, I hope, begin to see some of the problems concomitant to your station in life."

"I was always aware of my responsibilities." A drawl crept into his voice. "My unwillingness to accept them caused many of my rebellions. And a total ban just made me want to know what I was missing."

His father shrugged, but his mother watched him for a

while longer before she turned away.

Richard put his hand lightly over mine. He found it very difficult to be demonstrative in front of other people, even close friends and family, and I didn't ask for it, but when it happened it warmed me because I knew how much it cost him. "I have found a reason to put my family before myself these days." I understood his meaning, even if his father chose to take it another way.

"Perhaps you would care to go over the affairs of the estate with me while you're here." Lord Southwood sustained his interrogative stare. "I can't recall the last time you did that."

"Gladly, sir," replied his dutiful son. His duties had never meant much to him before, but now he was a father, responsible for more than his own desires, he might come to understand how much it meant to his own father. I hoped so. However badly they had hurt him, I found it hard to see his distance from his parents and the stiff formality that existed between them. We could try for cordiality. His father had been shocked when his mother had informed him that she had never told Richard about his children. Perhaps father and son could build some bridges while we were here.

We were served three elaborate courses. At Richard's request Lady Southwood had invited some of our friends and relatives, including Louisa Crich and Freddy Thwaite. Freddy was accompanied by his father, Lord Sambrook, whom I had never met before. Freddy was sensually attractive, and now I saw that although his father must be at least fifty, he exuded a kind of seductive desirability I hadn't seen in many men before. He watched every woman in the room with the knowledge that if he wanted her, she would come to him. I found his attitude distasteful, especially against his son's honest enthusiasm.

I was delighted to see my brother Ian, down from Oxford. He was well and happy—the only member of my family so little affected by our change in fortunes he hardly noticed it. He had completed his degree some time ago but continued at the University to study.

Totally oblivious to the tension engendered whenever Richard and Gervase shared space with their parents, he rattled on happily about his studies when I asked him. "I'm writing a paper which reconciles Plato's *Apology* with the *Crito.* They both discuss justice, but one is from a position of authority, and the other is a defence."

What could I say but "Oh", making him laugh? Gervase was also in the room, and he laughed too. "I know what you're doing," I said, fully on my dignity. "In case you've forgotten, Ian, you made me read both of them to you when you were struck down with the measles. That and the *Aeneid.* What I can't understand is why you're doing it."

"Because I'm deeply interested in it, and I have hopes I can advance understanding just a little bit by doing it."

"You had the measles when you read it?" Gervase asked. "What age would that be?"

"I was about eleven."

Gervase raised a brow, obviously impressed, and commenced to discuss the treatises with Ian, about his observations on the statuary he had seen in Athens and Rome on his travels abroad. Ian was absorbed, and when Gervase pointed out to him he had the means to see them for himself now, he grew even more interested. He admitted he had never thought of that before, and he would certainly consider it.

The only guest I hadn't met before was a Portuguese nobleman, Joaquin Aviz, Marquês of Aljubarrotta. He was about my age and darkly handsome, but without the threat Lord Sambrook carried with him. His eyes were the darkest I had ever seen, unreadable pools of warmth, and he held the kind of charm I had only seen before in Richard. He sat next to me and proved to be a gentlemanly person with an excellent command of English. He told me his mother was English, and he was encouraged from childhood to speak both languages. His French, he assured me with a smile, was vastly inferior. His mother was an old friend of Lady Southwood's, thus when he decided to pay a visit to his mother's country, he had been invited here. "A great honour to be invited to such an important family occasion."

"You are perhaps fortunate this child is a girl," I informed him. "Celebrations for a boy might well go on for a fortnight."

He smiled and said it would be an interesting event in any case. "There is remarkably good company here, and I understand some of it is your own family." He glanced up the table to where Lizzie sat next to Freddy Brean, busily enchanting all the gentlemen within easy reach. I smiled and followed his gaze. "My sister, Elizabeth. I'm very fond of her. She is in fact my half sister, as we have different mothers. It does explain why we look so different, however."

He looked back at me. "There is a resemblance. You both own a certain grace."

I accepted the compliment with a smile and a nod, where only last year I might have blushed.

Richard did his best to entertain Lady Kerre's very quiet daughter Charlotte, who was seated on his other side. She was a charming girl as far as I could see, but not blessed with too much in the way of brains.

After dinner, Lady Southwood took us ladies into the drawing room where the men soon joined us. Richard came straight to me. "Freddy asked if he could see Helen without delay. He says she's the only reason he came to Eyton."

I glanced up at Freddy Brean, Baron Thwaite, before I lifted the teapot. He smiled in that particular heart-stopping way of his, slightly crooked on one side. I returned the smile. "I don't see why not."

I sent upstairs for the baby. Whitehouse brought her, put her into my arms, and I held court.

A baby is a wonderful way to bring people together. There are always some people who claim they have no interest in them, but they seem to be rare. After all, at the very least these little scraps represent the future.

"She's the image of you, Rose," Freddy murmured.

"I still can't see it, and her eyes certainly don't come from my side." Helen's eyes had darkened over the last few weeks to the brilliant blue of my husband's. I was pleased for her. It would stand her in good stead one day to be in possession of those sapphire orbs.

Louisa was enchanted. "I think I must make my mind up this season. It seems to be the only way to get one of these." She extended her hand to Helen who met her regard gravely.

I caught Richard's soft expression as he watched. When he looked away, his familiar social mask fell back into place. I glanced up and caught his mother's expression. She stared at him in frank astonishment. Maybe she'd never seen the way he watched his daughter. To her, children were assets, nothing more. Not to us.

My room delighted me. It was very feminine, decorated in the Chinese style, with delicate wallpaper and heavily embroidered drapes that emphasised the theme. I had no time to go and see the room assigned to Richard, but I would have wagered it was all masculinity, mahogany and green perhaps. He confirmed it when he came through to me. "It's my mother's attempt to keep us in separate rooms. She hopes this room is too feminine for me." He tossed his robe over a chair and slid into bed beside me.

We began to share the same bed again about ten days after Helen's birth, when I asked him to, but marital intimacy had not resumed yet and I was getting desperate. He treated me like porcelain, and it was driving me slowly mad. At first ashamed of my body, I had worn nightgowns, and I still wore one now, although my figure, while a little fuller, had returned to an acceptable shape. I would have preferred to take it off. I would have preferred *him* to take it off.

He kissed me lovingly and caressed me, but when I responded and tried to arouse him, he gently moved my hand

23

away and drew me close to snuggle in. I sighed but accepted his decision. I didn't know how to persuade him. I hadn't the experience.

He propped himself up on one elbow, only the sheet covering him. I gazed frankly on his male beauty, the strong chest dusted with golden hair that caught in the light of the candles. I wanted him, but every time I tried to talk about it, he forestalled me. "I think you're more voluptuous like this." He drew his hand lightly across my stomach, over the fine muslin of my nightdress. It was the first time he had caressed me like that since Helen was born. I began to hope. "You just seem to be more—more luscious, more inviting. I love you however, whatever. Have I proved it to you now?"

I smiled. I had seen so many women impregnated and abandoned, their husbands amusing themselves elsewhere until the time came for him to plant his seed inside her again. Richard had loved me, cared for me, never left me, just as he had promised. "Yes," I said simply.

He turned, swung his legs out of bed and walked with an easy stride into his dressing room, returning after a few moments with a bottle and two glasses. I enjoyed the view, the strong, athletic body that had pleasured me so many times, unselfconsciously on display for me. He poured the wine, came back to bed and gave me one of the glasses. He touched his glass to mine in the toast he didn't need to articulate anymore, and we lay together at our ease, his arm around my shoulders. He had avoided lovemaking again. Disappointment sank deep into me, but that was the only thing that would, tonight. I had to be patient and learn how to tempt him beyond bearing. I had to admit, if only to myself, that I was tired after the conclusion of our journey and the relatively late night.

I could tease him a little. "If I had known that marriage was so delightful, I might have done it years ago."

He stared at me. "With somebody else?"

"Nobody else asked me."

"What about Tom Skerrit?" My childhood friend who briefly fancied himself in love with me. At least I hoped he was over it by now.

"He never proposed to me. No, that's not what I meant. I was afraid. I felt safer dressing dowdily when I propped up the wall at Exeter Assembly Rooms." I took another sip. "But I still wished for a beau or two."

"You have plenty of beaux now. Freddy adores you."

I thumped his shoulder. "How can you say so? He's a good friend, that's all."

Richard grinned at the vehemence of my rebuttal. "Oh, I think it's more than that, my love. I don't know if he'll ever marry. He prefers to keep that part of his life at arm's length. As I did once, such a long time ago it seems now."

I turned my head, kissed his shoulder in response and saw his loving smile, so I curled my leg over his and settled against him, my drink almost finished. He took my glass and put both of them down, slid down the sheets to hold me closer. "What do you think of the Kerres?"

I pursed my lips. "How well do you know them?"

"Not very well. My mother has known Lady Kerre forever. They were debutantes together, but when they visited I was in the nursery wing and later away from Eyton. I never spent much time here when I came back from the Grand Tour. Sir Barnett is my father's younger brother. The King knighted him for services rendered after the celebrations for the Treaty of Vienna. He apparently gave signal help with arranging the firework display." Which, I recalled, proved a signal failure when it rained on the night in question. However, the rehearsal evening had been a great success.

I settled my arm across his chest, feeling the tickle of soft hair. "They seem very pleasant, and they make a perfect family."

"That's what I mean. They behave so well together it's as though they have to work at it. It's like a concerto, where everything is carefully planned and brought together in the final work. But they don't look at each other very much, and they don't seem at their ease."

"But you come from a…" I paused, not knowing what to say, and went on, "…a family with problems. You were never close to your parents, so perhaps you're not used to it."

His finger traced delicious little patterns on my back. Such gestures were heaven and torture, because as soon as I started more intimate explorations, he'd gently deter me. "But I've seen your family together and you behave in a totally different way. You talk at the same time, your poses aren't at all studied, and you help each other in a completely unselfconscious way."

I smiled again at this reminder of my chaotic, but to me normal, family. "Do you think that's how our family will be? Would you like that?"

"It may very well turn out like that and I shall learn to cope. I don't know if I'll like it or not, but at least our house won't be so crowded." He found the close confines of the old manor uncomfortable, and our proximity to each other and the servants difficult to cope with. His kind, the aristocracy, lived in huge houses, and servants were all but invisible.

"You must come first. Above all, you must be happy in your own home." I settled my head more comfortably onto his shoulder. He pulled the sheet over us.

"Good night, *mi adorata*."

"Good night, my love."

Louisa Crich visited me the following afternoon while I was dressing for dinner. Louisa and I had become fast friends; her ebullient, irreverent personality complemented my more reserved approach. Lizzie joined her. I was surprised to see my sister, as she took forever to get ready, and here she was, ready before me. We chatted about the baby, about men and eventually I discovered the reason for the visit.

"You don't have to be as close to your husband as you are to Lord Strang," Louisa said.

She had found someone, I was sure. "Have you anyone in mind?"

She looked down at her lap, blushing, and lifted her eyes to me again. "I might have."

"Who?" I demanded.

"Sir Willoughby Fletcher is growing very particular in his attentions," she admitted.

I studied Lizzie. She met my gaze, eyebrows raised.

Sir Willoughby was an ascetic-looking gentleman, tall, pale-eyed and thin. I didn't like the way his Adam's apple stuck out, and I always felt wary of him, but I wasn't sure why. Richard seemed to get on with him well enough. Whether he was the right match for the lively Louisa Crich, I wasn't so sure, but people said much the same thing about Richard and me.

"Do you like him? Not every marriage needs love, but I am convinced liking is essential for its success." I didn't know if I believed that, but I had to say something. Lizzie stared, her blue eyes filled with shock.

Louisa still wouldn't look at me. "Well enough. I'm very fond of him, in fact."

"Have you told your mother?"

"She has an idea." Louisa looked up. "His attentions to me have increased lately, become more than the usual flirtation."

Her sincerity was indisputable, and I hoped his was the same.

Nichols returned and helped me into my gown. It was while she was putting the finishing touches to the pins and fastenings that Richard entered the room. We greeted each other with a smile, and I caught Lizzie's soulful sigh, quiet though it was.

I took one last glance in the mirror to check the green gown and emeralds I wore and was startled, as always, by the woman who looked back at me. I was at least comfortable with her by now, but she was still a stranger to the person inside. A fashionable, elegant creature, not at all like the hoyden I'd grown up with.

Richard moved to the door and opened it for us.

A piercing scream rang down the corridor from the guest rooms at the end. After one exchange of astounded looks, Richard took to his heels. I picked up my skirts and followed him as fast as I could, Lizzie and Louisa not far behind. Our feet weren't the only ones hurrying towards the sound. A collection of maids and guests were all racing in the same direction, and when we arrived, they were crowded around the door to a room about halfway up the long corridor.

I could not help but admire the lungs of the person emitting the ear-shattering shrieks. There seemed to be no particular message behind them, other than utter panic, but they showed no signs of stopping.

The crowd of servants outside the door parted to let Richard through and closed behind him like the Red Sea. I had to say, "Excuse me," and prod quite a few people before they turned and let me through, too, the elder Mr. Kerre and Lizzie behind me.

Inside was similarly crowded. Seated at the dressing table before the mirror was Lady Kerre, coiffured and made up for the evening, her mouth open like some unreasoning creature of the forest. She wore a thin white silk wrapper over her stays and petticoat which had fallen open, revealing acres of quivering flesh, vibrating with her screams. Everything shook.

Most people stood frozen by the deafening volume, but in my time I had dealt with hysterical maids and sisters in tantrums. I crossed the room to her and forced her to look at me by dint of placing two fingers under her chin and turning her to face me. My fingers sank into the abundant flesh, but I was careful not to press too hard.

"Lady Kerre!" I cried over the sound. But that seemed to have very little effect, so before any of the onlookers could protest, I swung back my hand and struck her on one side of her face. The slap could be heard above the wails, but the open-handed sting had the required effect.

The noise abruptly stopped, and Lady Kerre drew breath in a gasp that sounded as though she hadn't breathed for some time. From her other side, Richard grasped her shoulders, and when she turned away from me in reaction to the slap, he said, in his usual soft voice, "I'm sorry, but it was necessary. You would have fainted from lack of air had someone not done something."

After one horrified gasp, the lady seized him in both arms and clutched him to her more-than-ample bosom, forcing him to his knees. She burst into noisy tears, but they were far more bearable to the ears. Now I thought it would be my husband who was in danger of fainting from lack of air. She gripped him very firmly, but he made no effort to extricate himself until the lady's initial shock had subsided. Then he gently unwound her arms and handed them over to her husband, together with the rest of the lady.

I began to apologise to Sir Barnett, but the man lifted his hands in a gesture of exoneration and took over the onerous duty of comforting his wife. She melted into his arms in a flood of tears, the silk wrapper still in motion from her sobs.

Richard got to his feet, visibly gulping for air, and made use of the dressing table mirror. He straightened his neckcloth and smoothed his coat at the shoulders, making sure the effect was right before he turned back to the now-silent room. The screams still rang in my imagination. His quiet voice came as a relief. "Does anyone know what happened here? And could those people who have nothing to do with this please go about their business?"

The crowd of servants departed, murmuring to each other until only the Kerres, their eldest son, Richard, Gervase, Lady Kerre's maid, Lizzie, Louisa and I remained. As I watched the servants disperse, I saw one quietly detach himself from the rest and come to stand unobtrusively at the back of the room. Carier.

I moved past my husband to pick up an empty jewel case, but I didn't see anything adorning Lady Kerre's person. I glanced at Richard, indicating the empty blue velvet interior, and put the case back. Nothing on the dressing table would have filled that case.

"Sir Barnett...?" Richard said.

Sir Barnett looked up from comforting his wife and paled when he saw the case Richard had picked up. "My wife's diamond necklace. Do you see it?"

"I'm afraid not." Richard stooped and lifted the heavy lace that draped the dressing table, but straightened up again, shaking his head. "Nothing." He looked around. "Is Lady Kerre's maid present?"

The woman stepped forward from her discreet position at the back of the room and curtseyed. "My lord." She was a lady of mature years and serene appearance, her face serious and pale.

"Since your mistress is indisposed, could you tell us the series of events?"

The maid looked around. This was her moment as the centre of attention, her chance to be noticed. I saw her decision to make the most of this whirling through her head as easily as if she had spoken it out loud. I was used to reading people from the way they moved and slight changes in expression. My years of propping up the wall at balls were bearing fruit.

"It's the family necklace, passed down to my mistress from her mother. It has a large diamond drop on a chain embellished with smaller diamonds. I took charge of it myself, my lord, and I put it in the travelling safe we carry for such valuables. When I went for it tonight, the case was there but the necklace was gone." She stood stock-still and stared straight into Richard's eyes as she spoke. The practical tones she used contrasted vividly with those her screeching, hysterical mistress had used a few moments before.

Richard nodded. "When did you last see the necklace?"

"Just before breakfast, my lord," the woman replied. "Lady Kerre likes to...make sure it is safe, especially when we're away from home."

"It's sooo beautiful," wailed her mistress against her husband's shoulder. The irresistible picture came to my mind, of the lady gloating over her precious jewellery like an avaricious magpie. I dismissed it from my thoughts, but when I ventured a glance at my sister, I saw she was thinking the same as I. Her smile was too much like the one I was carefully repressing.

Richard put his thumb to his lips and sighed deeply. "The necklace is always kept in the case?"

"Always, my lord," said the maid.

Lady Kerre had turned in her husband's arms, and, remembering to pull her wrapper around her, gazed tearfully at Richard. "We should search everyone right away."

Richard rested his hand on the back of the chair and lifted his head to give Lady Kerre a direct stare. "Everyone? I'm afraid that would prove impossible, Aunt Sophia. My mother's guests wouldn't allow anyone to run through their baggage. The servants are all occupied. We must do what we can to limit the damage." He turned to Carier. "Can we discreetly search the rooms upstairs tonight?"

Carier nodded. "Yes, my lord. I can have them searched while you are at dinner if I have adequate warning of anyone approaching."

"That can be arranged. And our contacts—the people who find such items and sell them on. Can we send a message?" He meant the fences, the people who handled stolen goods.

"I will send someone directly, my lord." Carier's tone was expressionless.

Mr. Kerre, the eldest son of Sir Barnett and Lady Kerre, looked from Richard to Carier slowly.

Richard ignored him and turned back to his parents. "I'm very sorry about this, even more that it should happen here, in my father's house, but I promise to do my best to rectify the situation. For now, I suggest we carry on as usual and come back to the problem tomorrow." He addressed the maid, "Can you search this room very thoroughly tonight?"

The woman agreed and curtseyed.

Giles Kerre could keep silent no longer. "How comes it, sir, you know these things, you communicate with such people?" Mr. Kerre had begun to move forward, but at Richard's cool, direct stare he stopped.

Richard stood perfectly still while he answered, only his steady breathing making the jewelled buttons of his coat flash in the candlelight. "Most of my acquaintances know I take an interest in such matters from time to time. In the absence of any effective law enforcement organisation, we have to take what steps we can. I've built up stores of information I can call on. It is by no means exhaustive, but I hope my modest efforts might help." He didn't sound or look modest. "I will exert myself to do what I can." He looked every inch the gentleman of fashion, bored and haughty. "If the necklace was stolen by a professional, either it or its components will find their way to the usual channels. I think that eventuality is unlikely."

At the fatal words "its components", Lady Kerre buried her head in her hapless husband's shoulder and burst into a renewed bout of tears. His smart evening coat would be irredeemably stained if he didn't take steps to prevent her using it as her handkerchief. The resourceful maid gave him a large linen cloth that he proceeded to introduce to his wife.

Richard bowed to the company and offered the support of his arm to me. I laid my hand on his sleeve. We left the room, followed by the heartrending wails of the lady and the rising protests of her eldest son and her husband as they tried to quieten her. Lizzie and Louisa, who had remained unusually silent, enthralled by the events, followed us.

Richard paused at the end of the corridor, before we entered the one that led to the main staircase. "We can do very little at the moment. I think the necklace has either been mislaid or possibly stolen by an opportunistic thief. We'll probably find it before morning."

"How can you know that, sir?" Lizzie told him.

"A professional thief would have waited until Lady Kerre had no need of her jewellery. After dinner rather than before it. Then he would have time to get clean away. Or her, of course." He smiled. "Even the flower of English womanhood has a few poisoned blossoms." Richard began to walk towards our rooms, but he stopped. He turned and looked at my anxious face. "You mustn't let it worry you. This is a small matter, and with any luck, it will be easily resolved."

I smiled. "I know. Do you think Lady Kerre will want to come down after this?"

"I don't doubt it for a minute," he said, with a sardonic twist of his mouth. He was proved perfectly right.

Chapter Three

The day after the necklace was stolen was the christening. The necklace had still not turned up.

After a couple of hours helping my mother-in-law with the preparations for the christening, I went to see my daughter. When I was sitting in the nursery holding my baby, a message was brought to me. Lady Southwood sent a footman to discover where I was, "surprised" she said in her note, that I had left my post. I reluctantly handed Helen back to the nurse and sat at a small table by the window with a paper and pen. I replied courteously, but I disliked the tone of reproach in her words. I was not at her beck and call.

I hoped to send the reply by the same footman who stood waiting by the door like a life-sized lead soldier with a minimum of fuss, but my husband entered the room and stared at the man, waiting for an explanation. "Lady Southwood wished to send a message to Lady Strang, my lord," he said, his gaze steadfastly fixed at a point ahead of him, as though he saw something we couldn't.

"Oh yes?" Richard strolled over to the table where I sat. I handed him the note with a wry smile. He scanned it and put it back.

"There was no need for her to write," I said. "I was going back directly."

He put his hand over mine. "Don't let her do this to you."

I looked up at him. "Do what?"

"It's one of her devices. She will pester you with attentions until you do what she wants. She'll have another note sent if you're not back soon, you'll get tired of the job, and you won't enjoy it anymore. And that reminds me of what I came for—at least one of the things." He paused and smiled at our daughter. "I wanted to make sure that you're happy to do the tasks she has set you. If you're not, you mustn't do them."

I met his gaze frankly. "I'm quite happy, in fact, I'm delighted to be able to do one of the things I know I can do well." I smiled and was relieved to see the relaxation of his features.

I handed him my reply to his mother's note, which he read appreciatively. "She'll be livid."

"That wasn't my intention."

"Nevertheless, it will do the trick. She won't be pleased you're doing it on your terms, and not hers. You know she'll claim all the credit for herself?"

"I know." I gazed at my sleeping daughter. "But she can't claim the credit for everything, can she?"

When I looked at him again, Richard was smiling with real warmth. "No, she can't."

At his nod, the nurse brought our daughter to him. He touched Helen's cheek. She stirred in her sleep and moved towards him.

"She loves you," I told him.

He blinked, maybe getting rid of an inconvenient tear. "Nonsense. She hardly knows me. All she thinks about yet is sleep and milk. My love for her is entirely one-sided."

"I don't think so."

The peace was broken when our daughter opened her blue eyes and pink mouth at the same time, as though a clock had struck somewhere near her. The cry was reassuringly deafening, and I felt the pull inside again. I knew what she wanted. I nodded to the maid who took her over to Potter, who had appeared from her room, her hand at her bodice.

We watched her being fed, lifting her hand up to hold the swelling breast as she sucked, and I remembered the pleasure of feeding her. I had desisted recently, my attempts not a complete success, but I was happy to see her well fed. Perhaps I would keep it up for longer next time. I remembered how she gazed up at me when I fed her. It made me feel that she and I were still one.

This christening was held in the chapel at Eyton, performed by the local cleric, a pleasant, self-effacing man as different from my old adversary Steven Drury as he possibly could be. The sponsors were Lizzie, Gervase and Lady Georgiana, my lovely sister-in-law, who had arrived back at Eyton only the previous day from visiting her aunt in Cheshire. Guests packed the chapel, both houseguests and the more prominent of the local gentry, who would also join us afterwards for dinner. I wore cream lustring to set off the creamy whiteness of my baby's gown, which was pin-tucked, embroidered and adorned with the best Brussels lace, held together by breath alone, it seemed. Richard wore dark blue cut velvet and a cream silk waistcoat, heavily embroidered with a pattern of spring flowers.

I didn't powder. I hated the mess of powdering my hair, and I knew it didn't suit my cream-shaded skin as well as my own dark tresses, but I submitted when I had to. Being male, Richard could wear his hair short and for formal occasions don one of a multitude of wigs that were dressed in his absence. It didn't seem fair to me.

He looked superb, and from the envious looks of some of the ladies present, I wasn't alone in thinking it. He was always beautifully dressed but tended to simpler clothing for the country. This occasion, being more formal, demanded his best efforts. I had seen him look wonderful in an old country coat and well-worn leather breeches, but very few people ever saw him that way.

Helen behaved like an angel for most of the ceremony, until the rector removed her bonnet and trickled cold water on her forehead before making the sign of the cross. She took instant umbrage and ripped out a series of wild screams that drowned everything else, but from the movement of the chaplain's lips, I saw he continued with the ceremony, completely unflustered by this response. It was probably not unknown in his experience, but I was convinced no one could yell quite as well as my beautiful daughter.

When the rector returned her to me, I rested her head on my shoulder, on the soft cloth Whitehouse hurriedly placed there to protect my gown from the loving attentions Helen lavished on me. She hushed soon enough, but her gurgling and chuckling, which I was content to allow, punctuated the rest of the service. After all, it was her ceremony, not mine, and it was only right she should make her presence felt.

As this was a formal occasion, Richard didn't allow his demeanour to unbend for one moment. His performance was complete, the mask he had worn for so long carefully in place. It seemed so much a part of him many people believed it to be his true face, with nothing behind it. I knew better.

Verrio murals decorated the chapel walls, and old stained glass gleamed in the summer sunshine, casting bright colour on the guests below. Richard's late grandmother had embroidered the rector's vestments and the silverware was reassuringly old, presented to the family by King Henry VIII from one of the monasteries he had raided, gleaming in polished splendour. The smell of candle wax was almost soporific.

After the service, as I stood to leave the chapel, I got that strange feeling Martha used to describe as having somebody walking over your grave. I have no explanation for it, but I glanced at my husband, down at my baby and around the church, shimmering in the haze from the candles. I suddenly knew this was one of the important moments in my life, one I would remember forever. I must have stopped walking, for I felt Richard's hand on my elbow, and I looked at him again, smiled briefly, and continued out of the chapel. I wondered if he had his own moments and realised it would be too much of an intrusion to ask. I knew he would tell me if I asked him, but I also knew it was better to let him keep them for himself, so he would have something of his own, as I had now.

The local gentry were invited to a banquet, as many of the squirearchy as would fit around the great dining table. Local support was the basis of much of the power of the earldom, and they had a right to attend a great occasion like this. We did our best to court the gentry and make them feel at home. A General Election was imminent, one that Lord Southwood hoped would give Gervase a seat in the Commons, so the celebration did double duty.

We spent the rest of the day in music, cards and quiet conversation. The guests, mostly locally based, slowly drifted away. I excused myself early so I could go and see Helen, something I had wanted to do since I had parted with her.

As I left the nursery, I encountered Carier. I beckoned him into my bedroom and he bowed and followed me. Nichols was waiting, and as we spoke she removed my jewellery and restored it to its case. "Have you found anything out yet?"

He sighed. "It seems the diamond necklace was not the only thing to go missing, my lady," he told me. I glanced at him, surprised. "Several things have gone missing from guests' rooms, but the necklace is by far the highest value item."

"So it's a sneak thief?"

"I'm not yet sure, my lady. The other items were all lying about, easily purloined, but the necklace was locked away in a safe. It might be two thieves, or Lady Kerre's maid might not be as careful as she claims and left the necklace lying somewhere. I have two footmen and a maid searching the servants' rooms when they can do it without suspicion. I am hopeful I may discover something soon."

I nodded and dismissed him. I let Nichols unpin and brush my hair, and take all the elaborate clothes away, leaving me to slide gratefully between the sheets and slip into sleep.

Although Richard must have come to bed much later than I did, he was awake and watching me when I woke up. Strangely, that never unnerved me, because I normally hated being looked at. Richard frequently awoke before I did. I opened my eyes and drowsily reached for him, smiling my good morning, but still groggy with slumber.

He took me into his arms and asked how I did. I thought I heard amusement in his voice. "Very well." I snuggled into his warmth and glanced up at him. "You look fresh."

He kissed my forehead. "It's late."

"How late?"

"Ten o'clock, or thereabouts."

That surprised me, as we were both early risers as a rule. In London, of course, it was different, but anywhere else we were frequently up and dressed well before breakfast. We would have to send for something to eat, unless Carier or Nichols had done it for us.

"Do you think the christening went well? Compared to previous celebrations here, I mean. Did I perform to everyone's satisfaction?" It had felt like a play at times.

He grinned at my words, taking them a different way. "Considering where we are, my love, that's a very leading question." His hand moved a little lower, halted, and moved back to my waist. "Yes, I think it went well. You were your usual serene, beautiful self, and I was very proud of you. And Helen, of course."

I wouldn't have given these mornings up for anything. The spontaneous intimacy and the opportunity for private talk were priceless.

"I try to do what's expected of me."

I let my hand drift lower, but he put his own hand in the way and brought mine up to his lips. "Don't. Have pity."

"I feel perfectly well, truly I do."

He placed my hand firmly on his waist. "The doctor said six months."

I gasped. I hadn't realised he'd told Richard that because he hadn't mentioned it to me. It was barely six weeks since Helen's birth. Damn all interfering doctors. I wouldn't consult that particular one again.

"It's hard, but when I remind myself what the alternative is, it suddenly becomes easier."

"What's the alternative? Making love won't kill me."

"It might if you conceive again." He gazed at me, his eyes grave, not concealing his anxiety. "When you're feeling well enough, there are other ways."

"I *am* feeling well enough, Richard. I can't wait six months."

He smoothed my hair away from my face in a tender gesture. "I'll make it worth your while." He leaned over to kiss me.

At least we could still do that.

He drew back and I let him see everything he wanted to in my face. He smiled, a tender smile few other people had ever seen. Unease crept through me when I saw something else flash over his features. A doctor's dictate wasn't the only reason for his reticence. But for now I would be patient and wait for the right moment. It wouldn't be in six months' time, that was for sure.

"I've promised to go with my father today and familiarise myself with estate matters."

"Won't he be up late too?"

"What, him? Oh no, my sweet life, he is woken at seven if he hasn't risen before. He thinks the hours Gervase and I keep are deeply degenerate. With any luck he'll have gone without me, and I can keep you company instead. Unless you would rather have some time to yourself?"

"Oh no. Not if it's a choice between you and my own company. But I'm afraid they'll think I cling to you."

"Cling away." He kissed me again. "If it's not raining, I'll show you the gardens. We can talk in comfort, and perhaps I can steal a kiss or two. There's a little summerhouse at the end of one of the walks I know of. I always wanted to show it to you. Gervase and I used to play there for hours when we were little."

"What did you play?"

"Robin Hood," he admitted with a smile. "There was a little girl, the housekeeper's daughter, and we used to make her Maid Marian, or, if we were Knights of the Round Table, she became a damsel in distress. We had a wolfhound that was supposed to be a guard, but he wouldn't have guarded anything successfully. He was a huge, soft animal, and he used to be our dragon."

"What happened to him?"

He frowned. "I can't recall. I used to try not to remember and sometimes it worked. When my parents thought I was getting too old for such things, they had them removed with no explanation. One day they were there, and then they were gone. Toys, books, pets, everything was removed and replaced with something more suitable. I never knew what would be there from one day to the next."

"Oh poor little boys." I meant it. To do such a thing struck me as downright cruel. Then it occurred to me. When a fourteen-year-old Richard got a dairymaid pregnant, she was removed also. He didn't discover she had been pregnant until last year, so the pain of it was fresh with both of us. We were still searching for one of the twins. So they had given poor Lucy to him as a plaything and taken her away after she had completed her task. Richard had seen her as a human being, which, as far as they were concerned, was his mistake. When I looked at it in that way, the pattern was obvious. Richard's parents had set out to make the perfect earl and had nearly destroyed the sensitive man underneath. I'd met him just in time. "I still have a disreputable doll somewhere. I took her to Venice with me."

That got his interest. "I don't remember that."

"No, I was rather ashamed of her and I hid her. As you say, childish things should be put away."

"I didn't say that," he protested. "Will you show her to me?"

It touched me that he had used the personal pronoun. "Yes, of course. Nichols will know where she is. Don't you think me foolish?"

He smiled and kissed me again. "No."

"Richard, what made you trust me as much as you do? I know it's difficult for you to open up to people, why me?"

His eyes held gentleness. "Because you made it impossible for me to do anything else. Because, unlike anyone else I have ever met, you are without guile. Because I love you."

"I love you too."

He kissed me, but lifted his head when a knock fell on the door to the dressing room. It must be Nichols, or Carier, since no one else was allowed in when we were here. "Yes?" I called.

It was Carier. He bore notes for us from the Southwoods, one each. Nichols followed him in, pushing a trolley with the fragrant smell of breakfast about it. We lay in bed and opened our notes while our attendants went to our respective dressing rooms for our dressing gowns.

Richard's note was an expected one from his father. He would not wait above another hour for his son; it was fortunate he had paperwork to keep him busy, or he would have been long gone. Richard showed it to me and tossed it aside. "Interpreted, it means he's very pleased I've chosen to go with him, and he'll wait for me, so I'd better go." He gave me a regretful smile, but I was glad of it.

While his parents had treated him badly, his mother had been the instigator of most of the cruellest actions, and his father's sin had been more of omission—leaving it to her to deal with matters. Last year, when he'd heard that Lady Southwood had omitted to tell Richard about the twins Lucy had borne him, he'd been genuinely shocked. If Richard could maintain cordiality with his parents, it would hurt him less, I believed, and they would not hurt him anymore. I refused to allow it. I had Carier's compliance in this too. Although it would have been improper for us to discuss Richard, an unspoken agreement existed between us.

My note, from Lady Southwood, civilly requested my presence to discuss "the recent unfortunate events". Since she could not mean the christening, which had gone very well, she must mean the necklace. I showed Richard my note. "She has a right to know what we do. It's her house, after all."

"Yes, she does," Richard agreed. "Would you prefer to wait until I can come with you?"

I found my mother-in-law daunting, but I wouldn't hide behind my husband. "No. I'm sure I will do well enough."

Our dressing gowns were brought, and we made a hurried breakfast before we went about our business.

Nichols had laid out a blue gown ready for me with a light petticoat. I decided on side hoops, since the day was warm and the hoops kept the fabric away from the body, and wore only a shift and a single petticoat beneath. I was soon dressed and on my way to Lady Southwood's parlour.

I wasn't sure how much my mother-in-law knew about Thompson's, but I didn't think she took much of an interest. Had she been more concerned she would have known the network of special servants extended over this country and the continent—wherever there were servants, there was somebody we could call on. Merely by keeping a record of where these people were and who would be willing to help, Richard, Carier and Mrs. Thompson had built a network that rivalled anything the government could offer. The local authorities, the local constable and magistrate, could not hope to compete with this. The only people in authority who knew about this were the Fieldings in London and some government officials Richard had helped in the past.

I found my mother-in-law taking tea with Lady Kerre and

her daughter. After a gentle but thorough interrogation, I told them what we knew, which was regrettably little. We had found nothing in our searches and learned of a few other items that had gone missing, but discovered no sign of the necklace.

We were interrupted by a gentle knock on the door. When Lady Southwood sent the maid to find out who it was, she told us it was Carier.

Lady Southwood allowed him to come in.

Carier bowed low. "I'm sorry to interrupt you, but something has occurred, my lady." He didn't make it clear which of us he was talking to, but I knew. I also knew he wouldn't have interrupted us had it not been urgent.

Lady Southwood looked daggers at me, but I chose not to notice. "Yes?"

"One servant refuses to have his room searched," Carier told me. "He is being very awkward, my lady, and I believe he may be concealing something."

"Let's hope so." I was relieved to escape from this increasingly tense room. "Whose servant is he?"

"He is a liveried footman attached to the house, my lady," Carier replied. "His employment is of recent date. He is at present standing in the door of his room refusing to let anyone in. I put someone to watch him, and, in his lordship's absence, came at once to see you."

I stood and made my curtsey. "I will go see what I can do." The indignant gaze of the two older ladies followed me as I moved to the door. I left the room with Carier.

As we climbed the stairs Carier informed me the man was not from Thompson's. We knew little about him, but his references were good.

Carier opened a small, easily overlooked door and we passed into the world of the servants. They coexisted with us, complete in their own establishment. The change here was absolute. In my elegant French gown I felt like an interloper. The highly polished stairs were covered in rough matting to muffle footsteps, the pictures hung on the walls were prints, mostly of improving texts.

Carier led the way upstairs. We found ourselves in a narrow, whitewashed corridor. Several doors opened off both sides. What light there was came from a window at the end and some skylights. "The men's quarters, my lady," Carier explained.

"Do you sleep here, Carier?"

"I sleep closer to my lord in case he should require my attendance," said the manservant primly. I knew he'd ensure more comfort for himself than many of these rooms afforded. Because of Thompson's, Carier had a personal fortune that meant he didn't have to work at anything else if he chose not to. It was a measure of his affection for my husband that he chose to continue as his valet and bodyguard.

Carier led the way to a room at the end of the corridor. Most of the doors were closed, but this one stood open. It was easy to see the man who had brought me up here, as he was not properly dressed for his duties and stood between two immaculately turned-out footmen. I swept up to them in my best aristocratic manner.

I stopped and looked them over while they bowed. "So what is going on here?" I asked. "I hope you realise you have brought me away from my duties with Lady Southwood." Thank goodness. "I hope this proves important. Believe me, we have no interest in you other than recovering what has gone missing."

The man hung his head and mumbled, "I beg your pardon, your ladyship, I'm sure."

I was secretly delighted with my tactics and reminded of something Richard had taught me. If I behaved like the great lady, I would be treated as one. It didn't matter how I felt inside.

"So will you allow a search of your room if I remain here to oversee it?"

He lifted his head and met my eyes. I saw defiance there, and I decided to quell it. "Do you doubt my veracity?" I didn't know I could sound so haughty.

"No, your ladyship."

I stood back and indicated they should commence the search, but I stayed outside with the footman, as did Carier. The man stood with his hands clenched into fists and his legs apart, as if ready to fight, but he did nothing to interfere. Because he wasn't in his full uniform, he became more individual to me, and I could look at him as a man.

He was tall, as footmen are usually required to be, dark haired and swarthy complexioned, with deep creases running from his nose to his mouth. He wasn't very young and must have been in service for some time, if he had risen to this level in this establishment.

"What's your name?"

"Hill, if it pleases your ladyship." It didn't please me one way or the other.

I turned my attention to the bedroom. The men were very thorough in their search. There wasn't much furniture in the room, two beds, a chest of drawers and a table and chair was all, with nothing to cover the floorboards. Still, it looked more comfortable than some of the hovels I'd seen in my home village of Darkwater. The richest thing in the room was Hill's livery, hanging from a hook driven into the wall. The second bed wasn't made up.

The two Thompson's footmen busied themselves turning out the drawers. The contents were scanty, just basic clothes and some papers, letters from the look of them. I wondered if they were from a sweetheart or from his mother. They were tied together in a bundle with a piece of green ribbon.

The men left the contents of the drawers on the floor to be put away later, but I was pleased to see they didn't abuse them in any way. They stripped the bed and turned the mattress. They left the bedclothes loosely piled on top when they found nothing there. They lifted the prints on the walls and searched the shallow drawer in the table.

The footmen shook their heads to indicate they had found nothing. Perhaps Hill had wanted to protect his letters against prying eyes. Perhaps they were from a sweetheart after all. Hill's hands unclenched and hung loosely by his sides.

Carier stopped the men before they left the room. "Check the window."

I caught a movement out of the corner of my eye. Hill clenched one fist and released it again. I exchanged a glance with Carier. He'd seen it too.

One of the footmen opened the window. It opened smoothly, without a murmur. When he leaned out, he exclaimed in surprise before he reached out and pulled a large cloth bag into the room.

When he saw it, Hill lifted his head and began to move. He must have been strong, for his push nearly unbalanced me, which as it turned out was all to the good, because as he tried to shove me I thrust out my foot and tripped him. Carier, behind me, caught me and stopped me joining Hill on the floor. The man sprawled satisfactorily full length in the little corridor, and the footmen, quickly on his heels, were able to sit on him and secure his hands behind his back with a length of stout rope.

"Not too tight," I instructed. I had reason to know how much that could hurt.

Hill hadn't uttered a word during his attempt to escape, not even an expletive, and when the footmen hauled him up, he sat glumly on the floor.

I surprised Carier in the act of putting away a flintlock. He met my gaze almost guiltily as he dropped it back in his pocket. "My first duty is to ensure the safety of you and my lord. I was fairly certain it wouldn't be needed, but I like to be totally sure. My lady," he added.

"Never mind." I didn't think it necessary to tell him I had taken to carrying one of the wicked little stiletto knives Richard used with such skill. I had it as a way of carrying something of him with me, but I couldn't deny it might also prove useful from time to time.

With Hill suitably subdued, we turned our attention to the bag the men had hauled in. I sat on the hard chair in the little room while Carier loosened the strings which held the bag secure at the top. "They all have something like this," he explained, "to put their laundry in. I didn't see it, and I knew it had to be somewhere and that it was hidden for a reason." Very little escaped Carier's notice.

"Why the window?"

"It would be one of the places I'd use, my lady."

He upended the bag onto the bare mattress. I got to my feet. Winking at us was a diamond necklace. It had to be the one we were looking for.

Chapter Four

We stared in silence at the object on the tumbled bedclothes. It flashed fire in the summer sunshine, the only living thing in the room, it seemed. Carier broke the spell. He leaned forward and picked it up. He spread it out and we examined it.

It was a pretty thing, a chain of silver set here and there with diamonds in the shape of flowers, with a larger stone serving as a pendant at the front. The diamonds were an old cut; they had not been recut to increase their brilliance, and the flowers were of the more formal kind than was currently fashionable, but the necklace was undeniably beautiful. A few years ago had I been shown it I would have unhesitatingly declared it the most beautiful thing I had ever seen.

"Lady Kerre brought it as part of her dowry as a legacy from her mother," said Carier. "She treasures it, and she'll be glad to get it back." Carier continued to stare at the necklace. "Would you mind if we kept it until his lordship returns, my lady?"

"Not at all, but what should I say to Lady Kerre?"

Carier took a large, clean handkerchief out of his pocket and carefully wrapped the necklace in it. "She will ask, of course. Could you be evasive, my lady? I can keep the men outside quiet for an hour or two. With your permission, I'll have the man locked up here and set someone to guard him. We'll search the room for any weapons or means of escape and padlock the window shutters. I would lock him in the strong room downstairs, but it would mean rousing the rest of the household, and everyone would know."

"I'm sure your way is best," I agreed. "We must decide how to handle this before we make it public. There's the matter of the other items. I tried to pass it off downstairs as items taken as souvenirs, but they went before the guests arrived for dinner the other night, didn't they?"

He frowned. "I fear so, my lady. We must try to find them."

"What were the items?"

"Small items of some value, my lady. Snuff boxes, patch boxes, some other jewellery. All left lying to be taken."

"It looks like somebody else did that."

"We cannot be sure, my lady. It may be that Lady Kerre was more careless with her jewellery than she has led us to believe and the thief swept it up with the others."

It sounded all too probable to me. "I'd better go. I'll say the man was difficult and I came away when he was subdued. You can say you found the necklace when I had gone. Does that sound plausible?"

"Eminently plausible, my lady." He was very nearly smiling.

"Will you send word to me when my husband returns?"

"Of course, my lady."

I made to leave the room, but turned back on an afterthought. "You'd better use my safe for that thing." Although I trusted Carier, I didn't like to think the necklace might go missing again.

I nodded to the two men with their captive. I was glad to see he was quiet now. I went down the same stairs I had gone up, but went in the opposite direction to which I had come once I reached my part of the house again. I hoped to avoid the awkward questions of my mother-in-law and Lady Kerre.

I headed downstairs towards a quiet room where I could get some peace for a while so I could think. I was passing through the great hall, past the painting of an ancestor from the previous century, a Cavalier. The man had been a follower of the King and had died abroad in penury, like so many of his kind, but his portrait from kinder times was set here. Like all the Strangs, he was fair-haired, and his eyes seemed to be of the same porcelain blue that I saw every morning. Around him was gathered his vast family, all of them in the ravishing silks of the time, the foundation of a dynasty which sometimes seemed to me to encompass the whole of society. Several people, including the housekeeper, stared up at the work. Part of the housekeeper's privileges included any tips from tours of the public rooms of the house, and while I was surprised to see this while the family was in residence, it wasn't my house, and I concentrated on getting past them before they turned around.

Too late to attempt stealth, my unguarded footsteps made them look around from their contemplation of the picture. The housekeeper swept me a curtsey and following her example, so did the visitors. I was forced to pause in my flight. I acknowledged the curtseys with a gracious bow, and I stepped forward to greet them before I made my escape.

It was then I realised I knew them. The Sturmans.

I was at a loss as to what could have brought them here but I gave them a pleasant smile. "Why, Mrs. Sturman, how pleasant to see you. How are you all?"

There were three of them, the mother, father and their only daughter who had been and probably still was a friend of Miss Terry. Eustacia Terry had terrorised me in my younger days. She had laughed at my shyness and lack of style, and gathered the younger set about her. Miss Sturman had for a few seasons been her particular favourite, but she was by no means as vicious as her mentor. I still felt strangely nervous before them. I hoped it didn't show.

"Very well, your ladyship." Mrs. Sturman waited politely for me to say something else. I was trapped.

I asked them if they would like some refreshment, to which they naturally replied they would love some, so I glanced at the housekeeper who nodded to a footman standing next to the door to one of the rooms. He went away to arrange the refreshment.

"We'll be in the Green Drawing Room, Mrs. Gravelines," I told her. The lady bowed and left, and I took the guests to the room I had chosen to use. We climbed the great staircase. "Mrs. Sturman, what are you doing here, so far from home?"

"We have been to visit my sister in Scarborough, and we could not miss the opportunity to call on you on our way home." Mrs. Sturman's attitude was as critical as if she were still my social superior back in Exeter. She glanced at my simple gown, and for once I had nothing to blush for; it might be simple but it was in the latest taste and finely made.

While we walked she looked about her, but I had to confess I knew very little at what we were looking at. "I know the major points of the rooms, of course, but we don't spend much time here. We're here to celebrate the birth of our first child."

Mrs. Sturman's face unbent into a smile, and I remembered she had always been particularly fond of babies. "I'm glad to see you so well. We read about your happy event, of course. How is the little girl?"

"She thrives."

We had reached the Green Drawing Room. When Mr. Sturman opened the door for us, the sound of female voices met our ears. I recognised Lizzie. I could inveigle her into helping me to entertain the unexpected visitors. She was talking about something dear to her heart.

"Of course, if you must wear pink—" she was saying, but the chatter stopped abruptly as we passed into the room. I was delighted she was there, but she wasn't when she saw who came in behind me. She leapt to her feet and the piece of embroidery on her lap fell to the floor. She glared at me.

I gave her no chance to escape. "You remember the Sturmans, Lizzie?"

Also in the room were Louisa and my sister-in-law

Georgiana, all with delicate pieces of embroidery at hand, but they were really after a good gossip.

Introductions were made and we all sat. This was not a room casual visitors usually saw, being set aside for family use.

The maids processed in, carrying the tea things which they placed carefully about me, the teapot at my side and trays and stands of little cakes and suchlike on side tables around the room. Someone walking about now would have to be very careful not to knock anything over.

Lady Sturman watched the whole performance with a beady, critical eye, but she would find nothing amiss here. My mother-in-law was an exacting mistress. I glanced at Mr. Sturman and saw he had cheered up quite considerably. A good trencherman, that short, round gentleman. I exchanged a glance with Louisa. Her momentarily doleful expression, meant for me alone, was so comical it made me smile back at her.

My plan was to keep the Sturmans here for a while and escape again, by which time hopefully Richard would have returned and I could see him about the necklace. The servants would undoubtedly inform my mother-in-law of my visitors, but I doubted she would make an appearance while they were here. She disliked strangers and hated toad-eating. Not that there would be much of a chance of it with the forthright Sturmans, pillars of their own community and fully aware of their own importance in it.

"What do you think of Eyton, Mrs. Sturman?" I asked the lady, thus launching her on a critical appreciation of the house, or that part of it she'd seen so far. She certainly missed nothing. She seemed to know more about it than I did, but I had not read the various accounts of Eyton that appeared in the press from time to time; it made me realise I really must get to know it better. We could have used Mrs. Sturman as a guide. I watched her as she sipped her tea. She kept an eye on Louisa, who by now seemed fascinated by her; at least the smile on her face suggested she took some amusement from it.

Miss Sturman took in every detail. I watched her gaze travel up and down my gown when she thought nobody was watching. Mr. Sturman enjoyed looking too, but since he wasn't ogling but merely enjoying the company, nobody took offence.

"The music room was supposed to have been engraved by Grinling Gibbons," Mrs. Sturman informed us.

I fought an impulse to say, "Who?" and smiled and gave the maid Mrs. Sturman's tea to take across. She watched the way I did it critically, and it was only then I realised I was cultivating the movements of my hands, and I held them just so. I had developed these attitudes deliberately, but they were beginning to become part of me, so I didn't have to think about them anymore. It reminded me of how far I had come.

"He was supposed to have done some work at Chatsworth," the lady continued.

"If he was in the area, it would make sense to secure two such large commissions," Lizzie commented.

"I just thought the dusting must be a nightmare," I said.

Most of them laughed. "You're getting more like Lady Hareton every day, Rose," Louisa pointed out.

I couldn't accept that. "She is much better than I am at that sort of thing. I just tell someone else to do it and comment if it isn't done properly. Martha knows how to dust the music room. I would be terrified to break off one of the butterflies."

"So you have looked at it!" Mrs. Sturman said, as if she had caught me out.

I was forced to admit I had. "It's not entirely to my taste. I prefer something a little cleaner, simpler. I can appreciate the work involved, but there are other rooms I would rather spend my time in." There was a harpsichord in our suite for my own use, so I could avoid the carved butterflies.

"Which rooms do you prefer, my lady?" asked Mrs. Sturman.

It was the first time she had used my title. I tasted the sweetness of it. She seemed perfectly happy to use it, but in the past she had always dismissed me, and now she couldn't anymore. "The Blue Drawing Room is pleasant and the dining room is of course spectacular. But you must know we don't live here, we're only here to show our daughter to the multitudes." I smiled at the thought of Helen. I would go and see her soon.

"You have your own establishments?" Mrs. Sturman said, very sharp on the uptake.

"We have a house in London, one in Oxfordshire, one in Venice and some smaller places," I enumerated, embarrassed to have to list them like that.

From previous experience with the lady I knew Mrs. Sturman was committing them to memory so she could repeat them to her cronies once she got home, with appropriate comments. I wondered what they might be. Would I be "my dear friend Lady Strang" or "she's very grand these days, very puffed up"? It was impossible to say from her demeanour which approach she would use, as her attitude was what it always had been: one of superior indulgence, of a higher being watching the antics of the lesser mortals. It was common amongst many of the older ladies of my acquaintance, and it had made me determine it shouldn't be me, if I ever reached that age.

Louisa was unusually quiet studying the family as she sipped her tea. The embroidery she was working on had slipped from her silken lap, the embroidery I could recall having seen many times before, more a prop than a serious project. Her expression of quiet amusement hid a torrent beneath it, one that could erupt at any moment into the outrageous behaviour she specialised in. I watched her warily.

Lizzie, my more pragmatic sister, began to engage the Sturmans in gossip about Devonshire. She passed some little cakes around and left them at Mr. Sturman's elbow, where he could help himself at his leisure. "How does the house come along, Mrs. Sturman? I haven't seen it for a month or two now."

"Well I have decided to have an orangery put in," the lady began eagerly, but stopped short and laughed, an artificially high titter. "Oh how foolish of me. You mean the new Hareton House, of course." It was typical of her to think of her own house first.

"Your orangery sounds very pretty," Louisa ventured. I gave her what I hoped was a warning glare, but she ignored me.

Mrs. Sturman didn't notice anything, but sailed on as though we would hang on her every word. "Oh yes, but it doesn't compare to the vast enterprise going on in your home."

I recalled my little bedroom in the manor and sighed. I would miss it. While it had been there I could think of it as home, but now it had been demolished or incorporated into the new building, I had no home but Richard. I supposed the nearest I had these days was Brook Street, where I had indulged my own taste.

Mrs. Sturman proceeded to tell us about Hareton Hall. I hadn't known until now that James had definitely decided to call it that. James was Lord of the Manor of Darkwater, our local village, and now the new Earl of Hareton, so it would be logical to name the new edifice after his new title. It could hardly be called the Manor House anymore; it would be much too grand for that. I was interested in what Mrs. Sturman had to tell us, and I found her constant monologues restful, although I saw Lizzie was irritated beneath her polite smile, and Louisa was plotting.

"The house has the same aspect as before, but it is so much larger it isn't the same house. Lord Hareton is having the park landscaped too." She looked around to make sure we were all listening, like a schoolmistress with her pupils.

There was no stopping Mrs. Sturman in mid flow. "We are all agog to see inside," she confided in us, with a slightly roguish air. "I cannot believe how quickly work has gone. *Dear* Lady Hareton told me in her last letter it would be inhabitable very soon, although not all the work is finished." I hadn't known Martha was writing to her. "Cartload after cartload of things brought down from the house in Yorkshire and from London to furnish the main rooms, and at almost every delivery there are people outside the gates waiting to see what is arriving. The old wood is being remodelled, too, there are men there all day sawing and chopping." That was something I was very glad to hear; the wood held unhappy memories for me. That was where I was abducted, together with Tom Skerrit, just before my wedding.

The information flowing from Mrs. Sturman was beginning to reach overflow for everyone except the lady herself. Her daughter, a bright, pretty girl in the normal way of things, sat with her cooling dish of tea, staring into the distance. My gaze passed idly over her and I noticed something.

I had to wait until Mrs. Sturman stopped to draw breath, but eventually I managed, "Why, Barbara, you have a betrothal ring." For flashing on the third finger of her left hand was a pretty, and new, diamond. "Congratulations, I'm so pleased for you." I smiled at her in genuine pleasure. How could I begrudge anyone the happiness marriage had brought me? If it had been her friend Miss Terry, I would have feared for the man, but Miss Sturman was a gentler girl.

She seemed delighted and was finally able to say something for herself. Lizzie and I exchanged glances and smiled at each other.

"It came right out of the blue." Barbara rushed her words in her eagerness to tell us before her mother did. "Of course, I knew he was interested before. I was just worried he might have found someone else, but he came back just as single as he had left. Mama said I must make a push, so I tried to see if there was any interest." So far, it seemed very garbled, but I wasn't smiling anymore. I had guessed. "So I did, and it seemed there was. Indeed we are very happy, and we will marry in the autumn."

Lizzie looked at me and at Barbara, her bright gaze missing nothing. "Who is it, Barbara?"

"Oh, didn't I tell you? Why Tom Skerrit of course."

When the room stopped spinning, I was in the same place, in the same position, holding a teapot that was growing hotter by the second. I put it down hastily. Lizzie took over the burden of the conversation.

Tom was my dearest friend, and if I hadn't met Richard, he could have been more. Of course I didn't begrudge him any happiness, I longed for him to have someone of his own, but the news came as a shock to me. Finally I realised how he must have felt when he heard the news about Richard and me.

He was a squire, every inch of him, and he wouldn't be truly happy anywhere else but at his ancestral home, Peacocks. Barbara Sturman would suit him much better than a London miss or someone from another place who didn't know his terrain or understand his people.

Lizzie seemed delighted by the news, smiling and congratulating Barbara, so the rest of us followed her example, and we could at last get the conversation away from houses. "So you will be married before me," Lizzie said.

Mrs. Sturman turned a complacent eye to her. "I thought I heard you were waiting for a duke, Miss Golightly—Lady Elizabeth."

Lizzie flushed a pretty pink. "No such thing. Who told you?"

"The same person who told me you were taking London by storm." She picked up her tea dish and held it carefully in the approved manner, thumb and forefinger on the base and the little finger extended for balance. Satisfied, she took a sip.

"We did well last season," Lizzie admitted.

Louisa interrupted her. "Did well? I should say so. We old stagers had the shine quite taken out of us."

Lizzie shrugged. "The novelty of another three sisters hitting the marriage market."

"Two," said a soft, reproachful voice from the door.

Chapter Five

Richard came across the room and lifted my hand to his lips, and I smiled at him. "One was safely married." His touch fleetingly reminded me what I wanted from him, what he was denying me.

I recalled the dangers of our marriage trip. "Safely?"

He smiled warmly, not caring who saw. "Definitely." He turned to the rest of the room with a graceful gesture. "I believe I had the pleasure of dancing with you at the Assembly Rooms in Exeter, Miss Sturman."

She smiled and nodded in remembrance of it. He exchanged bows with Mr. Sturman, acknowledged Mrs. Sturman's curtsey with a bow and went to stand by the fire, there being no chairs left.

"You had a good day?" I asked him. He seemed in a good temper, so I assumed he had.

"Tolerably," he replied. "I've had a great many dishes of tea and glasses of homemade wine, so if you were thinking of pouring me some, pray don't. I am awash." I put the teapot down. "Helen is at present terrifying the nursery by demanding to be fed, but Potter is made of stern stuff and she refuses to feed her until it's the right time. I should leave it for a while if you were considering having her brought down."

"You've changed," I accused him.

His eyes twinkled. "Yes, did you think I would come to you in all my dirt?"

I had meant he'd seen Carier, and so must know about the necklace, but none of that marred the perfect surface of his self-control. His brief nod told me he'd understood my meaning before he turned his attention to the other people in the room.

His presence was having its usual magic, and I let him take control with some relief, as it gave me time to consider my best friend's betrothal. It must have been of recent date, because when Tom had written to me to congratulate me on the birth of Helen, he hadn't mentioned it. It was strange he hadn't written when he'd become engaged. Perhaps he hadn't liked to. I hoped it wasn't a spur-of-the-moment decision, one he might come to regret, because Tom would make someone a fine husband and it should be someone he had genuine affection for.

I watched Richard charm the female Sturmans. I was pleased to see Barbara's pleasant response without putting herself forward as she'd been wont to do in Exeter.

Richard asked after Miss Terry. Barbara Sturman smirked. "Still unmarried."

Richard noticed the ring. In fact, he'd probably noticed it as soon as he came into the room, but he pretended to notice it for the first time now. "And who is the fortunate suitor?"

"Tom Skerrit," she replied.

Richard didn't miss a beat. "You must both accept my congratulations." He took out his snuffbox, offering it first to Mr. Sturman, who took a generous pinch with thanks. Richard didn't care too much for snuff, but taking it was a marvellous opportunity for him to demonstrate a practised, graceful move, and it gave him some thinking time. "When did the happy event take place?"

"Just before we came away, my lord." Barbara's voice rose animatedly. "He came to see us and did everything that was proper. He sought an interview with Papa and then he came to see me. It was most chivalrous."

I thought that was a strange word to use, but I recalled Miss Sturman had filled her head with medieval romance, and might now be looking on Tom as some kind of knight in shining armour. I hoped he would prove so.

"We are to be married shortly after our return home," Barbara continued.

"Sir George is thrilled," Mrs. Sturman put in, her broad face beaming with delight. "He confided that he despaired of getting Tom up to scratch. Of course, once he had hopes in another direction, but we all understand why that never came to pass, and it was probably for the best." She gave me a coy glance. I tipped up my chin and met her gaze as calmly as I could.

"Undoubtedly," Richard agreed, his affability perceptibly cooled. He knew all about Tom's prior feelings for me, and it didn't concern him in the least, so if Mrs. Sturman was hoping to create some kind of trouble, she would be disappointed.

"I must write to Tom." I knew how they would expect me to react, and I was determined not to live up to their expectations. "I'm so pleased for you both. Who knows, in twelve months or thereabouts you might find yourselves in the same position as Lord Strang and I, parents of a nascent family."

Barbara flushed a pretty pink and glanced down at her hands.

Richard strolled across the room to stand behind my chair. He touched my shoulder in a seemingly casual movement, but I knew better than to think so.

Mrs. Sturman leaned forward eagerly. "We read about that of course, *dear* Lady Strang. My lord, we were so pleased to hear your lady had safely delivered." I preferred her slightly less-effusive reference to the event earlier. If I couldn't deter her, she might begin to make a remark about "popping them out like peas." I'd heard her use that phrase before in a similar context, and it would have been deeply embarrassing if she did it again here. For both of us, because Richard would depress any pretensions at familiarity in an instant.

I smiled politely. "I've had some letters from my particular friends."

"And some who were not," added Richard, equally gently, but with needle. The Drurys had written, as had Mrs. Terry and her daughter.

"It's only to be expected. The letters were kind, and we have replied to them."

"*All*," added my husband, with feeling.

Louisa smiled and moved a little so her silken skirts rustled gently. "You are always so aware of your obligations, but don't you find they take up too much of your time? Do you have to be quite so punctilious with people you never liked in the first place?"

She had struck, but with a gentler blow than I expected. She knew how I felt about some of the people at home. I'd told her about them, and as my friend, she had been most indignant on my behalf. If Mrs. Sturman tried to patronise her, she might find some problems, but so far the older lady's attentions were directed elsewhere.

"We had to reply," I reminded her gently.

"You used to have a secretary," Louisa persisted. "Aren't you thinking about getting another one?"

"Not immediately." Our experience of employing a secretary had not been a successful one, and I wasn't eager to repeat it just yet.

"Well if you did, he could answer all those tiresome letters and you would have more time to spend on the things that really take your interest," Louisa persisted. Even the Sturmans had got her point by now, but rescue came from another source, before my husband could deliver a set down to Louisa.

"I enjoy getting letters from my old life in Devonshire," said Lizzie. "If someone else answered for me, I'd miss the gossip."

Louisa smiled and let it be, only remarking, "I find life at home a dead bore. Mama says we must visit, but I'm determined not to spend above a se'ennight there."

"Where shall you go?"

"I want to go to Venice again, but we have to make an appearance at Bath, and there are a few other places I would like to go before the season starts again. And I suppose I must accept an offer sooner or later."

I thought the Sturmans would stay forever and considered asking them to dinner. Lady Southwood wouldn't like it, but she would be at her most coldly polite. It could be borne.

On the pretext of showing her some more of the house, Lizzie bore the two elder Sturmans off shortly after, leaving us with Barbara. I'd have to thank my sister later. Now my duties as hostess didn't have to be so proper, I could relax a little more. I felt Richard's presence as though he touched me, agony and delight at the same time. "Was it so very tedious this morning?" I asked him.

He moved to sit in the chair Mrs. Sturman had recently vacated. "Let's say I've had more entertaining days, but I've begun the lessons my father thinks I should have learned years ago. And canvassing is going on apace."

"I didn't know any of the seats were to be contested."

Richard shrugged an elegant shoulder. "A couple, but I think they are probably foregone conclusions. The people are making quite a meal of it, though, and we might have fun and games before the election is over." He picked up one of the little cakes and examined it critically. "Why don't you marry a politician, Louisa?" he said, glancing up at her sharply. "You were born for it, you know, and it would keep boredom from your door."

"I always thought you should go into politics," she retorted. "God knows you're devious enough."

Barbara's eyes opened wide.

Louisa gave Richard an enigmatic smile. "I can be devious in other directions. Don't you ever consider taking a seat? You can sit in the Commons until—until..."

"Until I succeed to the earldom," Richard finished for her.

"No, Louisa, I'll leave it to Gervase to fulfil the ultimate act of perfidy by entering the Commons. Once he's in that nest of serpents, I fully expect him to fulfil his destiny." He left it open as to what his brother's destiny was, but Gervase was a major shareholder in the East India Company and could not be innocent of double dealing and dissembling in the name of profit. Now he would do it for his country. He had told me once that he wasn't dishonest, merely pragmatic.

"I've always found Gervase much too honest, if anything," Lizzie protested.

Richard turned a beatific smile upon her. "That is his talent. And no one but myself and perhaps Rose can tell when he's serious and when he's playing the game." That was true enough. Richard covered all his actions with the smooth mask he had been developing since he was fourteen years old, but Gervase had a natural talent for it. He'd been forced into deception once it became clear that honesty was not what the world expected from him; honesty had got him into the greatest scandal of his life. Now he was wary of revealing his true feelings about anything at all. He loved me as his sister and had shown me nothing but kindness, but I sometimes wondered if he'd accepted me only because Richard wanted me so much. I couldn't read Gervase in the same way I could Richard, and he only let me see what he wanted me to see. I supposed Richard was like that to most people, but he had let me in.

"You would have made a very good politician, had you wanted it," I said now.

He considered me gravely, the twinkle in his eyes betraying his serious mien. "But would you have made a good political hostess, my sweet? Would you have enjoyed that?"

I caught the quick movement of Barbara's head at the endearment, but I didn't respond. Instead, I smiled at my husband. "No, but I'm not sure I'm going to enjoy being a Countess either—if I ever get to be one, of course."

"We must hope my father lives to a hundred." His voice

softened, became more intimate, and he was weaving his usual magic. In a moment I would forget there was anyone else in the room. "If you weren't recovering from the birth of Helen," Richard told me, "Gervase would have had you canvassing for sure."

"He will have a wife of his own," Barbara said, "and she will do all that for him."

Richard turned an amused, questioning look on her, and she subsided. By the suspicious glance she threw him I saw she had noticed something wrong but was unaware of what it was. I decided to put her out of her misery. "Gervase is a lifelong bachelor."

The blood rushed to her face as she realized what I meant. She put one hand up to her cheek. "Oh."

I wasn't about to justify the behaviour of my brother-in-law to her so I said no more and let her wallow in her embarrassment.

The others regarded her with amusement for a brief moment and began to talk about something else until a maid arrived with a request for Barbara to join her parents. When I asked, "Where are they?" we received the surprising information that they were sitting with Lady Southwood. I got to my feet. "I'll walk down with you."

We left the room, and I took Barbara's arm in what I hoped was a friendly gesture. "I'm sorry you were a little put out in there. You mustn't let it bother you. Gervase is very discreet these days."

"Should I keep quiet about it?" Barbara asked me, her eyes round with curiosity.

"You must do as you please. If you tell your mother, the whole of Devonshire will be agog with it, but Gervase is used to gossip. In truth, he may take a wife one day if he wishes for a political career, but his heart won't be in it."

"How can you live with him?"

I sighed. "I don't. I live with my husband."

"But to see him, to touch him..." She stared earnestly into my face.

I stopped walking. There was nobody within earshot. "Gervase is a very dear man. More than that, he is the image of Richard, so I can do nothing else but love him as a brother. What he does in private is not my concern, and it makes no difference to the way his friends feel about him. The authorities will condone it, as they do many others, as long as he is discreet. Barbara, my husband can be very hard if the mood strikes him, and if he discovers that gossip about Gervase emanated from you, he will take his revenge. I can't tell you what to do, but if I were you, I'd do nothing. And I wouldn't tell your mother."

She gave me a jerky nod of agreement. "You've changed, Rose."

"I've had to." We began to walk again.

"You have something about you that I never noticed before. I don't know if it's your new status or your new clothes, or something else." She flicked a glance at me. "Are you happy?"

"Blissfully," I assured her.

She was still doubtful. "Truly? Eustacia Terry said you were finding it all a bit of a strain last year."

"Did she?" I remembered last year when Eustacia had come to London. "What else did she say?"

"That you seemed a bit out of your depth."

I smiled. It hadn't been me who'd been out of control. "Perhaps she was right. It takes time to get used to things. Do you think I'm out of my depth now?"

"No."

I decided I'd like to keep in touch with her, if she wished it too. After Eustacia Terry's interfering the previous year, Barbara might help me to keep a discreet eye on her. I'd already had a Thompson's servant put in place. I rather relished conducting my own investigation. "How about you? Are you happy?"

She smiled up at me. "Oh yes." Something inside me relaxed. I wanted my best friend to be happy. "Tom and I get on very well, and I love Peacocks. His family have been very kind."

"Do you love him?"

She stared at me in what seemed like mild surprise. "What does that signify?"

I decided to be honest with her. "I want Tom to be happy. I know I have no right to interfere, but if I thought you were leading him on, or hurting him, I'd do something about it."

She gazed at me, her eyes wide Os of surprise. "You couldn't."

"Believe me, Barbara, I could."

She regarded me for a moment, then looked away, blushing. "I'm not sure what love is, but when Tom returned from London, we seemed to connect in a different way to what we had before. I'm very fond of him."

I nodded, relieved for the present. It seemed to be all right, and if this was Tom's free choice, I had no right to interfere. "I wish you both all the happiness I have found in my marriage."

She gasped. "But you don't love him, it was a dynastic connection. Eustacia said so, and it was put that way in the papers."

"Then it must be so." I didn't wish to say any more. Neither Richard nor I wanted to make our devotion to each other any more public than it already was. It was ours, and no one else's, but with the position he held in society, it was hard to keep anything secret.

We had reached the drawing room, and so I went inside and watched as Barbara made her curtsey to Lady Southwood, excused myself and went on my way. At last I could go to my room and hope Richard followed me so we could discuss the discovery of the necklace.

He was waiting for me when I arrived; he must have

excused himself almost as soon as I'd left the room. Carier was with him, holding a black box, and as I entered he opened it and revealed the necklace lying on worn velvet.

"It's very pretty." I reached into the box and held the necklace up to see the sparkle. "She should have the stones recut."

"It's paste," Richard said.

My gaze left the bauble in my hand. Startled, I looked at him, then towards Carier. "There's no mistaking it, my lady. It's paste true enough. You can see where some of the stones are chipped, and they wouldn't have done if they'd been genuine diamonds."

I lifted the necklace and examined it closely. To my dismay, I saw he was right. Several small chips marred the sharp edges of the facets where the brittle glass had broken away after a knock, in a way that a diamond would never do. I went to Carier and silently replaced the jewel in the box. "What now?"

Richard shook his head. "I have no idea. We may have been meant to find this one and return it to Lady Kerre. If she spotted it was a fake, she would raise a hell of a dust and it would be our fault."

I understood him at once. "Could someone have planned it that way?"

"Possibly," he admitted. "It may be a plot to discredit the Kerres. Either me, or someone who doesn't want Gervase to win the parliamentary seat. We know people who are capable of that."

"Not the Drurys!" I put my hand to my head and ran my fingers through my hair distractedly before I remembered the coiffure Nichols had carefully put in place earlier in the day. I let my hand drop. "They have no one here, surely."

"We can't be sure. We have a list of their associates, but we don't know if it's exhaustive."

"Oh, Richard."

He started and reached his hand out to me, then let his

arm drop back to his side. Was he feeling as raw and needy as I did? Did he need my touch as much as I needed his? Did he fear it?

Carier shifted a little and cleared his throat. "It might be a trifle premature to bring Mr. and Mrs. Drury into the picture at this stage. Although it is true that these days they seem to wish to discredit you rather than kill you, my lord, my lady. I shall, of course, put enquiries in place, but there are one or two matters we should also bear in mind."

Richard turned to his valet impatiently, spinning on one heel. "Which are?"

"The false necklace is not new." Carier lifted the lid of the box again so we could see it. "The silver is scratched and the chips on the stones are not sharp. This item has been about for some time."

Richard examined it again, running his fingers over the hard stones. "You're right." He straightened and looked at me. "That puts the Drury theory at one remove, but it can't be completely ignored." He came across the room and took my hand. Even that simple gesture sent a thrill of desire through me. "Don't look so worried, my love. If the Drurys were planning this, we've discovered the secret in time. But if it's an old necklace, it's been in circulation for some time. Perhaps Lady Kerre had it for a while, thinking it was the genuine item, or perhaps she had it copied so she could free some money. Who knows what vices lie beneath that soft exterior?" He smiled when he saw he'd lightened my mood. Even the mention of the hated Drurys troubled me, but usually I tried not to let it show. It disturbed me that they were still free to practise their own perverted amusements, although we were having them closely watched. They probably knew that too.

Now I smiled back at Richard and let my hand lie in his.

"Mr. Giles gambles," Carier reminded us. Richard frowned, considering the problem.

I grimaced. "So either he or his mother could have sold the

necklace to realise gambling debts? It wouldn't have done much good. If he gambles to excess, it wouldn't have fed his habit for long."

Carier bowed his head in agreement. "I fear you are right, my lady. I have seen military men wager their very weapons in a game of chance."

I glanced at Richard. "I'm glad you're not like that."

He released my hand. "It never appealed to me," he said with a shrug. "Although if it had, I'd have done my best to bankrupt my father." Richard took a deep breath and let it out again. "I think we must assume someone within the family had the necklace copied. I'm fairly sure we can discount the Drurys in this instance." Carier and I nodded. "I propose we confront my uncle's family at the same time, so we can watch their reactions carefully and they have no time to prepare anything. Perhaps we should tell my parents too. I'll send messages to all concerned to meet us in the music room tomorrow after breakfast, and I'll warn Mrs. Gravelines we are not to be disturbed. If that's agreeable to everyone?"

We agreed. In truth, it seemed like the most sensible arrangement, at least with the information we had, and the one least likely to attract any scandal. Lord Southwood was the head of the family, and the Kerres would think twice before alienating his regard for them. They might be more inclined to come clean.

"Now," Richard continued, "I think we should lock that thing away and go to see the unfortunate thief. We need to discover if he knows it's paste, and if he was in anyone else's employ, or just did it for himself."

"And to find out where he's hidden the other things," I added, remembering the other missing items.

Richard pursed his lips doubtfully. "It might not have been him."

"Two thieves in one house?"

He held out his arm so I could rest my hand on it in the

approved manner. "That isn't beyond the imagination. We have thirty or more indoor servants here and there are the attendants for all the guests as well."

I shrugged, still doubtful, but after Carier had locked the paste necklace away, he led us towards the servants' quarters.

We clattered up the stairs again and found things much as we had left them. The footmen we'd left on guard stepped aside to let us into the room, and there we found the man slumped despondently on the bed.

Without delay he stood and straightened in a well-trained attitude. It probably never occurred to him to do anything else.

Richard let him stand. He saw me seated on the hard wooden chair, the only seating the room had to offer. He took the bag from Carier and looked inside, searching for secret pockets, shaking it to see if anything rattled or the weight was more than it should be.

Nothing. Richard dropped the bag to the floor and finally turned to confront the footman. Richard looked Hill up and down at his leisure. I was thankful Hill's bow was a restrained one, as the room wasn't large enough for anything else, especially with the four of us in it.

"Where did my mother get you from?" my husband demanded.

"I was recommended by Lady Kerre," replied the man.

"How long have you worked here?"

"Just under a year, my lord."

Richard gazed at him for a time in silence, and he took a quick breath. "Why did you do it?"

"I didn't."

Richard indicated the laundry bag on the floor with one casual, graceful gesture. "Is this yours?"

"Yes, my lord."

"Was it worth it?"

Hill looked puzzled this time. "Was what worth it, my lord?"

Richard gave a "Tch!" of exasperation. "The necklace, man. How long would that have kept you?"

Hill met Richard's cool blue eyes and replied, "I didn't do it, my lord. I was on duty, and I can produce witnesses for every part of the day to say I was with them."

Richard regarded Hill steadily, but spoke to Carier. "Can we confirm that?"

"Easily, my lord," Carier replied. "I'll see to it as soon as we leave here."

"Good. We know the necklace must have disappeared before dinner, as her ladyship's maid remembered seeing it shortly beforehand. Can you produce witnesses for that time?"

"I was on duty during dinner, my lord." No trace of emotion marred Hill's harsh features.

Richard glanced at Carier and then down at me, where I sat. "Does anyone want to add to this?"

"Yes." I tilted my head to meet Hill's dark gaze. "If you are as you claim, innocent, who would have done this to you?"

Hill's shoulders sagged very slightly beneath his loose brown coat. "The servants here are very clannish, and they combine against the others."

Richard lifted a brow in surprise and glanced at Carier who nodded his confirmation. It was obviously something that had not occurred to Richard before, but had he ever thought about it, he might have worked it out for himself. That he didn't know surprised me until I realised why it was so. The gentry, the sort of people I was accustomed to, lived in smaller houses and so tended to watch the servants more closely. In Richard's world, servants were the invisible hands that looked after his house and his person. They had their own social structure, as rigid below stairs as it was above, two different kingdoms under one roof.

"You're saying someone else wanted to get you into trouble?"

"It's highly likely, my lord," replied the man. "I could give you the names of the ones who might have done it."

"That might help." Richard became brisk again. "In the meantime we have to keep you here. I shall explain matters to my mother if she misses you, but there will be someone at the door, so pray don't try to escape." He looked around the room. "You have this room to yourself?"

"Yes, my lord. I usually share, but Frederick has been excused while he visits his dying mother."

"I see. Is Frederick a friend of yours?"

"We get on well enough, my lord."

Richard sighed. "I don't think we can do any more here."

I stood and we left the room. Richard gave instructions that only one man should remain on guard, but it should be a Thompson's man. "My mother will be short of footmen if we continue to use them all on this."

"There's Bennett," Carier said, referring to Richard's groom.

"So there is," Richard agreed. "I shan't need him today. Put him to work here."

"Are we getting old and staid?" I asked Richard later as I lay in bed in his arms.

He let out a crack of laughter. "I never thought of that before, my love. Perhaps we are. Do you mind?"

I considered. "It's a sobering thought. But we're safely married, parents, and we don't flirt—well, not with each other, anyway."

He turned his head on the pillow so he could look at my face. "I shall have to remedy that. If a man can't flirt with his own wife, there must be something wrong. I thought you didn't like it."

"I could stand a little flirting now."

He smiled. "And you don't mind about Tom?"

"No, why should I?"

"Sweetheart, you're talking to me now. I know how you felt

about each other. If I hadn't come along, you would probably be ensconced at Peacocks by now. Don't you imagine I think about it sometimes?"

I had never thought of that. "You always seem so self-confident I didn't think it concerned you in the least."

He sighed. "The way I feel has nothing to do with the way I behave most of the time."

I reached down to touch him, something he used to love, but immediately he was there, putting his hand on top of mine and moving it up to his waist. "I thought I could make a good life with Tom before I met you, and you certainly catapulted me into something I never expected. Oh, not society, that would have come when James inherited the earldom, but all the other things." I paused. "I think he will do very well with Miss Sturman. I'm just surprised, that's all."

He nodded and leant forward to kiss my forehead. "And we're getting old and staid, are we? Well I might be over thirty, but I have a long way to go yet, and while I can't avoid getting old, I can avoid the sobriety." He moved his hand where it lay on my waist up to my breast and caught my armpit as he did so, raising me to an involuntary giggle.

That seemed to incite him further. He rose up on one elbow and moved his hand back down to just below my ribs. This time I convulsed with it, so he continued, reducing me to fits of laughter until I had to beg him to stop. So he did, and sobriety was forgotten, as was my desire for him. Perhaps that was why he did it.

Chapter Six

"My lady."

I glanced up to meet my maid's earnest gaze in the mirror. She was dressing my hair for the day, brushing it until it crackled before coiling it up into its usual loose bun. "Is there something bothering you, Nichols?"

She bit her thin lip. "Not precisely, my lady, but I have become aware that—something isn't happening between my lord and yourself. If you do not wish me to speak of it, I will not, but I may be able to help."

I gazed at her. Nichols was not an ordinary lady's maid. She was, it went without saying, superb with hair, clothes and all the other duties of an abigail, but she was also superb with most weapons. She was my bodyguard, effective because very few people were aware of it. She had learned in a hard school, and her skills were varied and surprising.

"Say what you wish, I won't mind."

She put down the brush and lifted the heavy swath of my hair over my shoulders to my back. "I would say nothing, my lady, but I can see it is making you unhappy. Is it because my lord doesn't wish you to make a child too soon?"

I dropped my gaze. "Yes. That's it." Not many women would allow a maid to speak so freely, but I would have been stupid not to listen.

"There are ways, my lady, some of them more reliable than others. My lord probably knows the less reliable ways." He knew some, but he had told me they weren't sure enough. "While no way is totally certain, there is one which is under the woman's control. May I tell you?"

She told me. I felt as though a great weight was lifted from my shoulders. If Richard accepted this, I could love him again. Really love him. Feeling much lighter at heart, I finished dressing and went downstairs.

Richard had sent notes to his parents and the Kerres, requesting an interview in the music room after breakfast. He also sent a verbal message to Gervase by Carier, to tell him the facts in more detail and to ask him if he could spare half an hour. Consequently, at eleven that morning we were all duly assembled in the room with its heavy carvings and family portraits, all servants dismissed.

It would be too dramatic for Richard to enter after everyone else and produce the necklace with a flourish, but it must have been tempting. Instead he arrived just after his parents and sat in one of the comfortable armchairs, placing the black jewellery box on the table next to him. I sat on a sofa by the window, ready to watch, and Gervase joined me there, obviously with the same intention.

Richard refused to say anything about the necklace until the Kerres had arrived, preferring to converse about the state of the home farm and the healthy appetite of our daughter, whom we'd visited earlier that morning. Carier remained stolidly behind Richard's chair, saying nothing. Lady Southwood flicked a guarded glance at Carier.

The Kerres entered in a group, the expressions on their faces varying from apprehension to anger. I studied them all as they were sitting down. Richard sat completely still, negligently supporting his chin on one hand, the elbow on the arm of the chair, his legs crossed carelessly before him.

When they had seated themselves and the initial conversation died down, he finally spoke. "I'm sorry to break up your day, but I thought you should know as soon as possible, without all our guests being aware of the situation."

He picked up the black box. With a careless flick he opened it to reveal the necklace, shining inside the velvet depths. "This is the necklace you lost?"

Lady Kerre came forward in a rustle of silk, swooping down on the box and its contents. "I'm so relieved!" She gazed at the object in delight. "Where did you find it?"

Richard ignored her question. "Please make sure it's the one you lost."

Sir Barnett, Giles and his younger brother Amery all made small, sudden movements. Lady Kerre looked into the case again. "Yes, this is it." She fingered the jewels. "It came from my mother, I would have been very sorry to lose it."

I felt a pang of pity that she should have lost it. Or perhaps she had not; perhaps *she'd* had it copied.

"It's paste," Richard announced. His gaze swept up to Lady Kerre. Gervase and I watched everybody else.

The reply was instant and vehement. "It can't be! I've had it since my mother died ten years ago."

Without looking anywhere but at Lady Kerre, Richard reached his hand up and Carier silently placed something in it.

"Are you sure?" Lord Southwood demanded. He must be realising some of the connotations of such a discovery. Lady Southwood sat silently, her mouth pursed in disapproval.

"I'm sure," Richard assured him. "Carier noticed it, but it's unmistakable." He placed the quizzing glass in Lady Kerre's trembling hand. "Look at the stones, ma'am. The edges are chipped. That wouldn't happen with diamonds."

We waited in silence while Lady Kerre verified his statement. Everyone in the room seemed to hold their breath while she stared through the glass, which was probably of more worth than the necklace, being set in an elaborate gold frame that was undoubtedly real. Only Miss Kerre seemed relatively unaffected, sitting quietly with her hands folded in her lap. Lord Southwood drummed his fingers on the little table at his side. Giles gripped the arm of his chair with one powerful paw, while his brother Amery was frowning, the furrows etched deeply into his pale forehead. Sir Barnett was more perturbed than I had seen him, the careless attitude I had noticed in him before completely absent now.

Eventually Lady Kerre looked up, her delight replaced by fury. She stared at Richard, pulled her hand away and deliberately let the box drop. It crashed to the floor at her feet and the necklace bounced with the impact, falling back half in and half out of the box. It lay there, glittering deceitfully.

She handed the quizzing glass back to Richard who gave it back to Carier. "You're right, Strang. That's not the necklace I inherited from my mother. Has the thief had it copied?"

"He wouldn't have had the time," said Richard dryly. "The chips are old ones, rounded with wear. No one knows except us, the thief and a couple of trusted footmen who are taking turns ensuring the thief doesn't escape."

Lord Southwood turned a baleful eye to his son. "And you didn't think to tell me?"

Richard met his gaze full on. From his reddened features and the deep frown engraved into his forehead, it seemed Lord Southwood was working himself up into one of his rages, but this didn't seem to concern Richard at all. "I'm telling you now."

"Arrogant cub!" his father exploded, only stopping when his wife moved quickly to put her hand over his.

"Later."

Lord Southwood subsided.

"Maybe," Richard told him, deliberately provocative now. He was using this situation as an opportunity to needle his father, something I was sorry to see. It could do nothing but sour the burgeoning relationship between them, when I'd hoped they were arriving at some kind of truce.

Lord Southwood leaned back in his chair and took several deep breaths. Everyone except Richard was afraid of Lord Southwood's rages. He'd dismantled a room before now. This self-control was so rare as to make Gervase gasp. I glanced at him and saw his look of utter astonishment as his father said, in quieter tones, "I merely would have preferred to be consulted first."

Richard inclined his head, seemingly unmoved by his father's capitulation. "Of course, sir."

Lady Kerre turned, leaving the box and its contents disregarded on the floor, and took her seat next to her husband. "Who was it?"

"One of the footmen attached to the house," Richard told her. "Rose and Carier discovered it in his possession yesterday." All eyes turned to me, and back to my husband again. "The man denies it, says someone else put it there. Carier made some discreet enquiries and it seems the man was on duty during dinner, in plain sight for anyone to see, so it may be that someone else stole the necklace."

"Why couldn't he have stolen it before dinner?"

"Preparations," Richard said. "Footmen must wear their best livery and be inspected beforehand. They help to lay the table, to carry the dishes from the kitchen to the preparation room. Dinner doesn't produce itself like a conjuring trick."

"He could have slipped away and stolen the jewels," Lady Southwood said.

Richard sighed. "Until we discover the truth, I propose to keep the man confined to his room. It will take two footmen away from their duties. I'm sorry for it, but I've put my servant Bennett on to it, and I'll try to cause you as little inconvenience as I can."

Lady Southwood inclined her head in a mirror image of her son's gesture a moment before. The gloss of her flowered silk skirts shimmered as her hand moved in her lap, but otherwise her pose was one of absolute tranquillity.

Not so the Kerres. "We could not think of it!" cried Lady Kerre, back in a passion again. "We must report this to the authorities and let them deal with it. This cannot go unpunished."

Lady Southwood shuddered, but Lord Southwood replied. "We should discover what we can first. Otherwise, the house will be overrun by people who have no business here, prying into matters that don't concern them in the least. Strang has my confidence."

Richard concurred with his father's objections. "We would have to give the officials all the relevant facts. They'd need to know that the necklace is paste."

Lady Kerre fell silent and Sir Barnett cleared his throat noisily. Their two sons fidgeted. My money was on the eldest son, the gambler, but I'd watched him closely and he showed no signs of guilt or discomfort. He might just be a good actor.

"I suppose we could leave it in your hands for the present," Sir Barnett said reluctantly, "but I would be extremely loath to think this man would get away with it. Who knows when he might do such a thing again?"

"Indeed," agreed Richard. "I'm inclined to believe he is the thief, but in fairness to him and in the interests of justice I'd like to determine the truth. Besides, if he is innocent, the true thief is at large and may strike again."

Sir Barnett nodded in agreement. He leant forward in his chair, his great hands clasped together before him, and stared at my husband. "How long will it take?"

"Not very long, I should think," Richard replied. "There remains the problem of the necklace itself." Richard turned his attention to the object on the floor. "Did you know it was paste?"

"Of course not." Lady Kerre glared at the necklace with loathing. "It wasn't when I inherited it."

Sir Barnett glared at his two sons, one so defiant and powerful, the other passive and ascetic. "I will discover who did that. I don't think it has anything to do with the theft. If you, sir, would concentrate on that, I'll look into the other matter."

His wife looked at him apprehensively, and his mouse-like daughter showed real fear in her eyes. Sir Barnett stood and his family stood with him, some of them with speedy obedience, one with sullen defiance. He bowed to Richard. "I appreciate your help in this matter, Strang. If you would care to keep me up to date with developments, I would appreciate it. Come, Lady Kerre, children." It seemed a misnomer, to call a strapping man like Giles Kerre a child, but he followed his father, his head high.

We watched the procession in silence, but when the door closed behind them, we let out a collective sigh of relief. "That was interesting," remarked Lady Southwood.

"Very," Richard agreed.

"I'm relieved the necklace wasn't copied in this house," Lord Southwood said. "If that had happened it could have caused a great scandal."

Richard met his father's direct stare. "Perhaps someone hoped we would come to that conclusion and replace the jewels for them."

We all fell silent, the sounds of a busy household filtering through the closed door. "Too Machiavellian," said Gervase, who up until now had remained silent. "Do you really think anyone would think as deviously as you do, Richard?"

"Some certainly do, and while it's only an outside possibility we should bear it in mind." Richard turned to his father. "Sir, you know them better than I do. Do you think they would be capable of that kind of thinking?"

His father was gratified to be consulted, and I was pleased he had thought of it. Richard saw my smile, for he glanced at me directly once, briefly, before turning his attention back to his father. "I don't think so," Lord Southwood said. "Sir Barnett is full of bluster but doesn't have two thoughts in his brain at the same time. Lady Kerre is a silly woman, and although her husband bullies her, I don't believe she would think of such a scheme on her own. Giles is the best of the bunch, in my opinion, but he gambles and would sell anything not nailed down for another turn at the tables. Amery cares for nothing but his books and he's certainly clever enough, should he take the idea into his head, but he's never shown any interest in anything less than five hundred years old."

"Pity his future wife," said Gervase.

Richard said nothing. He was thinking, a small crease between his brows. Eventually he turned to me. "Did you notice anything, my love?" His mother shifted in her chair; Richard's affection towards me when we were *en famille* unnerved her.

I shook my head. "Nothing really. Except that Sir Barnett seemed defensive, and his sons watched him closely. Charlotte knows nothing, I'm sure of it. She just sat there; she didn't react to anything particularly, except when you said the necklace was paste. I suppose she had hopes of it coming to her, one day."

Richard's eyes gleamed, and he smiled at me. "Perceptive woman. I think someone in the family knows about the jewels being paste, and I think it's one of the men."

In that, we were in general agreement. "My money's on Sir Barnett or Giles, but we can't totally exclude Amery." He turned his head so he could address Carier, still standing quietly behind his chair. "Can we make enquiries about Amery?"

"Certainly, my lord, but it is likely to take some time."

"I would like it done. We should know more about him. After all, he has an outside chance of becoming Earl of Southwood one day."

"Oh no." His mother's remark was involuntary, obviously from the heart. "I couldn't bear that. Amery has no taste."

"At least I won't be here to see it," said his father, but I noticed he didn't broach the prickly subject of our offspring, as he would have done a year ago. He wouldn't dare. He knew now that if Richard sensed I was upset, he was likely to pack and leave at a moment's notice and not return.

Richard suggested we go out riding later that day, a pastime I always enjoyed. Lord Southwood also thought it a good idea, as Richard could show me the boundaries of the estate. I had no horse, as I'd not been allowed to ride during my pregnancy, but there were plenty of hacks in the stables, and Richard promised to find me something suitable. The rest of the house party was engaged elsewhere, so it was only Richard and me.

I was not vain, but I knew I looked good in a riding habit, and I had a new one I was particularly pleased to wear, in dull crimson cloth. Even Richard could find no fault with this one, although I remembered one he took a positive dislike to. He'd disposed of it by bleeding all over it, but I had been amply compensated for it since.

Outside the front entrance of Eyton, the sunshine blazed down. We stood at the head of the steps and I saw the horse selected for me.

It was a fine animal by anyone's standards, a little eager, but obedient to the groom. She was a beautiful chestnut hack of about fifteen hands, standing just in front of Richard's large brown Strider. She was tacked up with my sidesaddle, a new one bought for me just before I became pregnant, so at last I could to try it out. Delighted, I turned to Richard. "She's beautiful. Who does she belong to? I must thank them later."

Richard smiled back, the private, warm smile. "She's yours if you want her. I sent to Black's last week, and they came up trumps."

"Oh Richard, thank you!" I flung my arms around him, and he returned the hug before I recalled our public situation, in front of the house where anyone could be watching, and released him hurriedly. He didn't look in the least disconcerted but smiled, his eyes bright with pleasure. Another step forward. Richard hated to let his private life show, and that included his devotion to me, but I hoped that one day he might find more freedom.

I loved riding. When I'd lived in a small house with a large family it was one of the few ways I could be on my own without tiresome chaperonage or equally tiresome relatives. Much as I loved them I needed some solitude sometimes, and I'd ridden about the countryside on my own as much as was seemly. If I saw a neighbour, I often pretended the groom was just behind me, but more often than not, I would dispense with one.

Bennett was to accompany us today; a horse stood saddled for his use behind Strider, but Bennett was a stolid and, for the most part, silent servant, totally loyal to Richard, so we could count ourselves as alone.

I turned a smiling face to him. "How do you keep these secrets?"

"I'm used to it. And it's worth it to see your response."

"But you give me so much."

He moved his mouth closer to my ear to say a few words for me alone. "And all you give me in return is a happiness I never looked for and complete devotion. Believe me, my love, it's a poor exchange on my part."

I felt his warm breath on my ear, and I relaxed into it for a brief moment, but, eager to meet my new mount, I pulled away and started down the steps. Even Bennett's features were relaxed into something that on his weather-beaten face would pass as a smile. I touched her, felt her response and knew she was mine. "What's her name?" I asked Bennett.

Dourly he replied, "Rosebud. But you can change that, my lady, if you wish." I thought he might wish me to.

Richard watched me. "You haven't needed a horse to ride before this. Otherwise I'd have got you one long ago. Or maybe two."

"I can't wait to go out on her." My hand rested on Rosebud's nose. A silly name, but I was tempted to keep it, if only to see Bennett's expression when he or I referred to the animal.

Our ride was wonderful. Rosebud was a strong, clever horse and I loved her within half an hour. I would have done so anyway, because Richard took such pleasure in my responses to his gifts. Sometimes his total attention to my happiness frightened me.

This ride seemed like a perfect opportunity to broach the subject of renewing our intimacy. I needed him, and with what Nichols had told me, I had more ammunition. When we reached the outer part of the estate, we stopped on the edges of the Home Farm. Bennett took care of the horses while we walked a little way, admiring the view and enjoying the summer weather. Since there was no one about, I took off my riding jacket, as did he. We left them slung over the saddles and strolled arm-in-arm, looking out over the fields, sheep dotted over the landscape beyond the ha-ha.

"We should do this more often," he commented as we came to a standstill.

"We should," I agreed. "And I shall wear breeches and show you how well I ride astride a horse."

He stared at me. "Can you?"

"It was the only way I knew how to ride at one point. But my father's second wife, Lizzie and Ruth's mother, made sure I rode the proper way. At least she tried to."

"What was she like?"

"My first stepmother?" I gazed out over the fields to the peaks of the Pennines far beyond. A few clouds drifted high in the sky and the air was still and clear. "She was a good woman. She cared for us and brought us up in the proper way. A daughter of the gentry, past her first youth and happy to accept my father's offer. My own mother died in childbirth..." I paused, because I didn't want to spoil today with sad memories, but spoke again after a moment. "She was a sickly woman by all accounts, and should never have had another child after James, but she did and succumbed to the fever after Ian. I don't think the birth was well managed, either." I hoped I had limited the damage I could have caused by speaking thoughtlessly. I wanted Richard to think of childbirth and what went before it as a natural, joyful time, not a time for fear and death.

Richard seemed fully at his ease, looking out at the landscape and listening to me.

"My father married again. He needed someone to care for the house and his children. In the next few years she gave birth to Lizzie and Ruth. I had to look after my brother Ian because Lizzie was born so soon afterward. Ian was a sickly child, but he thrived with a little care, and we were very close as children. When we caught the measles, he made me read the *Aeneid* to him." I smiled at the memory of both of us smothered in red blotches, banned from the rest of the household who managed to catch it anyway—all except James. "That made him determined to learn more. He's the only one of us to go to school, the rest of us were educated at home by a governess and what we could pick up in our book room and those of our friends, but Ian always tried to teach me what he'd learned." I broke off, startled by the freshness of the memories, and turned to my husband. He was still staring over the fields. "You shouldn't let me ramble on like that. It can't be interesting to you."

"On the contrary." He glanced at my face and then turned his gaze back to the green fields and distant peaks beyond them. "It's fascinating to hear about an upbringing so different from mine. It sounds as if there was a lot of laughter in your household."

There hadn't been much laughter in his upbringing. "Yes indeed. Not too long after that, James married Martha and they started breeding too. My father always said he would build an extension, but he never got around to it, and, later on when he married again, he left us all to cope on our own."

"Didn't you mind?"

"Oh no. Papa was always more remote from us, and he and

my third Mama were so much in love it would have been a shame to put anything else between them."

"And she never quickened?"

"No, I don't think she could have children. She was a widow when Papa married her, and she hadn't any children from her first marriage, either. It was a blessing as far as we were concerned. Any more and we would've had to encroach into the servants' quarters."

He gave a crack of laughter. "Whereas we could have fitted our family into one corner of Eyton."

"Was it so hard?" I shouldn't have said it, but he didn't seem to take offence or tense as he had the few times before when I had spoken to him about it. Perhaps here, in the open air, it was easier for him to talk to me.

"No. We had nurses and a governess who loved us—all dead now, I'm afraid—and we had each other. When Georgiana arrived, Gervase and I had someone to look after, as well. Gervase and I had a tutor we both hated, but he beat the rudiments of Latin, Greek, literature and so on into us, and thank the Lord, it didn't stop Gervase following his love for them. In fact, Mr. Heath sometimes found Gervase reading the classics in the library rather than attending one of his sessions. He still got beaten, but I think it confused the man to have to do it."

"Didn't you complain to your parents?"

He seemed genuinely puzzled, frowning. "What good would that have done?"

I hadn't thought about that. He was right, it wouldn't have concerned them. His father's main objective was to bring up a future Earl of Southwood, not a son. As long as the punishments didn't affect Richard's health, his father wouldn't have minded, and his mother was the coldest woman I had ever met in my life.

We turned to go back to the horses, but before we did I plucked up all my courage and took both his hands. He looked surprised but let his hands lie there quietly in mine, waiting for me. I heard a bird calling.

"Richard, I want to love you."

It wasn't long before he understood me. "It's too soon."

"It might be for some women, but you and everyone else took such good care of me I'm perfectly well again. I want you, Richard, I can't bear it much longer, certainly not six months."

"I don't want to risk you at all. I can't bear the thought of losing you." The pain in his eyes spoke for him.

"I had an interesting conversation recently. Have you heard of the sponge?"

Richard shook his head.

"How did you prevent your mistresses conceiving?"

Being Richard, he didn't blush and he didn't look away. We'd agreed on perfect frankness, but it was a moment before he replied. "The married ones didn't care, but I did, so I— withdrew. It worked, but I know it doesn't always work."

"And the unmarried ones?"

"Only the ones who took care of such matters for themselves. I used— Never mind."

I saw a blush mantle his cheeks, and I wondered just how innocent he thought I was. I'd heard of the devices worn by men when they slept with a woman, but they were used more for protection against disease than against pregnancy. They could be washed out and reused. For that reason, respectable women eschewed them, but this new method had originated in the French court and was entirely discreet.

"There's a new method. A small sponge soaked in brandy, lemon juice or vinegar. It is said to be extremely effective."

He raised a brow. "Really? I've heard of lemons, but not this."

I hadn't heard of lemons. I would have to ask Nichols. Ladies' maids handled such matters all the time. "So we could use that. I have sponges, and a small piece could be dedicated to something other than bathing. And if I fall pregnant again, it's not too tragic, is it? It's better done while I'm still relatively young and healthy. And just think how relieved your father would be."

"I don't want you podding babies for him." Distaste curled his lip. "All my life I was told what I was to be, and I don't want that for any child of ours. The course of my whole life was planned out for me from the day I was born. I used to pray I would wake up one morning to find Gervase the eldest son, so I could do something else. But they never told me about you, the possibility that I'd meet someone who would make all this bearable. You make up for all those years of duty and expectation, and more." He brought his mind back round to the subject again. "Of course, if we have a son, he would be brought up to appreciate his station in life and taught his responsibilities, but not so much he wanted to run away rather than hear any more about it. Do you know I was taught the history of the Kerres long before I knew anything about any other kind of history?" I shook my head. "Family pride came close to ruining my life."

He dropped my hands and moved to put his arm around my shoulders. "What family has learned from its mistakes?"

"We can try."

"I suppose we can." He turned his head to look at me.

With his face so close, it was natural to kiss him. It felt very peaceful, out here in the warm, sunny day, but if anyone but Bennett had seen us, they would have thought we'd run mad. His lips caressed mine, his tongue explored my mouth softly, leisurely.

When he eventually withdrew, Richard was smiling. "Are you sure? I don't want to bring you a moment's discomfort."

"Yes. I want you, Richard. It's killing me to have you next to me at night, holding me and feeling you harden and not do anything." I stopped, biting my lip.

"I thought I'd hurt you." He looked down. "I was afraid."

I knew that was the truth. Fear had governed his actions. We couldn't live in fear. "I'm perfectly well, and now we have a way of controlling our fertility, will that help?"

He nodded.

"Oh, Richard, I've missed you!"

Careless of who might be watching, he drew me close and kissed me again, pulling me against him, letting himself reveal more passion than he had in months. I felt him hard against my unhooped riding habit. I'd known he had reined in his desires, but not how ruthlessly he had done so. I should have guessed. His kiss was needy, as needy as my response. "I love you so much, Rose, I would do anything to keep you safe."

"You can't keep me completely safe." I smoothed my hand up his chest, delighted when he didn't move it away or draw back. "You cosseted me so much when I was expecting Helen I thought I'd go mad."

"I know. I saw the look on your face sometimes, but I couldn't help myself."

"Perhaps when we're on our twelfth child, you'll be more used to it."

I had wanted it to be a tease, but Richard shuddered. "If we have four girls and you are quite well we might try once more, but not after that. I'm a selfish man, Rose; I married you for myself, not to service the needs of my family. If we have no more children or nothing but girls, I will be perfectly content, but not if you wear yourself out with trying. I'll burn Eyton down before that happens, destroy the centre of the inheritance and give the rest away."

He was deadly serious. I too had seen women worn out and prematurely aged by repeated pregnancies their bodies could hardly bear. Deep down I knew I didn't want that for myself, and I was grateful I had a husband who wouldn't expect it.

"I love you." My heart was full, I was unable to say any more.

He kissed me again. "I love you too. I'd do anything to make you happy, sweetheart."

Hand in hand, we went back to where our horses contentedly cropped the grass while they waited for us.

Chapter Seven

We went upstairs to change when we got back and very soon afterwards Richard came into the bedroom in his shirtsleeves and his riding breeches, although his boots had been removed. "Carier says there's been a development," he told me. "If you have some time to spare, perhaps we could talk about it."

"I'll come through to you when I'm ready."

I dressed in a pretty, lightweight gown of pale yellow Indian cotton, and went through to Richard's bedroom. He was still in his shirtsleeves, seated at his dressing table, his wig on its stand next to him, buffing his nails while Carier went about the business of tidying up. He smiled as I came in, and Carier stopped in his work, putting Richard's riding boots quietly down on the floor next to the door to the dressing room. He held a chair next to the fireplace for me and stood straight with his hands by his sides, reminding me of his army days.

Richard put his nail buffer down. "Carier has discovered something. It makes the picture a little clearer."

Carier relaxed his pose. "Indeed, my lord. The household naturally split into various groups who felt their loyalty was to each other rather than to the house as a whole..."

"He means they feel they should stick together, and we in the family are seen as a necessary evil," Richard put in with a wicked grin.

"Not all, my lord," Carier said with a great deal of dignity.

"Present company excepted," added my husband.

"We also have some Thompson's men in the house, whose loyalty is to us before all. However I made my enquiries, as I usually do, on my own behalf. The man Hill is well liked amongst the other footmen, but the housemaids are wary of him. They claim he has roving hands and no sense of fidelity."

"Now who would have thought that?" wondered Richard.

He was rewarded by a black look from his valet, who, nevertheless, continued to give us the information he had received that morning. "When accused of the crime, he could muster servants who would vouch for him, but I interviewed a Thompson's employee in private, who told me what really happened. Not all the footmen were on duty that night, one had leave because of a family crisis. When he returned from the village, he donned his livery and exchanged places with Hill for half an hour, while Hill went upstairs with one of the maids." Carier glanced at me to see if I would take offence, but I shrugged and smiled to show him I hadn't. "It seems likely he went upstairs and stole the necklace instead."

"And the other things," I added.

Carier inclined his head. "Maybe, your ladyship, but we haven't yet found them."

"So he did it."

"It certainly seems that way." Richard examined the surface of a nail, and, dissatisfied, plied the nail buffer again. "But why?"

"Gain?" It seemed to me like the obvious reason.

"It seems a singularly foolish way of getting money," Richard remarked. "If it had been real, the necklace, broken up, would fetch quite a sum, but to steal such a thing is extremely risky. This house is full of treasures that wouldn't be missed for a day or two."

"Did he seem stupid to you?" I asked Carier.

"Not at all, my lady. Although we cannot discount him taking the necklace in a moment of rash impetuosity."

"Yes we can," said Richard. "He must have made his arrangements beforehand with the other man to take his place, otherwise he would have remained in the village overnight. My mother gave him the night off. Have you found a housemaid Hill might have trysted with?"

"No, my lord, all of them were on duty that night, in full view of at least two others. It might have been one of the maids-in-waiting here, but they were all busy attending their mistresses, and in any case, none of them would stoop to a footman."

"There are enough ladies of my acquaintance who wouldn't deny a footman's attentions," Richard remarked conversationally.

Carier looked at me, but I only grimaced. It was true, footmen were chosen because they were tall and strong, a great temptation to any lady inclined to take her amusements outside the marriage bed.

"Not ladies' maids," Carier said firmly. "They look for something more than a casual friendship. They scorn footmen."

There was a pause. Richard put his nail buffer on the dressing table and looked up. "So there was no maid. He was lying, and the only conceivable reason he should lie would be if he was doing something he shouldn't have been doing. The evidence is damning. Even Fielding would condemn him."

"We should confront him."

"No time like the present," said my husband cheerfully.

Carier helped him into his coat, and we went upstairs to the attic. This was almost familiar territory by now, but the absolute contrast between the two parts of the house, the feeling of "theirs" and "ours" was still as fresh. Even in my simple cotton gown, I felt like an interloper.

The man sitting on a hard chair outside the room leapt to his feet and bowed as we approached, assuming the usual position of a footman, bolt upright and staring straight ahead of him, but Richard nodded to him as we passed, an acknowledgement not usually given nor looked for.

Inside, all was much the same. The man sat slumped on the bed, staring into space, but he got to his feet when we came in. Again I sat on the one chair available and craned my neck to look up at him.

Richard leaned against the table, folded his arms and stared at the man. "We know you did it and how you did it. We have *some* loyalties we can call on." He waited. Hill didn't reply, so Richard waited some more, but the man seemed determined not to speak, so Richard continued. "We know you paid someone to take your place for half an hour." The man caught his breath. We all heard it, but Richard was still talking. "We know you didn't have an assignation with one of the maids, as you told him, as none were available that evening." Hill was staring directly at Richard now in helpless disarray. Richard kept his attention. "So you were stealing the necklace. We'll have to hand you over to the authorities, but we can temper the argument in your favour. If I speak for you, things won't be as hard. Without my word, you could hang."

Hill put a hand to his face and sighed heavily.

"I want to know why you stole that necklace," said Richard. "If someone paid you, who it was, because I don't think you did it on your own. If you tell me that, I'll speak to the magistrate for you and use my influence to mitigate your sentence. I might even persuade my father to speak for you."

The man before us dropped his hand and stood straight again. His shoulders slumped after his one effort at defiance. "I beg your pardon, my lord, but can I trust your word, if things are as you say?"

"Yes," Richard replied crisply. "I shan't even take offence at your doubting it."

"May I have some time?"

"You may have until just after breakfast tomorrow morning," Richard told him. "I wish to bring this matter to a speedy conclusion."

Hill bowed slightly, and stayed on his feet while we left the room. The footman outside was also standing as we went down the wooden stairs to our part of the house.

It rained later, so I stayed in my sitting room, practising on the harpsichord. Richard came in at one point, so I stopped practising and played for him. Afterwards he smiled his thanks, but remained seated on the chair by the fire while I sorted out some sheets of music and looked for something else to play.

"Would you like to try one of those new pianofortes?" he said suddenly.

I looked up. "Those German keyboards? I've read about them. I don't know if I would like them, but I'd certainly like to try."

"I'll see if we can get hold of one," he promised. "It shouldn't be too difficult."

"Not with our contacts." I met his eyes and smiled. "They're not as resonant as a harpsichord, nor as responsive as a clavichord, but I've read the sound they make is completely different to either. I must say I'm intrigued."

"I should like to hear what you make of it," he replied.

I found another piece of music and my hands were on top of the keys, just about to apply the pressure for the first note, when we heard a knock on the door. I put my hands in my lap, shrugged at Richard and called, "Yes?"

We hadn't expected Sir Barnett. My heart sank when I realised he might be wishing to press us on the matter of the wretched necklace. The thing was all but complete, and I'd been looking forward to going to Oxfordshire for some peace, almost immediately after the public ball Lady Southwood had planned for a few days' time. This had been such a pleasant afternoon, and very soon we'd have to change for dinner. If we hadn't been in tacit agreement to put it off, we might have been in our rooms now, but I'd decided not to powder my hair, which would save some time and Richard could hurry when he needed to.

We were enjoying the peace of these few hours alone together, so unusual in a large house such as this one, but it had been disturbed now.

At Richard's invitation Sir Barnett sat on a chair opposite him. This was only a small room meant for our private use, so the only other chairs were hard ones, giving me the excuse I needed to retain my seat by the window, beside my instrument. From there, I could observe without being observed.

"I'm sorry to disturb you," Sir Barnett said, receiving a gentle smile from Richard in return. So he had noticed. I hadn't been sure Richard's uncle would have recognised his intrusion, as he seemed very agitated and not at all like his usual bombastic self. His customary neat appearance had been sent into disarray. His wig was too far forward on his forehead, his waistcoat was done up wrong. In anyone else I'd have called his expression anxious, but having never seen it before in this man, I couldn't be sure.

Richard gave him his drink and he accepted it with thanks. As he brought mine over, my husband lifted one eyebrow on the side facing away from our unexpected visitor. I smiled in return. I had my ideas why the man was here, but it was best to wait and see.

Sir Barnett drank deeply and put his glass aside as Richard sat, crossed his legs and waited. The older man cleared his throat. "The truth is—" He picked up his glass and put it down. He looked up at Richard. "It seems to have complicated matters, so I thought I had better clear it up, but I ask for your confidentiality in this."

I smiled, trying to look reassuring. "We can promise that, as long as you're not about to confess something criminal." I folded my hands on my lap. Sir Barnett's fidgety behaviour was making me feel nervous, as though it was contagious.

Sir Barnett nodded. "You must be aware," he began, but his voice was too loud, and he was forced to clear his throat again in an effort to moderate it, "that my son Giles has certain habits that have become difficult of late."

Richard put down his glass. "You mean his gambling?"

"Yes, Strang, I mean his gambling." For some reason, the flat, plain statement didn't please him. "I don't scruple to tell you in the last year or two he is hardly ever out of the gaming hells. When he is, it's to attend a race meeting or to take part in some highly reprehensible wager." His voice rose as he spoke, and when he finished Richard didn't respond immediately, but let the sound echo around the room. Sir Barnett looked down at his hands and looked back up at Richard again.

"It is very unfortunate," Richard agreed, "but there are other sins. My father would have gladly changed places with you in the past." He smiled, but it wasn't with any real amusement. Wild wouldn't have begun to describe his behaviour before we met.

Sir Barnett snorted. "I can't help but agree with you. But now, you seem to be taking your responsibilities as a sensible man should, and my son is getting worse. You're much of an age, Strang, you and Giles, and I hoped his early excesses would settle in time, much as yours have done."

"They become tedious after a time." Richard could have given Sir Barnett a set down, but it wouldn't have been advisable at this point. I thought I knew what he was about to tell us, and his first words had confirmed it. Giles had stolen the original necklace.

"I envy your father now," Sir Barnett said. "His family is everything it should be."

I saw Richard's still expression, indicating to me that he had deliberately frozen it. His pose was now one of perfect negligence, set and poised. He inclined his head, inviting Sir Barnett to continue.

Our visitor took a deep breath. "A few years ago Giles's behaviour became entrenched. I tried to remonstrate with him, to point out no one's fortune was bottomless, that he would run us into the ground, but he lost his temper. We didn't see him again for six months, by which time he had run through his allowance for the next two years and all the valuables he possessed. He seemed contrite, but he'd only come home for more money. When he received it, he disappeared again." He sighed and stared down at his hands, a deeply troubled man. To know his heir would most likely run through his whole fortune in a few years after his death must be extremely disturbing.

"Did you consult with my father?" asked Richard. After all, Sir Barnett would have inherited the estate after Gervase, and Lord Southwood was the head of the family, so it was a reasonable thing to ask.

Sir Barnett seemed to think so too. "All he could suggest was that I lock Giles up."

Richard's expression changed and I knew the horror he must be feeling inside, echoing the sick coldness in my stomach. If his father had been capable of suggesting that to Sir Barnett, perhaps he would have considered the same fate for Richard, to confine him somehow until he agreed to conform. That would have killed him. "That sounds like my father. What did you do, sir?"

"I couldn't lock up my own son, although the debt collectors might do it for me. I won't bail him out forever. I did think of sending him abroad, but I couldn't trust him out of my sight. I gave him money and sent him away. That was when he approached his mother. She gave him some of her jewellery, and I became concerned when I discovered it. If he realised he could get money that way, he wouldn't stop to ask in the future." He looked up at Richard and sighed once more, his expression reminding me of a bloodhound. "So I took the necklace away. I told my wife I was having it cleaned for her, and I had it copied. I also took away one or two other things over the next few weeks and had them copied too. I daren't tell her, because Giles is the apple of her eye, but luckily she seemed to accept the new, fake jewellery as real. I have the originals safely locked away at home." He shrugged. "My wife isn't a very noticing woman."

"So she *did* bring the paste necklace here?" I asked.

Sir Barnett gave me an apologetic smile. "I'm afraid she did. She's fully aware of what Giles is doing, and she worries about it as much as I do."

"You will have to tell her now," Richard said.

"I've already done so." Sir Barnett's hands lay quietly on his lap. He seemed to be more relaxed, now he'd made his confession. "She's vexed, but I've made her see the sense of my actions."

"So the fact that the necklace is paste has little bearing on the theft?" Richard suggested.

"It would seem so," Sir Barnett replied. "We brought the paste necklace with us, and it has now been returned."

"You would like us to say the necklace has been returned and the thief caught?"

"It would seem the sensible thing to do."

Richard looked away, towards me, the light of amusement sparking in his eyes. He turned back to Sir Barnett, perfectly grave. "You know Hill was recommended to my mother from you?"

"Is Hill the thief?" Sir Barnett appeared visibly startled by the revelation.

"The necklace was in his possession when we recovered it," Richard replied. "He denies it, but we think he's lying."

"He was always a good footman. I remember him well. Fine physique the man had, I used to put him up on the carriage."

"Did you ever suspect him of dishonesty before?" Richard was watching him closely.

"Certainly not." The reply was instant and indignant. "If I'd ever suspected him, he'd have been dismissed without a character."

"Of course," Richard said quickly. "I was merely wondering why he should do such a thing now."

Sir Barnett looked at him with narrowed eyes, perhaps suspecting what Richard meant. "It may have been one temptation too far."

"It may be that," Richard agreed, although we knew it couldn't have been an impulsive action. He turned brightly to me. "Perhaps we'll see Oxfordshire as soon as the week after next."

"As a member of the family I think I can say how pleased we all are to see this reconciliation with your father." I wished Sir Barnett hadn't said that. "Your interest in the estate is commendable. I only wish one of my sons would take such an interest." He sighed heavily.

"Does Amery not take an interest?" Richard shook back the heavy ruffles at his wrist and picked up his glass again, taking a bare sip of the ruby liquid inside. Sir Barnett sighed again. "His interests are solely in the antique. I despair of him ever finding a bride, just as I despair of anyone taking Giles seriously."

Richard put down his glass and came to me, holding out his hand. "And now, if we don't go and dress, my mother will be forced to wait dinner for us, and you know how much she dislikes that."

I took his hand and let him help me to my feet. Sir Barnett stood too. "I hope the matter we have discussed will go no further."

"You can rely on our discretion," Richard assured him. "Although I might have to tell my father."

Sir Barnett nodded. "Of course." He looked as though he bore all the cares of the world, his shoulders bowed, his face furrowed in a frown. He straightened up, and he let the lines on his face smooth out as he put his chin up and bid us good day.

I sat between Richard and Freddy at dinner, a delightful combination. They sparked off each other, and since both seemed to be in good spirits tonight, I was greatly amused by some of their fantasies. They recalled teaching me the elegancies of the minuet when we were in Venice, and lamented one of them wasn't female, so they could make the perfect partnership. They vied in making elegant, female gestures which Richard couldn't help but win, as his delicate, exquisite gestures would beat Freddy's more masculine efforts every time, but Freddy was game, showing a delicacy belied by his large, strong hands and his square-jawed features. His crooked smile was delicious, but I think he knew it, and was not above playing on it. He'd been born with an attraction and would never have to try too hard, but although I liked him very much, I could see the man he might turn into when I looked at his father.

Lord Sambrook had lost his looks, but he still had that attractive something. When I saw the way he talked to Louisa, it seemed as though he was giving her his whole attention, and he took her seriously, agreeing with her and letting her talk. I realised that would make a man immensely attractive to a woman, and I wondered if he knew he was doing it or if it came from instinct.

Lizzie was getting on famously with the Portuguese Marquês de Aljubarrotta. I had hoped to hear from Thompson's about him by now, but perhaps enquiries had been sent abroad for him, increasing the delay. He was a handsome man, tall, dark haired and skinned, making a piquant contrast to my fair-haired, angelic-looking sister. His attentions to her were more marked tonight, and they seemed to be sharing a private joke at one point. He seemed pleasant, but I'd never heard of him before, and although Richard and Lady Southwood knew his mother, there was no account of him or his fortune available. Lizzie had developed expensive tastes in a remarkably short time, and it would take quite a lot to keep her happy these days. The Marquês looked prosperous enough, but as we had learned in the last few days, the richest appearance could belie the reality beneath. On her other side, Giles Kerre was vying for Lizzie's attention, but the way she leaned towards the Marquês made her preference obvious.

It was a hot night and we were as lightly attired as fashion and decency would allow. The myriad candles added to the heat, and I wished, not for the first time, that some form of lighting was available that didn't make it hotter, but I couldn't think how that could be. I vaguely remembered something Ian had said to me about Newton, but I couldn't ask him because he sat at the other end of the table, conversing seriously with Amery and Gervase, on some scholarly topic by the look of it. Ian and Amery were scholars pure and simple, but Gervase's extra interests gave him another dimension, made him a more complete man. I wished my brother would show more of his sense of humour and his kindness in public, but he was too shy, I think, or he simply didn't care. Gervase caught my eye and he lifted a quizzical eyebrow, as though to say, "Look what I've been landed with", but he looked as though he was enjoying the company.

At one point, Freddy borrowed my fan to demonstrate a move and nearly knocked his glass over, but a white-gloved hand came from behind him and silently put it straight. It was true; we didn't notice the individual footman once he was in livery. It would have been easy for Hill to change places with someone else.

Freddy sheepishly restored my fan to me and attracted the attention of Lady Southwood at the end of the table. "Nearly, Thwaite," she commented quietly, and Freddy dropped his eyes in mock apology. "By the way, Strang, I hear you have solved our little problem."

Richard smiled and raised his voice a trifle, just as his mother had. She wanted to ensure everyone knew the matter was resolved, but he had other motives. A hush fell. From the commotion Lady Kerre had made on the night of the theft, it had been impossible to keep it a secret, and everyone must be keen to find out what had happened since.

Richard leaned back in the chair, his eyes hooded. "We recovered the necklace, and Lady Kerre has it in her possession once more." He glanced across the table to the lady in question, and she raised her glass and smiled at him. No one would have known she wasn't delighted to receive the tawdry finery back. "It was a servant," Richard informed the company. "We will shortly hand him over to the authorities. However, I'm not entirely convinced that is the end of the matter." He ignored his mother's change of expression, from satisfaction to displeasure, as though he hadn't seen it. "I think he stole the necklace at the behest of someone else."

"You think there's a gang at work?" Lord Southwood snapped.

Richard shook his head. "No, but it wasn't a sudden impulse drove this man to steal—he's been a faithful servant for many years. He planned the theft, and if we'd taken everybody at their word, he'd have been the only person to take the blame. He paid another servant to take his place, who has also been dismissed." He shot a glance at his father, who nodded in confirmation.

I became aware of a tension behind me, and I looked up at the other side of the table to where a footman stood, immobile, but all too human. Richard still spoke, holding the attention of everyone present. "I believe he was doing this for someone else, that's why I haven't handed him over to the authorities yet. We'll find out who was paying him first." He leaned back and picked up his glass, the red liquid glinting in the candlelight.

This created quite a stir and considerable speculation. It took attention away from my husband, so he could watch them.

"I've seen you admiring that necklace," Gervase said to his sister Georgiana. "Could you have wanted it that much?"

Georgiana shook her head and smiled quizzically at Gervase. I guessed the opposite had been the case, that she hadn't admired it at all.

"I think everyone here could have done it at some time or other," she said, looking up the table at Richard. "But perhaps it was someone from outside? A professional thief?"

"Why should he pay anyone else?" Richard responded. "On

the day in question he could have come in with the other guests or posed as a servant and stolen it for himself."

Georgiana shrugged and leaned back in her chair again.

Lady Southwood raised one finger and, galvanised into action, the servants began to remove the covers. When the table was bare and only fruit, sweetmeats and wine remained, she waited for barely one toast before she stood and led us ladies out of the room. She wasn't pleased with Richard.

Once in the drawing room she asked me if I would play for the company and offered to turn the pages for me. Knowing what was coming, I chose a simple, pretty piece and let my hands do the work while I talked to my mother-in-law.

"He said he would make things right over dinner," she murmured. She stood to one side of me so I couldn't see her, but I knew the expression that would be on her face, one of frozen polite indifference because she was seething underneath.

"We need to know who paid Hill," I replied, as quietly as she. I paused while I negotiated a piece on the keyboard, then I continued. "The best way to find out is to challenge him—or her."

"Why at dinner?"

"He left it until the end," I pointed out, "and it's the only time when all of the guests are present."

"But Lady Kerre has her wretched necklace back, why does it matter?"

"The footman." I seemingly concentrated on the keyboard, but in reality all my thoughts lay elsewhere. "Hill could be hanged for this. We want to know who was responsible for leading a respectable servant astray, and perhaps that will mitigate his sentence."

"We? You share Strang's sentiments?" She sounded impatient.

"He's my husband. His wishes must always be paramount with me," I replied primly, the image of the docile wife, but I spoiled it a little by adding, "I hate injustice as much as he does."

I didn't need to look at her to see the tightening of the lips. "I'm still thankful Richard married you instead of that Cartwright female, but I wish you would lead him into more tranquil paths. I always said he would send me into an early grave, and now I know he will."

She leaned over to turn the page for me, her hand steady. I continued the piece in silence, knowing anything else would only add fuel to the fire. Her ladyship had looked forward to a satisfactory conclusion, but we weren't at all sure it was resolved.

The tea was brought in and I moved away from the instrument to help serve it. I was glad I could take a seat at another table, where the caddies, hot water and teapot were brought to me and I could concentrate on doing a mundane task as well as possible. I'd discovered this to be one of Richard's secrets; everything he did was done superbly, adding to the whole effect of exquisite perfection. It was almost obsessive, but it was something he could drop at will, although some of it was so ingrained in him it had become instinct. So I took care to open the caddies gracefully, something I'd have had no patience with two years ago, but being married to Richard had given me the impetus to rival him in grace. I poured the hot water carefully, without a splash.

Lizzie, Georgiana and Louisa were there. "You know," said Lizzie thoughtfully, "people tried for years to make you a lady, but I never thought you'd achieve it. Now you have."

"My heart wasn't in it, but being married to Lord Strang means everybody looks at you, and I didn't want to embarrass myself or anyone else. Anyway, I'm enjoying it now."

"What, being the centre of attention?" demanded Lizzie.

"No, not that." I still didn't enjoy being stared at. "I'm not that changed, but I like the clothes and the amusements. I love the opera, and I'm one of the few who takes any notice of the performance. I read about the fashionable life in the papers, when we were still at home in Devonshire. I thought it all frippery and fashion, but that's just the trimming. The substance is the estate management, the use of power."

"And what have we women to do with that?" demanded my sister.

"We're at the centre of it. Do you think the public ball is just for Helen's arrival? Of course not. It's for the tenants to meet me and reassure themselves I would be a proper countess in the fullness of time, for the local dignitaries to exchange views, maybe to form new alliances. Gervase is going into the House of Commons in the autumn. The seat is assured, but the support of the local gentry is very important to him."

Louisa took her cup from me and regarded me frankly. "Does Strang let you into estate business?"

"I'm to go with him to meet the land steward soon."

"So you *are* more than love's young dream," Lizzie pronounced with a great deal of satisfaction.

"We were rather hoping no one would notice," I admitted, to a general laugh from everybody sitting nearby.

"We either know Richard Kerre or we know you," Louisa commented. "Those of us who knew him before have seen such a change as to realise what was in the wind, and the people who knew you before say you have changed as well. It's hardly a secret, my dear, and the world is now looking for a fall."

"That's what we were trying to avoid. It really is no one's business but our own."

"That's just naïve," Louisa said. "Lord Strang is a public figure, and likely to become more so. He's never been one to search for the shadows. At first, society accepted some sort of dynastic arrangement had been achieved, but most of them were there to see your wedding, and the adroit way you slipped away afterwards."

"Or tried to," I grimaced, for that had not gone according to plan.

"Well that was one secret you managed to keep," Louisa

remarked. "To the world, you had a narrow escape not being on board the yacht when it caught fire, that's all. Some of us saw you in Venice and we wrote home. You came to London. That's when your secret finally came out. But Richard isn't despaired of, you know. There are still some hopeful matrons angling for him." She was referring to Richard's previous affairs with all the young married women he could persuade. Some were not so young.

I grinned. "I know, I see them, but they must look elsewhere now. I have him and I'm keeping him."

Lizzie frowned doubtfully. She'd always been wary of Richard. "What guarantees have you got that he won't go back to the way he was before?"

I loved my sister, and I knew she was only thinking of me in this. Otherwise I might have lost my temper. "I have none. But if the worst happened I would still be his wife and the mother of his children." It was true, but it was a future I couldn't contemplate. "Besides, he didn't give up all that philandering for me, you know, he grew bored with it."

"*Bored?*" Louisa repeated incredulously. She put down her tea dish. "How does a man get bored with that? I think he was just being polite, my dear."

I lifted one shoulder in a light shrug. "I think he was bored."

"I was surprised when I met him, to find such a polite, considerate man where I had expected to find a supercilious libertine," Lizzie said grudgingly.

"He could be that," said Louisa.

"He frightens me," said Georgiana, surprising me. She had never shown signs of that before, and I knew how fond Richard was of his sister.

"I didn't know that, Georgiana. What can possibly frighten you about Richard?"

They stared at me. "He has a will no one likes to cross," Lizzie suggested. I watched and listened, sipping my tea. It was interesting to hear what my husband seemed like to other people.

If they hadn't drunk so much over dinner, they wouldn't have been talking quite so freely in front of me. "He looks at one—so—when you make a mistake." Georgiana imitated Richard's expression of faint surprise I'd seen him use on occasion, but never to me.

"He's capable of the worst snubs in society," added Louisa with feeling. "I've seen him turn his back in such a final way everyone knew that particular liaison was over." That last comment chilled me as the others had not. I was so deeply in love with him I knew I would never get over such a rejection, unlikely though it seemed.

Lizzie watched me as she sipped her refreshed tea. I knew it, so I kept a serene mask. "I wish I'd known him before."

"No you don't," Louisa assured me. "He was terrifying. He had a reputation as one of the most reckless men in society, he would do anything for a dare, he didn't even need it to be a proper bet. Get hold of the archives at Whites' and see how often his name crops up there." I regarded her questioningly. "They note down the bets that take place," Louisa explained. "Act as honest brokers, so to speak."

I nodded to show her I understood. "So tell me—what did he do? I've never spoken to anyone except Gervase, and he was away for Richard's wildest years, so he's no wiser than I am."

Louisa looked at me, assessing me with her clear grey eyes fixed on mine. "You must have heard of some of the things he did."

"Only hearsay," I replied. I knew more than that, but I wanted to give them a clear field.

"Well," Louisa began, folding her hands over her fan and leaning forward slightly, "there was the time he managed to seduce two rivals in the same week. Bets were high on that one because the two ladies hated each other, and if one had found out about the other he would have been spurned, reputation or no. He did it, and he told them about each other at one of the Duchess of Queensberry's balls. The Duchess banned him from any more of her gatherings for a year after that. The two ladies confronted each other on the dance floor, and the spectacle was wonderful, but dreadfully embarrassing, of course, to their husbands." Louisa was getting into her stride now. Lizzie smiled in delight as she listened to stories a single, well-brought-up miss should not be aware of. "He's taken on impossible races in that phaeton he drives, and overturned himself more than once, but provided a great spectacle for us all. He drives very well, but I wouldn't have liked to have gone up with him, because he never seemed to care if he went over or not."

I could have told her why he didn't care. One of his aims was to put a period to his existence, because he had nothing to live for and his death would have spited his father. Thompson's had saved him, it had given him an interest that wasn't purely destructive and vicious, although he had initially gone into it to help Carier.

"Perhaps he was bored," I suggested.

"Well he seems to have found an interest now," said Louisa acidly.

Lizzie smiled, put down her tea dish. "This is a good estate and likely to get better. There's much to interest a person here."

I suddenly realised something I should have known before. This estate was near to the border, where Derbyshire met Yorkshire, and the Hareton estate was close too. It would make sense, if James was selling, for Lord Southwood to take a look. I wondered why Richard hadn't told me. I was glad it wouldn't include the house. Hareton Abbey was a monstrous house, far too large and badly built to make a home, but it was entailed, and so couldn't be sold. Much of the land was disposable, only the Home Park was included in the entail. James had no desire to return to that miserable place and no other property thereabouts, but I had good memories of some of my time there.

"He's never taken much interest in it before, but he says he must, since he's now a family man."

They all smiled and I saw the power a baby has over a man. I hadn't seen much of Helen that day, and I'd missed her.

I found Lady Southwood and got her permission to send for my daughter. A maid was despatched and soon Potter arrived bearing Helen, the expression on the maid's face showing she was put out by the disturbance in her routine. I ignored it and took my daughter into my arms, smelling the milky perfume all new babies carry with them. The other women gathered around.

"I was doubtful about your leaving off swaddling bands," Lady Southwood said, "but I think you were right. She's growing well."

It was a new fashion, and one I agreed with. My baby would be able to kick and wave her chubby hands about all she liked. Helen seemed particularly sunny tonight, smiling at all of us. Although the nursemaid assured me it was just wind, I knew better. When the gentlemen joined us, they declared themselves charmed by the scene that greeted them.

Richard took her little hand, as he usually did, and then he took mine. The people standing near to us, his mother, Lizzie and Gervase could also see his face. He didn't trouble to hide his expression, one of soft loving contentment.

I was glad Lizzie had seen it. She truly cared for me, and it was the only way I could show her how well Richard did too. She still had her doubts about him. I knew she thought it wouldn't last with him, but I hoped to prove her wrong, and to do her justice, I think she wanted to be proved wrong.

Helen smiled and gurgled at everyone, taking proffered hands and submitting to a cuddle with Lizzie, Georgiana and Louisa in turn. Most of the others preferred to look on, but I noticed the softened expression in the face of the Marquês when Lizzie took Helen from me.

My baby's little face crumpled and as quickly as she had smiled for the guests, she burst into tears, so Potter came forward, but I decided to take her myself.

I carried her to the nursery where I watched as she was fed, her linen was changed and she was put to bed. She fell asleep almost as soon as she was laid down. I stopped for a while and watched her sleeping peacefully, loving the tranquillity it brought to me, and I went back downstairs.

Chapter Eight

The rest of the evening passed in chat, music and cards, and after supper Richard and I made our way upstairs. When we had bid everyone who was going our way good night, and we were alone, I linked my arm through his and we passed companionably through to our rooms. No one knew what we had planned for that night, but inside my stomach was churning. What if it was different? If he didn't like me anymore, for some reason?

At the door to my bedroom he kissed my hand and left me, as most husbands did, and went farther down the corridor to his room. Anyone watching us would have assumed we'd remain separate for the rest of the night.

With many couples that would be the last they saw of each other until the morning, but not us. I went through to my room, where Nichols waited for me. She helped me to undress, brushed out my hair and held the towel while I washed. She'd washed my hair that morning, and it still shone.

One of the things I appreciated about my maid was her ability to be silent when I needed it, and to converse without too many *your ladyships* and the like. Tonight we were quiet, and she went about her duties efficiently, hardly raising a sound from the floor as she moved to the dressing room to take my clothes away. I used the precaution she had suggested. There was no need to mention it to her. What I required, a small sponge and a bottle, waited for my use in the dressing room.

I wore only my dressing gown. It was the one Richard had bought me in Venice that I had put away during my pregnancy. I was pleased to be able to get into this one again, a delicate confection of ivory silk and floral embroidery. He'd bought it in the week between his arrival in Venice and mine.

I leaned back in my chair and closed my eyes, remembering that time and how overwhelmed I was by the intensity of his loving and the intensity of my response, the trouble we'd shared there fading into the back of my mind. Partly because of that time I trusted him wholly now and respected his needs as much as he respected mine.

I heard the door from his dressing room open, but I didn't open my eyes. I smiled as I breathed in that sharp perfume he always wore, and felt his lips gently touch mine. I opened my eyes and met his blue gaze, saw him smiling at me. "You're here."

"So I am," he replied. "Are you tired, my love? Would you like to go to bed?"

"No I'm not tired, but I would like to go to bed." It was an echo of our first night in Venice, an indication he had been thinking about it too.

I went into his arms. We stood for a long time, holding each other, before he gently loosened his hold and took my hand to lead me to the bed. He undid the fastenings on my dressing gown and undid his own. Neither of us wore anything underneath. I touched his hair, short, with a natural wave. I thought it gave him an angelic look. "Will you ever wear a nightcap?"

"I doubt it. The absurdity would make us both laugh too much to get any sleep."

"You could wear a nightshirt with it," I pointed out. "Most men do."

"And you're classifying me with most men?"

I smiled. "There you have me."

Softly he kissed me and pushed my dressing gown off my

shoulders. I let it slide to the floor.

I thrilled to see his gaze ignite. "I can't believe I have you."

"Believe it. It's true." His voice excited me right to the marrow.

He slipped off his own gown and drew back the light bedcovers that were all we needed on this warm night. Candles burned on the dressing table and on each of the nightstands so we could see each other. I got into bed and held out my arms for him. He came to me gladly.

"This time," I whispered to him, my mouth close to his, "I want to make love all night. I want to see the sun rise, and know I've been with you every minute, every hour." We would make tonight count.

He moved to hold me close, to make love to me, to show me his love in the most physical way, but the way that brought spiritual fulfilment sighing in its wake, that made the difference between love and sexual congress. This would be our time, our night.

I was determined to make this night memorable. Since it was summer and the fire not lit, I had a supply of candles on hand, so I could see him whenever I wanted to. My hair was brushed into a shining sheet of waves, a chestnut sea for him. I left it loose, to fall below my shoulders for his pleasure.

He took his time. He touched me, loved me, as though this were the first time and we had come fresh to each other, except by now he knew what I liked best, what would give the best response, the most intense sensation. I no longer felt awkward with him, indeed I hadn't felt like that since our first night together.

He touched me, kissed where he had touched, my mouth first, deep and sweet, our bodies pressed together, my breasts against his chest, our legs entwined. "You have the sweetest taste in the world, my love, my only love."

I touched him in return and ran my hands over his lean strength. "My heart is yours, my body and everything I have."

He slid down, cradling my breasts in his hands before he kissed each one and took my nipples into his mouth to taste and nip. He could have done that all night and I would have begged for more, but he left them with reluctant kisses, to touch and lick further down, lingering at the soft space inside my hip, where I was particularly sensitive. His hands on my hips prevented me from wriggling out from his grasp, and his low chuckle told me he knew the reaction he had on me.

I gasped as he reached the inside of my thigh, lingering, softly kissing me. Every touch sensitised me even more. I could hardly bear his touches, but I wanted more and yet more. The longing was killing me, but it was exquisite torture, and I whispered, "Please—oh yes," as he finally reached the place I yearned for him to be.

"I have missed this so much, sweetheart. Your taste has haunted my dreams." His murmurs heated me and when he parted me with his thumbs, his breath washed over me and I shuddered. I wanted him here, now. But he stopped to kiss, to lick, to taste. His low murmur of "Mmm, brandy," told me he'd detected what I'd used to dampen the sponge. His tongue swept inside me in one luscious lick, then hardened and penetrated me in a parody of what was to come before he left me again to take that knot of precious sensitivity into his mouth and lavish attention on it.

I went beyond speech for a time, I don't know how long. His hands and tongue worked skilfully, driving me to height after height, until eventually I shuddered and cried out, past anything but sensation. I grasped his shoulders as he came back up to me to kiss me, the taste of that other place still lingering on his mouth.

He would have joined with me, but I pushed him so he was lying on his back. I was determined to repay him, to love him in return. I took a moment to look at him, so beautiful, so supple and athletic, and smiled when I saw him returning the compliment, eyes feasting on me, bright with love and desire. He lifted his hands and cupped my breasts, but released them as I moved down his body to reacquaint myself with what I had missed recently.

I kissed him in the places he liked, his nipples, teasing the tips with my teeth until he groaned, just under his ribs, his flat, firm stomach, moving slowly, tantalisingly down, touching and caressing all the time. I was rewarded by his soft words, rising to an "Oh. Oh, my God, oh, Rose, my love."

He touched my hair, drove his fingers into the loose waves. I loved the control, and I licked the crown of his shaft, tasting the salty essence of him, stroking him with my tongue before I sucked him into my mouth and drew him as deep as I could. I released him with a break in the suction that made him gasp and arch, and I drew him back. I didn't care if he exploded now, in my mouth, because we had all night. Plenty of time to regroup. But he tugged me up, grasped handfuls of hair and dragged me back up the bed to lie over him.

He rolled so I was underneath and drove into my eager body with a low growl of need. The explosion in both of us was almost immediate, neither of us able to stop. It took us both, powerful, instantaneous and completely engulfing. All we could do was stare into each other's eyes and ride the storm. Together.

We held each other tight for some time afterwards, exchanging small kisses until we recovered ourselves enough for me to slide to one side of him and lie close.

"I'm sorry, sweetheart."

"What for?"

"It was too quick."

I laughed and kissed his neck. "It couldn't have been anything else. It happened and it happened for both of us."

He smiled at that. "Sometimes I can hardly believe my luck. This intimacy means so much to me, I don't know how I could ever have contemplated living without it."

"I feel the same." We kissed, long and lingering, enjoying the freedom after months of restraint. I let my hand move down to his stomach.

He laughed and put his hand on top of mine, brought it back up the bed and kissed the fingertips. "It will take a little longer than that, sweetheart."

"We have all night."

His voice softened at my reminder, became more intimate still. "So we have. Do you think we'll be allowed to sleep late tomorrow?"

"I don't care. If we want to, we will."

He let go of my hand, moving to kiss my mouth. His tender smile was one only our daughter and I ever saw. It transformed his face from his usual aristocratic disdain to a sensitive man who could be easily hurt. He exposed everything for me to see, gave me everything he was, and even after the hurts he'd suffered, he trusted me to keep them safe. No wonder he preferred to keep that hidden; it would make him a target for every malicious member of society. He looked so open, so dear.

He stroked my cheek. "If anything makes you unhappy, you must tell me at once."

"So you can be unhappy too?"

"So I can prevent it."

"You may not be able to."

"Then I'll share your unhappiness and help you to bear it."

"I'm happy now. You weren't there when I was unhappy."

"In Exeter?"

It all seemed a very long time ago now, but in reality, it wasn't quite two years. "In Exeter. And in other places. Without you, I would have deteriorated into an old maid, even when James inherited the earldom. I was good at blending into the walls, and I'd had my confidence eroded, unwittingly by Lizzie and deliberately by Eustacia Terry and others. And by myself, I know that now. I didn't want that, but I didn't know how to stop it happening."

"A season in London would have stopped it," he assured

me. "You wouldn't have been short of offers. Men of my age look for more than fleeting prettiness and good manners in a wife. You'd have found somebody. I was fortunate to get there first."

I found the peace of this leisurely talk, of the quiet around us, priceless. "And you're forgetting Tom," he reminded me. "Once he realised how he felt about you, he would have made you an offer, and from what you say, you'd have taken him. I came very close to losing you before I even met you."

It was true, I had forgotten Tom. "In that case my life would have been worthwhile, but not as fulfilling. I wouldn't have known this." I slid my hand up from his waist, up his chest to his shoulder, loving the freedom to touch him, his freedom to touch me.

"Are you sure?" It was an insecurity only I was allowed to see.

I smiled and kissed his other shoulder. "I couldn't be more sure."

"And you don't mind Tom marrying someone else?"

He was watching me closely. I shook my head. "No, my love, only that he should be happy in his marriage. I wasn't sure, you see, because Barbara Sturman was one of Eustacia Terry's particular friends, and that was how I knew her."

"I see."

"When I talked to her properly, I was reassured. She's much gentler than Eustacia. I may not love Tom as I love you, but he is dear to me and I want him to be happy. She and Tom have the same background—always a good basis for a marriage, don't you think?" I quirked a smile.

"Not always," he answered, amusement colouring his voice.

"Something else happened with us. Your parents were forced to accept your choice, and when James inherited his title, it suddenly became acceptable."

He stroked my hair, gazed into my eyes. "It would have made no difference. I was determined to have you, if you wanted me too. And they would have accepted it, as it was their only way of ensuring their precious heir. I told them that. You or no one."

"Didn't I prove I wanted you?"

He smiled delightfully and leaned over to kiss me again. Emotion rose in me, together with the heat of desire. I returned his kiss with interest and felt his tongue touch mine as he rolled over me, found his way inside and began to move in that rhythm we had made our own, as, no doubt, thousands of other lovers had done before us.

But they weren't my concern now. Tom, the necklace, everything was forgotten as the sensation spread through me and I marvelled again that such a seemingly simple thing could lead to such exquisite delight. "Oh, Richard!"

"My sweet love."

In this as in everything else, he moved with grace and precision, bringing artistry to our lovemaking in an effort to pleasure me to his utmost ability. I ran my fingernails lightly over his back. He paused and let his breath out in a hiss, and then resumed the dance, thrusting harder than before. I cried out when the first peak hit me. It was almost like losing consciousness. The intensity surged through every part of me and I arched my back, pushed against him.

I opened my eyes to see his smile of triumph and smiled back, still panting slightly. "Do you know," he said in a voice lowered into a soft, velvety murmur, "how beautiful you look now? No man could resist you like this, no one would ever pass you by for someone else."

"You're all I want to see. No one else."

He laughed and pulled me up to him for his kiss, which went on so long that I prayed for it never to stop. His movements became slower, more sensuous. He laid me down and bent his head to take my breasts into his mouth one by one, running his tongue over my nipples until I sighed, transported by sheer sensation. I touched him, gave myself over to the freedom he had denied me these past months, reacquainted myself with the smooth muscle of his powerful chest.

He supported his weight on one elbow and used the other hand to caress me where we joined. I called his name and pulled him to me, clamping my legs around his so I could hold him tight while my body took control.

When he withdrew, he chuckled at my protest. He turned me over, kissed my neck, my shoulders and my back, moved his hands over me before he entered me again. I was his now, I could do nothing but his will, but his intent seemed to bring me all the passion I had missed so much. His hands slipped around to my front, and he eased me onto my side, kissed my neck and said to me, "My heart's delight, I love you, I love you."

He moved, slowly at first, but became more insistent, pulling me hard against him as my responses increased and became more incoherent, finally ending in one loud, "Yes!" as my senses swam once more.

This time he didn't pause, but carried away by his own needs, continued to push me further into that world where nothing else mattered, relentless, uncompromising in his purpose, making me feel helpless, until with one shattering, wordless cry, he pulled me tight to him and lay still, panting while his shaft throbbed inside me, releasing his essence into me.

I felt a small kiss at the base of my neck and heard a faint chuckle as he came back to himself. "You make me work hard, my lady."

I laughed in my turn and turned over so we could hold and look at each other. His face was relaxed, that faint strain gone from his eyes and his mouth. "Long enough for you this time?"

"No, it's never long enough."

I laughed to see his warm smile and hugged him close. "Am I too greedy?"

"Whatever I expected in a wife," he admitted, "it wasn't this."

"What did you expect in a wife?"

"At best?" He looked at me, his eyes saturated with love. "A partner. Someone who would help me to bear the station I had to fill. Someone who wouldn't be completely repellent in bed, who I could make children with. Someone I'd known most of my life, one of the girls from the families we're distantly related to." He kissed the tip of my nose. I lay still, listening to him. "Not someone I would want to stay with all night, every night. I knew I wouldn't be as...active as I had been as a single man, but I did expect to keep a mistress or two, and in return I would condone the occasional lover."

"So I can take a lover?"

He laughed. "Would you find the time? Aren't I enough for you?"

"You're a feast." I met his loving gaze, his eyes' usual cold blue suffused with warmth. "I can't imagine anyone coming close to what we do together, so what would be the point?"

Softly, he kissed me again, his lips only just meeting mine. "What we do is as different to what I did before you as that paste necklace is to the real thing. We make love. We turned what was a pleasurable activity into something almost spiritual."

"Isn't that blasphemous?"

"I don't think so," he replied seriously. "God made this for us, as he made everything else, so surely the act of procreation should be like this. I don't know. I know I love you, have always loved you, and will always do so."

"I love you too." There was a pause. "I never imagined it either. I wanted to be useful to someone, to find a friend, and if anyone had told me it would be you, I'd have been appalled." He chuckled. "I'd read about you, and before we went to Hareton Lizzie collected every piece of information she could find about you and Gervase. When I first met you, I was astonished and shocked by what I saw. I'd never seen anyone quite like you before."

"No one had," he commented. "But I'm like other men underneath it all, aren't I?"

I let my hand move down to touch him and heard his responsive sigh of pleasure. "How would I know? To me you're all men, all things. I didn't know if what we did in that nursemaid's room was normal, if I could expect that every time."

He paused and let himself relax into what I was doing for him. I moved my hand rhythmically, up and down, feeling the magic begin again as his shaft hardened under my fingers. "Did you know you were the first virgin I ever had?"

"How did you know how not to hurt me?"

I suppose I was naïve; he laughed. "You can read about it, and men do exchange knowledge about such things. Some even boast of their conquests."

"Did you?"

"I didn't need to. I merely made no secret of it." He smiled and touched my face with one finger, his breath catching in his throat when I firmed my grasp on him. "But that was before you. I took great care of you. I touched you, felt where I should go, what I should do, and I knew I must be gentle. Even then I hurt you."

I smiled back at him. "Not much. And what you've brought to me since makes up for it a hundredfold."

"Thank God the woman I fell in love with loves this as much as I do. Or do you? Is this all an act, to please me?"

He was teasing me, but I replied, "Do you think I'm that good an actress?" I let him go and swung myself on top of him, propping myself up on my elbows. I pushed my now-tangled hair back behind my ears. "I never expected this, but when we first met—no, the day after, when you were helpless and hurt—I saw the man beneath all the affectations, the finery. I wanted you although I didn't know it was desire. My body seemed to recognise you first."

He smiled and shifted a little under me, sliding his now-hardened member between my thighs, touching my cleft but not going any further. "And there you were in that hopelessly outmoded but obviously new riding habit, standing next to your sister who was so lovely she could make the sun come out at night, and I knew I wanted you, knew I had found you at last. I was horrified."

That made me laugh. "Did you fight it?"

"Not for long. You wouldn't let me. If you hadn't been so openly responsive, the moment might have passed and I might now be married to Julia Cartwright."

Even the name made me shudder. "Don't let's talk about her now."

"No." He looked at me, his gaze sweeping over what I was revealing for him, his smile telling me he was enjoying the sight. "I don't want to bring either my error in judgement or her noxious husband into our bed anymore. Let them do as they please, so long as they leave us alone."

I could do nothing but concur with that. I bent my head to kiss him, feeling his hand still on my breast crushed between us. I sat up, and his hand followed me. His other hand held my waist, and he lifted his knees, giving me something to lean on. I sat up and looked at him, decided to tease. "I was told tonight about some of your exploits."

His look never left mine. "Which ones?"

"When you seduced two rivals in a week and spurned them both at a ball."

He smiled reminiscently. I had not expected that, especially in this situation. "They deserved it. They had started their own book on which one could get me first, so I obliged. After I put a substantial wager on the winner. But she was only a winner by an hour or two."

"Don't you miss it?" I looked down at his face. I found it difficult to connect those stories with this person I knew so well.

"No," he answered immediately. "It was pleasure engendered from a mixture of boredom and desperation. I didn't care. You made me care."

"I didn't mean to."

"I know. But there's nothing to miss. I have so much here I can't imagine ever wanting anything else. You shouldn't listen to them."

"I want to know what you were like before."

He shook his head, serious now. "No, no you don't. I spent twelve angry years trying to destroy myself. I'm not angry anymore, I have all I want, and it fell into my life before I went looking for it."

I smiled and watched him. He lowered his eyes to look at my body and back up to my face again, taking his time, his loving gaze lingering on me. I delighted in the pleasure he took in me. "It's like they're talking about a stranger. I don't know that man."

"If you had known him, you'd never have taken me seriously. You'd have watched, as others watched, without coming close."

"I'd have run away. I didn't like hurt or distress and you went looking for it."

He frowned. "I wouldn't have let you. I love you too much to let you go." His face cleared as he looked up at me. He reached his hands up to hold my breasts. I moved into his hands and lifted, so he found his way back home. I sighed in contentment as I felt him fill me. Our immediate needs, the desperation was gone now. This was loving. "And now?"

"Now," he replied, "I don't care what anyone else does. I have you, and I mean to keep you. Whatever it takes, I'll take care of you and love you. Remember what I told you. This is love, this is making love, and whatever anyone else says can make no difference to this."

He began to move slowly, sensuously, and I responded, my movements an echo of his. I kept my eyes on his face and watched him until his hands slipped down to my waist and I leaned back against his knees, putting my hands behind his legs to pull myself onto him.

This always engendered some of the most intense feelings in me, and I cried out, hearing his murmur of "Yes, that's it, oh, my love, yes," from below me. I didn't stop moving, but I felt the waves engulfing me as they took me up, and I gasped his name as I reached the apogee of ecstasy.

I opened my eyes and saw him taking his pleasure from my joy. I determined to make him feel the same thing and began to move more insistently. I felt his response and watched it in him.

I loved his body, and I could see it clearly now. He was lean and firm, and because of his fair colouring, the fine downy hair that covered parts of his body hardly showed, but softened his skin to my touch. His chest was bare, but well muscled. The muscles flexed in his arms when he pulled me to him, the scar on the upper left arm gleaming in the candlelight. I laughed and moved over him, hearing his soft murmur as he responded to me.

I kept moving. I lifted myself off him so he could help us both reach the highest point of our loving. Both of us called out at the same moment, shaken by the same reaction, and wet warmth filled me once more.

I stayed there for a while, leaning back against his still upraised legs, and I opened my eyes and smiled at him. I leant forward and let myself sink into his arms so I could kiss him. "It's been so long," he said, his voice soft.

"We'll have to practise," I said back to him and heard his throaty chuckle.

"We might get it right one day."

A flicker alerted me to the fact the candles were beginning to gutter. I sat up again to light some of the fresh ones from the drawer before the old ones went out and I would be forced to use a tinderbox. I wanted to see him, memorise the loving expression he only showed to me in private.

Richard swung his legs out of the bed, presumably on his way to his dressing room, but he stopped halfway across the room. "I'll get us something to drink. I think there's some wine left in the sitting room." He picked up his robe and slipped his arms through the sleeves. He went out, and I got out of bed, the better to light the fresh candles. I replaced them all, on the nightstands, the dressing table and the mantelpiece, and went into my dressing room, finding everything quiet.

As I leaned over the washstand to wash my hands I looked up, and suddenly, in the tousle-haired woman in the mirror, I caught a glimpse of the girl I used to be—a sullen, confused person who withdrew more into herself the more hurts she received. No wonder Tom never realised how he felt about me. I hadn't been a figure anyone could have admired easily. Perhaps Richard's outré appearance had startled me into dropping my usual expression of sullen compliance, and he saw me as I should have been. As I was now.

I brushed my hair hard until it crackled, restoring it to some semblance of order, and turned to go back into the bedroom, hoping he would be waiting for me there.

Then, tearing through the tranquillity of the quiet house came the sound of two shots—and another two.

Chapter Nine

Panic-stricken, I looked around for my gown and realised I had left it in the bedroom. I hurtled through to my bedroom, seized my gown and was still thrusting my arms into the sleeves when I ran out of the room towards the sound. All I could think about was my child and getting to her safely.

"Here."

Someone else had been thinking. I grabbed the pistol from my maid and thrust it into one of the pockets.

To my relief I saw Richard as he too raced towards the source of the shattering noise, but at the sound of the bedroom door opening he turned and shouted to me, "Go back!"

"No." I carried on.

He waited for me and seized my shoulders when I caught up with him. "Go back. There might be danger."

"All the more reason I should come. What about Helen?"

"The shots came from the guest wing. Helen isn't there. I've sent a couple of footmen to safeguard her, just in case."

My relief was profound. I hadn't thought about the direction of the sounds, but he was right. The guest wing was a long way from the nursery, which was on a different floor and in the other direction. Since no more shots had followed the first ones, we could assume the danger was contained.

But I still wouldn't leave him alone. I was a fair shot. "I'm not going back."

I dipped my hand into the pocket of my gown and brought out my pistol.

Richard showed me the wicked stiletto in his hand. He cast a look over his shoulder as we saw doors open and other people come out of their rooms. "Just keep behind me and promise to go back the minute I tell you to." I heard the resignation in his voice when he realised I wouldn't wait in our room. I promised him that.

I met Lizzie as she came out of her room, becomingly attired in a ruffled dressing gown and lace cap. I noticed she'd stopped to find her slippers too, and wished I had mine. Richard and I were barefoot. "What's going on? What was that noise?"

"I don't know." I moved on, and she followed us.

The sound had come from over our heads, and I headed for the servants' quarters, fearing the worst. Richard was just in front of me.

At the foot of the stairs we heard a commotion, women screaming and men shouting, though I couldn't distinguish any individual voices. Carier pushed through the throng of people at the foot of the stairs and gasped, "This way, my lord."

"Is it safe for Rose?" Richard demanded, taking my hand.

"Yes, my lord, but it's not an edifying sight."

"You know me better than that, Carier." Keeping a firm grip on Richard's hand, I let him pull me through the people gathered at the stairs and climbed up, past more people. I was hard put to it to keep my dressing gown about me, as I hadn't had time to fasten it, and with such a press of people, it kept catching and pulling, but I kept my hand in Richard's, afraid I might lose him if I let go.

We made our way past the servants gathered outside the room and met a footman, one of Thompson's by his stoic demeanour. He was blocking access to the end of the corridor, where Hill was confined. Finally I managed to fasten my gown.

The shots had come in two pairs, so there must have been

more than one because I doubted there had been time in between the shots to reload the weapons.

On the ground, just behind the guard, was a man, blood spreading from the wounds on his chest and beginning to seep over the floor. It had already saturated his clothes. He sat, his body slumped to one side, as though he'd been standing against the door and had slid down it, confirmed by the trail of blood down the wall behind him.

Richard bent to lift the man's chin and look into his face. "It's Derring. One of my mother's footmen. He's worked for the family for years." Sadness coloured his voice. I lifted the skirts of my gown to stop it getting soiled with blood and looked at the poor man.

The door behind him stood open, so Richard stepped over the body and looked inside. He reached inside the room and handed out a folded blanket, which I took and shook out to cover the unfortunate Derring. The commotion outside was still going on, but inside there was a chill, not at all in keeping with the hot summer night. I pushed Richard and he moved aside to allow me entrance.

Hill was in bed. The light sheet had been thrown off him, and his nightshirt had ridden up, as they do in sleep, exposing his manhood grotesquely, though it was no good to him now. He'd flung one arm out and the fingers touched the floor. The other arm lay across his chest. The room was illuminated only by the full moon outside, and I thought Hill looked peaceful, lost in slumber.

Of course, the reality was different. The bleached-out colours were soon thrown into relief when Carier entered with a branch of candles, which he set on the table opposite the bed. The three of us studied the figure laid out on the bed in silence until Richard moved to lift the sheet over the lower part of the body, covering the exposed bottom half of the man and restoring some of his dignity.

He couldn't have been asleep when he'd been shot, he must

have been roused by the noise outside, as his eyes were open, staring ahead of him fixedly, but he hadn't had time to get out of bed. His assassin must have been upon him very quickly. I thought back to the time between the shots and wondered if he might have known his murderer, and that was why he hadn't risen from his bed.

He'd been shot through the head and the chest. The blood still flowed sluggishly, soaking the sheets under him. Richard shut the footman's eyes with steady hands. "Pride goeth before a fall."

I took Richard's hand, more for my comfort than for his. He seemed to come back to himself and turned his attention to me, his gaze sharp. He drew me to his side and looked up at Carier. "Find Nichols. I want my wife taken back to her room." Carier nodded, but as he turned, I saw Nichols at the door.

I looked at Richard wordlessly. "I promise I'll come soon," he said gently. "There's nothing you can do here, so go back to bed and try to rest." He turned to Nichols. "Perhaps her ladyship would like a hot drink."

Richard put his arm around my shoulders and led me to the door, giving me up to the care of my maid. I said nothing, but looked behind as I left and tried to smile. He watched me leave.

The crowd outside parted to let me pass, a hush falling over them that soon picked up again when I had gone. The cries and shouts had muted now to general talk, questions and speculation. The crowd of guests gathered at the bottom of the stairs talked. I didn't take it in at the time but I had never seen so many people in their nightclothes in one place at the same time before. It was the kind of trivial observation that sometimes intrudes when tragedy is present.

I halted and waited for silence. Lord Southwood, at the back of the crowd, watched me carefully, and I addressed my remarks to him, as the head of the house. "Two of the servants are dead. Richard is up there, but there's little anybody can do tonight." My voice shook, and I said no more.

I saw my father-in-law's nod of understanding and was relieved when he took control. "It seems there's nothing more we can do tonight," he announced, in a matter-of-fact tone.

A sharp, female voice cried, "We could be murdered in our beds!" Lady Kerre, of course.

"My son would have advised us if that were the case," said Richard's father. "If it would make you feel safer, there are locks and bolts on all the doors."

Lady Kerre burst into noisy tears, and suddenly I felt dizzy. I reached out my hand and Nichols was there, her arm about my waist, supporting me firmly. I felt someone else on my other side and recognised my sister Lizzie by touch alone. I kept my gaze fixed on the floor in front of me in an effort to steady myself. I wanted my daughter.

I set off before anyone could stop me, taking the stairs up to the next floor two at a time and racing to the nursery.

The nurse met me at the door, which was, as Richard had promised, guarded by two burly footmen. She put her finger to her lips and led me to the crib where Helen slumbered peacefully. I touched her cheek and left the room, going to the nurse's room to speak with her. "Nobody is to enter here without the express, written permission of myself or my husband," I said. "Nobody."

The nurse nodded her agreement. "I've locked the jib door, my lady. Nobody can get in here without using the main entrance." People often forgot the private servants' door. I was glad that she thought of it.

My daughter's safety assured, weakness swept over me, and I shuddered as I left the nursery. Lizzie and Nichols waited outside for me. They must have guessed where I was going.

They helped me back to my room where I sat on the edge of the bed and propped myself up with my hands, while I tried to regain my composure. Nichols lifted my feet and helped me onto the mattress, where I could lean against the pillows she banked up behind me. I soon began to feel better. Unthinkingly I loosened the fastenings on my gown and let it fall open. Nichols moved to help me take it off and covered me with the sheets, afterwards leaving the room.

Lizzie was looking at me in blank astonishment. "Rose," she said, in a voice higher than usual, "you're naked."

I had forgotten. "So I am. We usually sleep that way." Although it hadn't been exactly sleeping.

"And you share a bed every night?"

"Oh yes," I replied.

The practical side of Lizzie's character began to take hold. "Don't you get cold in the winter?"

"We have the fire, and each other. I can't say I've ever noticed."

"Rose, this is shocking, whatever would Martha say?" She didn't look shocked. She looked thrilled.

"Why do you think we never let anyone in the bedroom except Nichols and Carier?" Shock added irritation to my voice.

She looked at me doubtfully. "I'm not sure I'd like that kind of intimacy."

"I would find it difficult to live without it."

"You've changed, Rose."

"I have," I agreed. For the better. "I've never been so happy. I'm loved and cared for, and I love and care for someone else."

I remembered my resolution earlier in the evening. Anything rather than think of that awful room upstairs. "Lizzie, are you fond of the Marquês?"

She blushed, dropped her gaze and looked up again, staring at me icily. "Yes."

"You're sure?"

"I'm sure," she said, and after a pause added, "so is he."

A thought struck me when I remembered how soon Richard and I had managed to find our way to a bed together. I sat up and hugged my knees. "Do you think you would like this kind of intimacy with him?"

Her blush deepened, so I persisted. "Have you already?"

"I wouldn't do anything so foolish."

"I did," I reminded her.

"It passes my understanding how you ever let him do such a thing. He seduced every woman in society—"

"Only the married ones."

She glared daggers at me. "But I do feel strongly for him." She didn't mean Richard.

"Does James know?"

"Martha does. I met the Marquês in London first, and Martha noticed my particularity at once."

I remembered my courting days. "Martha misses very little." My motherly sister-in-law had monitored my courtship as carefully as she could, despite having to cope with her new station in life and the rest of the household. She would do the same with Lizzie.

"What do you know about him?" I asked her bluntly.

"Only what he's told me." She shot me a sharp look. "You're making enquiries, aren't you?"

I was spared the necessity of making a response by the entrance of Nichols, bearing a tray with two glasses of hot milk. She set one beside me and one on the little table at Lizzie's elbow. Then she took up a hairbrush and calmly began to put my hair to rights. I leaned forward to make her task easier and the sheet slipped down, exposing my breasts. It didn't concern me, as Lizzie had certainly seen my body over the years. Nichols finished my hair and left the room, and I reached for my glass of milk.

Richard came back. He stopped on the threshold, lifting a surprised eyebrow at Lizzie, but smiled and bowed before coming over to the bed and taking the hand I reached up to him. "I was stupidly weak, Richard. I'm fine now. I checked on Helen, but afterwards, I felt dizzy. It's only a momentary foolishness."

"I checked on her too." He smiled reassurance. "She slept through everything. I'm ordering the men to remain at her door until we're certain the danger is over." He searched my face visually, anxiously examining my expression. "Whatever my mother thinks, you're not getting up for breakfast tomorrow. Or rather, today." He picked up his watch from the nightstand, commenting, "Nearly three." As he straightened up he lifted the sheet and pulled it over me, smiling with amusement. "Spare Lizzie's blushes, my love."

I looked at Lizzie, and she had indeed turned a dull brick red. I knew them both so well I'd forgotten they didn't know each other very well. I grinned ruefully. "Drink your milk," I told her. She buried her nose in her glass.

Richard left the room, returning with the decanter he had been on his way to fetch when we'd heard the shots. Neither Lizzie nor I wanted any, so he poured out one glass for himself. "Now I'll tell you what happened, then I'll walk you back to your room, Lizzie."

"What if someone sees you?"

"I'll call Carier or Nichols as well. She mustn't go back to her room alone."

Lizzie looked indignant, but she realised the sense of what he said. It was nearly three in the morning, and she was in her night things. Richard's reputation being what it was, scurrilous stories might circulate quicker than the morning papers. She smiled ruefully instead. "I only came to help Rose."

Richard gave her a warm smile. "I greatly appreciate it. She looks in much better spirits now." He turned his attention to me. "Do you want to hear any more about this tonight, or would you like to leave it until the morning?"

"Just a little more." I didn't want any more, but I knew I had to hear. I was ashamed of my weakness, so I tried to ignore it.

"Well then." Richard took a large gulp of his drink and put

down the glass. "Derring was shot with a pair of guns that are no longer on the scene. One of the bullets passed right through him and into the wall. It's the size of shot you'd find in a pistol. The murderer must have taken the weapons away with him, since we haven't found them. That meant the pistols the murderer carried were useless, having been discharged, but he acquired Derring's weapons before he entered. We can presume that Hill sat up in bed in alarm. He was shot with Derring's weapons; we found them on the floor, behind the bed." He paused, his expression grave. "Both the bodies are decently covered, and I've left a couple of armed guards there, with instructions *not* to sleep." He picked up his glass and finished his wine without a tremor. "And there we must leave it until the morning."

A knock came on the door. Richard glanced at us and answered it himself. After a murmured conversation, he opened the door to reveal the Marquês. The man entered and bowed to me and then to Lizzie, his dark eyes warming at the sight. Lizzie, dressed for the day in her best silks, was a sight to behold, but like this, her hair tousled around her shoulders, wearing a night rail and loose silk wrapper, she could be said to appear positively seductive. The Marquês, in a brocaded banyan which reached down to his ankles, his short, dark hair free of wig or cap, also showed to advantage.

He crossed the room and took her hand. "You are well?"

I exchanged a look with Richard, my brow raised. He smiled back and nodded.

"I will take you safely back to your room. I don't wish you to return on your own with a murderer around." He glanced at Richard. "I mean no offence. It is the truth."

"Yes it is, and we regret it deeply. We will find whoever did this."

The Marquês turned back to Lizzie. "I do not doubt it."

Nichols came in. Although she was also in her night things, she was perfectly decent, a large cap covering her hair and a practical, heavy dressing gown covering the rest of her, despite the warm night.

"Miss Golightly needs to go back to her room," Richard told her. "The Marquês will escort her. And I want the doors to this suite locked tonight and the keys removed from the housekeeper's room—I won't subject her ladyship to any danger."

Nichols curtseyed and left the room. Lizzie kissed me good night before she left with the Marquês. They made a very handsome couple.

When Nichols returned, she put a set of keys into Richard's hand. "I couldn't see any others missing, my lord."

Richard took them with a word of thanks and dismissed her.

Once we were alone, after locking the door he threw off his robe and came to bed. He folded his arms around me, but then he drew back to look at my face. "My love, you're trembling."

I couldn't help it. "I'm sorry. It's so missish."

He put his hand on the back of my head, much as I had seen him do when he held Helen. "I don't think it's at all missish. You saw something particularly gruesome tonight."

"I've seen things like that before." I tried hard to keep my voice steady, but failed miserably.

He held me while I wept and made soothing noises. "It's shock, my precious, just shock. I knew I shouldn't have let you see."

"No, no!" I cried through my tears, "I won't be treated like a weak woman, please, Richard. I don't know why it should have affected me like that, and I don't think it will happen again."

"I might know." He stroked my hair with one hand and kept the other arm tightly about me. "You saw those men walk around the house, thought nothing of their presence. To see their lives snuffed out so quickly is always a shock. I want—need—to care for you. I don't want you affected like this."

My tears were subsiding now, and I sniffed, regaining control. I eased away from him and reached across to my nightstand for my handkerchief. I sat up, blew my nose and wiped my eyes. Richard slipped out of bed and went to his dressing room, returning with a cool, damp cloth he insisted on holding to my eyes. The coolness helped.

I took the cloth away and gave it to him. He dropped it on his side of the bed. "I'll probably put my foot on that in the morning," he said in a resigned tone, and moved to take me back into his arms.

I settled my head comfortably on his shoulder. "Truly, my love, it was only a moment of weakness, nothing more." I looked up and met his eyes. "Do you think there is any danger?"

"I don't think there's a madman with a fresh brace of pistols stalking the corridors of Eyton. If I thought that, we'd be on our way to Oxfordshire now, despite the late hour. I think the murderer achieved everything he—or she—set out to do, but there's no harm in locking a few doors until we're sure."

"I think so too." I paused. "Richard—"

"Yes?"

"I'm sorry this evening turned out as it did."

"Not as sorry as I am. But we have other nights." His voice was soft, full of tenderness, and I saw it reflected in his eyes.

"More than Derring or Hill can say."

"Sadly, it is." He let me go, got out of bed again, and pinched the candles out until there was only one left. He got back into bed by its dim light, and finally extinguished that one too. We were left in the dark with the faint smell of beeswax drifting about us, and I held him close. To my surprise, I heard him chuckle. "I was only thinking of your naturalness in front of your sister and myself. Didn't you realise what you were showing her?"

"She's seen me naked hundreds of times before—Oh." But not in the marital bed, and not so comfortable with my husband. Very few people of our station slept together and not many were so familiar with each other's naked bodies.

"Yes. Another witness to our jealously guarded privacy."

"Do you mind?"

"Not if you don't. Lizzie may be a gossip, but like all good gossips, she knows when to keep quiet. If it had been Louisa Crich now..."

I finished the sentence for him. "It would be all around London as soon as she reaches it."

"Before that. She can write, you know."

"Lizzie won't say anything," I assured him.

I felt his fingers under my chin as he gently pushed it up to kiss me. "Good night, my love. I'll be here when you wake."

"I know. Good night."

Richard had risen before I awoke the next day, and Nichols brought a tray in for me shortly after. Richard came in as I was still eating, and I poured him some coffee. "You're an angel," he declared, taking the cup from me and dropping into the chair opposite.

"A fully recovered one. So what have you been doing while I was sleeping the morning away?"

He sighed. "My father has sent for the constable, and we've agreed to leave things as they are for him to see, but we'll have them put to rights later this afternoon. We've sent messengers to Hill's and Derring's families, so we can expect them to arrive soon."

"What about the other guests?"

He put a hand to his forehead.

"Shall I say?" I thought it might give him a little respite, and I could guess how it had gone. "Correct me if I'm wrong. Some are still in their rooms. The Kerres want to leave. Freddy has asked you if he can help." I paused while I called the other guests to mind. "Louisa and Sir Willoughby want to leave, and I don't know about the Marquês. Ian and Amery probably haven't noticed."

At least I had made him smile. "Perceptive woman. Mostly right, my love, but Sir Willoughby seems fascinated by it all and has offered to help, and the Marquês has also asked for my advice. I want them all to stay until we know who has done this."

"Have you sent to Alicia Thompson?"

"It was the first thing I did. I sent a rider, so he should be there late tonight or tomorrow morning, ostensibly to send two more footmen, but she'll send two men from the box as temporary cover." The box was where we kept the names of the special people, the servants loyal to us first, who would perform any task, within reason, that Richard asked of them. "I've asked for Sharman and Cole, two brawny fellows with brains as well, but I don't know if they're available."

He put down his cup, leaned back and closed his eyes, so after I had refilled the cup for him, I threw on my gown and put my hands on his temples, rubbing them gently for him. Then I tried to ease his tight shoulder muscles.

He opened his eyes and smiled his thanks. "You make everything much more bearable."

"It's what I'm here for," I replied. "I'll get dressed and do what I can."

"Are you sure you're up to it?"

"Of course I am. It was only a moment of silliness."

He put one hand up to cover mine. "Not silly at all. Shock affects all of us from time to time."

He dropped his hand and shut his eyes while I tried to ease away his tension. "We should go to see Helen."

"I'd like that. I'll wait until you're dressed and we'll go together."

I left him to his coffee and went to find something to wear. Nichols found a gown of pale blue silk for me. It didn't take long to wash and dress. She even tamed my hair in record time, so I was back with Richard within the half-hour.

He'd fallen asleep, his head propped on his high-backed chair. The coffee had gone cold. I was tempted to leave him there, but I knew there was too much to do, so I touched his arm. His eyes opened. "We'll have an early night tonight."

He raised his eyebrows. "When we have early nights I seem to get less sleep." He held out his hand to me.

I took it. He got to his feet. "I've managed on less sleep, but the rest was very welcome. Shall we go and see Helen?"

After a welcome respite with our daughter, we were descending the main stairs to the great hall, thinking we should consult with Lord Southwood, when the cacophony of voices told us he was there. Two voices, raised in argument, one of them his lordship's, the other one unknown.

We saw them when we rounded the bend in the stairs. Two men, one in the expensive attire of the man of fashion, the other in a homespun coat and bob-wig, but both with angry, red faces and open mouths, neither waiting for the other to finish speaking. The noise was dreadful. They were making so much noise they didn't hear our approach.

We waited once we had reached them, and eventually Lord Southwood stopped trying to drown out the other man. The one voice remaining wasn't about to give up easily, though, and continued for a while until he realised nobody was listening.

"My son and daughter-in-law, Lord and Lady Strang," announced my father-in-law. "This is Mr. Hampson, the constable."

The man bowed and we acknowledged it. "You should know my wife has a dislike of angry voices," Richard said mildly, thus putting both of them in the wrong and forcing them to beg my pardon. The difference in station wasn't apparent in their apologies; both were sheepish.

I held my hand out for Mr. Hampson to bow over. "Was there a problem?" I asked, as sweetly as I could manage.

Lord Southwood cast a dark look in the constable's

direction. "He wants all the servants gathered in the kitchens so he can interview them about the unfortunate events of last night."

I retrieved my hand. "I see. Won't that be difficult, with dinner being prepared and the household going about their duties?"

Lord Southwood answered with admirable economy. "Impossible."

I turned to the constable. "Mr. Hampson, we know you must do your duty, but shall we take this in order? Wouldn't you like to see the—scene first? Then, if we release servants from their duties six or so at a time, would that do?"

"My lady, one of them could easily give me the slip that way," the man protested.

Richard took a hand. "Not if Patterson supervises it. He has a register of all the servants presently at Eyton."

Hampson looked from Richard to Lord Southwood and back again. The situation must be difficult for him. He had to investigate this matter properly, but was at a distinct disadvantage here. It must be like stepping into a small kingdom. Richard suggested a course of action to him. "As you can imagine, my mother is anxious to restore the situation to more like normal."

"It's been left as it was?" Mr. Hampson seemed incredulous.

"It did happen in the middle of the night, and in any case, we thought you might prefer to see it as we found it. We have dropped blankets over the corpses, but this weather is too sultry to leave them for much longer. The maids need to clean up." Richard was calm. Now Hampson's feet were set on the path, it seemed inevitable he should follow, but Richard had made it possible for him to do it without loss of face.

A footman was despatched with the constable to show him the way. We watched him go, clumping up the stairs in his heavy outdoor shoes. "We'd better get a housemaid to clean those stairs." White marble wouldn't have been my choice, and

Hampson's shoes, fresh from the great outdoors, made their mark.

"That should keep him busy," Richard remarked when the official was out of earshot, and he turned to his father. "What did you tell him about the necklace, sir?"

"Just that the man had been found in possession of a valuable piece of jewellery belonging to one of the guests here," his father replied, in milder tones. He had a virulent temper, but it was soon over. That display in the hall had been power rather than temper, because in his rages, everyone except Richard was afraid of him, and Richard was only courageous in the blast because he didn't care.

Richard nodded. "It's all he needs to know—why the man was being held."

Lord Southwood humphed. "He had the effrontery to ask why we hadn't sent for him before."

"Did you answer him?"

"Of course not." Lord Southwood looked surprised we had to ask.

Richard smiled at the predictable response. "I thought not. He'll ask again. He looks like a persistent kind of man."

"Either this one takes his job seriously or he's making the most of his access to this house."

Richard grimaced. "We'll have to see. Meantime, I've sent enquiries to London, and we should know more soon. Also for some footmen for you. You'll be feeling the want of them."

Lord Southwood stared at both of us in silence. We suffered his scrutiny until he said abruptly, "Come with me," and he led the way to the back of the hall and into the estate office.

Neat stacks of papers covered the large rent table, but no one worked on them today. Lord Southwood found me a chair, the only upholstered one in the room, presumably where the steward sat when he received visits from the tenants. Richard sat on a hard chair set near to the window, and Lord Southwood found himself a similar chair on the other side of the desk.

"I know you two are together on this, and I know you mean to make yourself busy, Strang, but I'd like to be kept well-informed this time." Richard, considering his father closely, merely nodded. "I need to know well in advance if there's any scandal to be scotched. We can't have Gervase's entry to Parliament in November overshadowed by family scandal. God knows we've had enough of that."

"But now your two prodigal sons have returned respectable and—in one case at least—wealthy." Richard's soft voice filled the small room. "I understand your concerns, sir, and this time I share them. If I discover anything that directly concerns the family, you'll know it first." He paused and glanced at me. "Or second," he added, smiling briefly. I returned the smile.

Lord Southwood sighed, but it wasn't a sigh of sentiment. It sounded more like exasperation to me. "Can we be frank? We're all thinking that Sir Barnett and his family have more to do with this affair than we would like. Are we not?" He glared at us challengingly.

Richard let silence fall before he replied. "I'm afraid so. It seems self-evident." I bowed my head to show I concurred with this. "Hill used to work for Sir Barnett," Richard continued, "and yet they haven't mentioned that once, as though they want us to forget it." Lord Southwood lifted an eyebrow but said nothing. "The necklace belonged to Lady Kerre, and why else would someone want to kill Hill? It must have been something to do with the necklace."

"I thought you were going too far last night at dinner," his father commented grimly.

"It was deliberate, sir. I knew there was more to that business than a simple theft, and I wanted to confirm it." His face grew more serious. "Although now I wish to God I hadn't."

It was spoken calmly, but I knew the torment he must be going through inside, and I was angry with myself for not noticing it before. However, he wouldn't want to talk about this in front of his father, so I stayed silent, resolving to speak about it to him later. I smoothed the silk of my dress, an action I couldn't rid myself of when I was disturbed. Richard glanced at my hand and away again.

Lord Southwood didn't notice, but he did mark the last statement. "I did think it was somewhat rash at the time, but no one could have foreseen such a bloody result." He leaned forward and rested his elbows on the table. Despite his relatively lowly position, his air of absolute authority could never be mistaken.

I couldn't imagine what to do. "If they are involved, what can we do? We can't conceal something as serious as this."

They turned their heads to stare at me, a most unnerving prospect. "We don't have to make it public," said Richard. His father stayed silent, but didn't look as though he disagreed.

This situation illustrated the difference between us, my sort, the gentry, who worked within the community and to improve matters locally, including supporting the law, and the aristocracy who preferred to deal with their wrongdoers themselves, who didn't understand that it could be anybody's business but their own. I'd have to make up my mind which side I was on, and I knew without even thinking about it that it would have to be the same side as Richard. If I couldn't persuade him, I'd have to accept it, but for the first time, I felt apart from him, not wholly in accord.

"So you think Sir Barnett or another of his family could have done this?" I asked.

Richard sighed and touched his brow with one elegant hand. "Yes, I think it's highly likely."

His father echoed the sigh. "I agree. And after you and Gervase, Sir Barnett is the heir to Southwood. What do we do if the constable looks as if he's getting close to the solution?" Risking public exposure and damaging scandal.

"I don't think that will happen," Richard said. "We told him the necklace has been returned to its owner, but that leaves him without a reason for the killings. We must give him one."

Lord Southwood grunted. "Can't we just send him away?"

"He won't give up easily, that one," Richard said grimly. "Rose, you're an excellent judge of character, what do you think?"

He nonplussed me by his direct consultation. I didn't know my hand was at work on my gown again until I looked down and saw it. I stopped at once. "I think he's a man who takes his position seriously. Toadying is the last thing he would do. If he feels he has any opposition, he will set himself up against it, just on principle."

The two men looked at me again, then at each other. Richard smiled. "Didn't I say she was good?"

"You did," said his father, a speculative expression on his face when he looked at me. It was probably the first time he had seen me as anything other than a brood mare. "Very succinct, very pertinent. I begin to think you'll make an excellent Countess, my dear."

"Not for a long time I hope," I said.

"That kind of summation of character can be very useful," said his lordship.

I could do nothing but thank him. A footman knocked and entered the room. "Mr. Hampson asked if he could see you, my lord."

"Do you want us to stay?" Richard asked.

Lord Southwood nodded. "If you don't mind."

When the constable was shown in, it was to a room where we were, to all intents and purposes, attending to estate affairs. Lord Southwood had produced a pair of spectacles from somewhere and had a paper in his hand. He took the spectacles off and put the paper back down, looking enquiringly at the man. He made one bow to all of us.

"I have seen the bodies, my lady, my lords, and extracted everything I can from them." That sounded distinctly unpleasant.

"What do you make of it?" asked Lord Southwood.

"For one thing, either a pair of guns are missing, or the pair that were found on the scene were reloaded," the constable replied.

"What difference would that make?" drawled Richard, once again every inch the bored aristocrat. He took out his snuffbox and went through the elaborate charade of taking snuff. Mr. Hampson couldn't take his eyes off him, but Richard decided not to notice.

Eventually Hampson tore his eyes away from the exquisite performance and gave his attention to Lord Southwood. "It means someone must have gone to the room with loaded guns, ready. Someone went there with the intent of killing those men."

"Why not take four guns?" demanded Lord Southwood.

The constable shrugged. "Perhaps he didn't expect the other man to be there." This was a very good point. Although he knew the room was guarded, the murderer might not have expected the guard to be either armed or incorruptible. It might have been a she.

"Do you think the assassin was crossed in love?" Richard was deliberately obtuse now. "Perhaps a jealous lover shot him."

"I saw no evidence of that." Hampson met Richard's innocent gaze. "You say the man was under guard because he had stolen a valuable item, my lord?"

"Yes, that's right, but the piece has been returned to its rightful owner."

"Who would that have been?"

Without a tremor, Lord Southwood replied, "My wife."

I couldn't understand why he had said that at first, but after a moment, I understood. It would leave the Kerres to us, take his attention away from them.

Hampson lifted his chin. "I was told the necklace belonged

to one of the Kerres."

"We *are* Kerres," Lord Southwood reminded him.

Hampson frowned doubtfully, but he obviously didn't want to accuse his lordship of being a liar. "Did everyone know the piece was returned?"

Before his father could reply, Richard chipped in. He crossed his legs, creating a rustle of cloth that attracted attention and, as though he had all the time in the world, he drawled, "Servants come and go all the time. If Hill did have an accomplice, he may not have known the piece was back where it belonged."

Hampson shot him a sharp glance, but Richard returned his gaze blandly. "That had occurred to me also."

My husband gave him a gentle smile. "So pleased to be of help."

"So you think I should look for an accomplice?" Hampson, looking suspicious still.

"You must do as you please, as long as you find out who has done this dreadful thing." Richard seemed to lose interest in the matter, turning his head to gaze out of the window.

I smiled at Hampson, but I didn't make it too friendly. After all, this was my family now. "Is Patterson arranging for you to interview the servants?"

"Yes, your ladyship. I will see them in the butler's room downstairs."

"Very good. Do you need someone to show you the way?"

"No, my lady." He took his cue and left, after bowing to us.

Richard turned back from his contemplation of the outdoors. "Lizzie is taking a walk with her Marquês, and her maid isn't too close behind them." I frowned. "My love, you can hardly complain. We shook off as many servants as we could while we were courting."

His father cleared his throat. "You could hardly keep your hands off each other."

I blushed; Richard laughed. "But you've had your reward, sir. And there might be more to come, who knows?" He didn't look at me, but I was acutely embarrassed. I'd lost my parents years ago, but this wasn't the way I'd have talked to them.

Lord Southwood saw nothing amiss but made a kind of "humph" noise I took to be approval.

Richard smiled at me, a particularly warm smile Lord Southwood must have seen. "Sir, I think I can put the man off the scent."

Lord Southwood stared at his son without expression. "How?"

Richard leaned back in the hard chair, as much at ease as if he were sitting in his own drawing room. "We'll tell him one of the servants has gone off. If we're subtle enough, Hampson will assume the man was an unknown assailant and infiltrated himself into the household without our noticing."

"Your mother would have noticed."

"We don't have to tell him that."

"No." They stared at each other for a time, assessingly.

It was only then that the resemblance between them struck me. Facially Richard and Gervase favoured their mother, with the angular features, the startling blue eyes. But there was a distinct resemblance in the attitudes of the men, and the details of their physical appearance. They shared the same shape of nose, for example.

I wondered what our son, if we had one, would look like. Suddenly I longed to find out. I knew it was a little too soon after the birth of Helen, but I wanted to do it again, to see another miracle. But I would have to be patient for a while yet. Richard wouldn't allow my health to suffer by bearing children too close together.

Lord Southwood took a deep breath. "That should work. You'd better see to it."

Richard stood, so did I, and we left together. Outside, he gave me a quizzical glance. "You're going to find Lizzie, aren't you?"

"I'm going to try."

"Such a prude." He laughed softly. "It didn't do us any harm."

"We don't know anything about the Marquês."

"We will soon. Meantime, can't you leave her to her flirtation? After all, you knew more about me than was good for you, and that didn't deter you."

I had to admit the truth of that. "I suppose you're right. I shall go and do something useful."

He paused, more serious now. "I think we have something to discuss. You weren't wholly in accord with us there, were you?"

"I had my doubts, but I have no right to doubt you." I had promised to obey him once.

"You have every right. Can you go upstairs in a little while? Order some coffee and I'll join you in about an hour."

I agreed, and he went off to find the servants he intended to bribe.

Chapter Ten

For the first time, I felt uneasily apprehensive waiting for my husband, and I fortified myself with a small glass of brandy. I was determined not to fall out with him, but I needed to get these things sorted out in my mind, or they would eventually come between us. Perhaps this was how many couples managed, with private disagreements smoothed over in public, but I didn't want to become like that. I would do my best to prevent it.

When Richard entered the room, he waited until I poured his coffee before he said anything. He studied me closely, ignoring the cup I set on the small table by his side. "You're doubtful about this, aren't you?"

I took a breath. "Yes. I'm sorry."

"Don't be. You have every right. It was what we were talking about the other night, the differences in our backgrounds." He picked up the cup and drank a deep draught of the steaming liquid.

"I suppose so." I remained standing, trying not to twist my hands together. "It's just—I was brought up to respect the law, and the men who upheld it. If such a thing had happened, we'd have called in the authorities and asked them for discretion, not—not—" I broke off, lost for words.

He wasn't. "Lying to them," he finished for me. I nodded miserably. He drank his coffee before he said anything else. "How do I explain?"

"You know I won't say anything—" I began, but he interrupted me.

"That's not the point. I want matters understood between us. No lies, no misunderstandings, Rose. We won't always agree, who does? But I want you to know why, and that it's not some form of ingrained superiority. *Droit du seigneur*, if you like." He looked at me again, his eyes sharply observant.

I sat in the chair opposite and folded my hands in my lap. "In my father's case it's what he's been used to all his life. Since the Commonwealth, we know it's important everyone is seen to be equal in rights and under the law, but we're not. However much you want it, it's not true. People look to us, the aristocracy, not for an example, but for excitement and scandal. They *want* us to fail. When we do, it's trumpeted around the kingdom, and we're never allowed to forget it. Remember how easy it was for you to find out about me from your fastness in Devonshire when you knew you were going to meet me." He paused, waiting for confirmation. I managed a nod. "And not everything about me was true. If you'd believed all that, you wouldn't be here now."

"I remember." My voice was too thready. "But this has happened; don't we owe the families of the victims some justice?"

His face shadowed. "We owe them a great deal. But not their reputation and ours dragged through the papers and scandal sheets. If Kerres were involved, it will be dealt with. Justice will be done."

"How? Do we kill them ourselves?"

He shook his head grimly, staring at his hands. "If need be." He lifted his head and met my steady gaze. "Have you forgotten what we did in Devonshire?"

I sighed heavily and wished I could have kept my doubts to myself. "I can never forget that."

"I told you at the time it left its own scars, but sometimes it has to be done. The law doesn't always do it."

"What do you mean?"

He seemed to speak easier now the subject didn't directly concern him. This, criminal justice, was a subject that interested him, had for many years. "The law is a mess. The sentences are clear-cut; you can be hung for stealing a loaf of bread, or a diamond necklace, or for murder. But it doesn't happen like that in practice. First, there's the benefit of clergy. If a condemned person can read a preset piece, he or she might be excused their first offence. Some can fool a judge for three or four such offences before someone recognises them. If there have been too many hangings recently, the sentence will change to transportation or the charges reduced to allow something lesser to take place. Too many hangings are as bad as too few." He leaned back in his chair and met my eyes again. "Someone arrested for a minor offence might perish in jail. Jail fever is a terrible thing. Judges can catch it, and it's killed some."

I shuddered, and he smiled, but there wasn't any amusement there. "The law is haphazard to say the least. It's the injustice of the law of our land that drives me on, it kept me going when I had nothing else, to work for a better system, true justice. If someone steals your valuables, it's up to you to bring the prosecution. That leads to terrible injustice and is one of the reasons smuggling is so rife. Sometimes it's best to circumvent the official channels to bring the required result. If we hadn't done what we did in Devonshire, Eustacia Terry and her mother would have been condemned publicly and lost all their belongings. They'd be left destitute."

"It might have saved us much trouble," I said, remembering Eustacia's games in London last year.

"But she had the right to create that trouble," he replied gently. "I don't do this for my own good, my love."

I didn't know what to say. I had to persevere. He might not want to discuss this again. To give myself time I picked up the coffeepot and poured out two more cups. He smiled his thanks when I put the cup by his side again, but he didn't attempt to touch me. I was glad of it. I didn't want to be reminded of what we had shared last night. Not now.

"You know how it affects me, to take a life," he said.

I looked into his face. I saw no subterfuge there. He was open to me, allowing me to see him as he was, no masks, no pretence. "You suffer. I'm glad I'm there for you. But shouldn't we all abide by the same rules?"

"That's what I believe too, but the law doesn't bring it, does it? I think that's the nub of my argument. Every case should be dealt with in the same way; everyone should be the same under the law. It's a naïve hope, I know that, but it's a philosophy my simple mind can grasp, and strive for."

At last, something we agreed on. I sighed in relief as though a physical weight had been lifted from my shoulders. If the fundamental belief was the same, we could work at it, come to an understanding. "Can't we improve it from within?"

"It's one way, but I haven't the patience to persevere in that way. I can't spend years toiling away in Parliament while people suffer. I'm hoping Gervase will help me, but he has his own concerns. He's seen different kinds of injustices, in the financial world, and he hopes to reform them."

"Really? I hadn't realised, I'll have to talk to him about them."

"Another of your concerns, my love?" He too must have seen the common ground, for he looked more at ease now, and his smile was softer.

I shook my head in response to his question. "No. It's something I know scandalously little about, and maybe I should know more."

"Taking your studies seriously?" He put down his cup. "Do you remember once I said to you that you should be yourself?" I nodded. "It was true and it still is. I'm delighted you want to discuss this with me, pleased you don't take my word for everything. I need someone to do that, and no one has done it before now. This is part of sharing, my love. Never stop. I've always considered the responsibilities I'm expected to undergo a burden. When I was little, I used to pray I'd wake up and find myself the younger twin, but it never happened. With you as my partner, suddenly it doesn't seem so bad."

He stood and held out his hands to me. I rose to join him and laid my hands in his. "I'm very lucky," I told him. "I want to share, to be useful, but many husbands deny that to their wives. I'm your property in law. I never belong to myself, you can do almost anything to me, and you choose to share." I met his gaze full on. "I've always said I'll love you whatever you do, and God help me it's true, but now I've seen a little more of the world, I think love can be killed, can't it?"

"Yes it can. Men take lovers to humiliate their wives. They beat them and despise them, even though some of them had a good beginning. Their words are discounted and they are nothing but pretty accessories. It's partly carelessness, partly thoughtlessness, partly arrogance. I promised myself that when I won you I wouldn't do that. It's good to hear I'm succeeding."

I smiled up at him. "I told Lizzie last night I've never been so happy, and I meant it. I don't care who knows, but like you I don't want to advertise it to everyone."

He pulled me closer and kissed me very gently. "So we have some agreement? Can you live with what I do, so long as it's just and fair? Will you promise to tell me when it isn't, when you see something wrong?"

"If you want me to."

"Always." He drew me to him and held me. "Always."

With my head on his shoulder I could say with truth, "I think we've found something here we can work with. I don't feel so troubled anymore."

I drew back, and we looked at each other, taking pleasure in what we saw. "But your father will do this for the family."

"For dynastic imperatives," he confirmed. "The reputation of the family must be kept clean, at all costs. Of course, there is something else."

"What's that?"

"I would hate to see you dragged through the mire. This isn't a family imperative. I want to protect what I love most in the world. If this were to come to court, we would be in the public eye, and you'd hate that."

"We could always go back to Venice and live quietly for a while," I said with a smile.

His returning smile carried memories. "I have every intention of going back there. One day."

"One day," I agreed. I had it with me always.

We were about to leave the room when a soft knock fell on the door. Carier came in at Richard's "Enter." He was carrying a cloth bag, and he didn't look too pleased, so we sat again and waited to hear what he had to say.

His bow was perfunctory. "My lady, my lord. We've been clearing up upstairs. I thought I should oversee it, and it's as well I did." He opened the bag and slowly drew out two pistols. He laid them on the small table at Richard's elbow. "It seems, my lady, my lord, we may have the murder weapons. I discovered these a little further along the corridor, in an empty water can. The murderer must have tossed them away after the deed for fear of being caught with the weapons in hand."

Richard handed me one of the pistols and picked up the other himself. They were a good pair, silver mounted and of excellent quality.

Richard turned the flintlock over in his hands, examining it closely. "King's," he said when he read the maker's name. "London. That tells us nothing of any use. They could have been stolen from a guest, used by a guest or brought in to be used."

"Do you recognise them?"

Richard looked at the pistol again and shook his head. "No. I certainly haven't a pair like these, and I don't remember seeing any in the house either. I think they must belong to one of the guests. Carier?"

He held up the weapon. Carier took it, and the one I was holding. "You've cleaned them," Richard commented.

"Yes, my lord, I could see nothing to be gained in leaving them as they were. They have been well looked after; they only needed a wipe to remove the"—he looked over at me doubtfully—"blood. The man was murdered at fairly close range, so they were soiled."

I smiled to reassure him. "I've not changed, Carier. It was only a moment of weakness. The bullet hit a blood vessel?" Carier nodded. I had seen a vessel pierced by a pitchfork before—the blood could spray a considerable distance.

"I'm extremely glad to hear it, my lady." Although Carier's vocal range was limited, I knew he meant it. I'd proved an able assistant to him in the past when he'd been called upon to minister to the injured. Still, I was glad to rid myself of the flintlock, which until recently had been resting close to the body of a dead man.

"They're very good quality," Richard commented. "I'd like to wager there's an empty case somewhere."

Carier considered the problem, a deep crease furrowing his brow. "I will set a search in place. Since we can restrict the search, it shouldn't be too long. I can have it done while you are at dinner tonight, if that is satisfactory."

"Perfectly," Richard answered. "Meanwhile, would you like to lock them up in my safe? The ball is tomorrow and there'll be any number of strangers and their servants milling about."

"Yes, my lord." The admirable man exited quietly.

Richard turned to me. "That was an unexpected stroke of luck. I think it excludes the servants unless one of them stole the pistols." He resumed his seat.

I remained standing, thinking. "But why didn't the owner of the pistols not say they were missing?"

He leaned back in his chair and smiled. "That, my love, is why I need you so much. I was thinking much the same, but you were quicker to articulate it. Either they haven't been missed, or the owner hoped the loss would go unnoticed. I'd guess whoever it was didn't expect there to be a guard set on two dead bodies. Perhaps he—"

"Or she," I put in, loath to let my own sex go unnoticed.

"Indeed," he agreed. "Or she. It might have been sheer, blind panic. The job done, the murderer leaves the scene and only later realises what has been left there."

"So whoever did it wasn't used to murder."

He smiled in genuine amusement. "Who is? Yes, my sweet, I know what you mean, there's no need to elaborate. I think we should ask all the guests to check their gun cases, but not yet. Let Carier look first, and we'll see."

I had to agree with him. It was so important to find out where the pistols had come from. They were fine examples and must surely have been missed, so their absence was being concealed for a reason. I thought of something else. "Whoever used the pistols must know by now that we have found them."

He sliced a sharp look at me. "So they will. Considering all this happened through my own arrogant stupidity—"

I wouldn't let him get away with that; he was far too hard on himself. "How can you say that? He—"

"Or she," he reminded me with a wicked smile.

I accepted the correction. "Or she, might have been planning to do this anyway, and who's to say you had anything to do with it?"

He frowned. "What I said at dinner last night probably pushed them into it. He or she would have thought Hill was about to tell us, from what he said. I meant them to."

"It's not your fault," I protested. "Richard, you mustn't blame yourself, please. You did what you thought was best; you're not responsible for the consequences."

I think he took comfort from my protestation, I hope so, but he wasn't entirely convinced. "I could have stopped it."

"Why? How? Did you know, are you omnipotent?" A muscle in his cheek twitched, but he said nothing, so I continued. "Who knows what might have happened? Whoever it was would still have tried to retrieve the pistols, they knew from what you said last night we hadn't found them. But they would have found out anyway, wouldn't they?"

He sighed and leaned his elbow on the arm of his chair, pillowing his cheek in his hand. "The only one responsible is the one who did this. The best thing we can do is find out." I went over to his chair and leaned on the arms, bending down to put my face closer to his.

He stared at me for what seemed like a very long time, sighed again and spoke to me at last. "I'm not afraid of death, but I am afraid of leaving you."

This wasn't at all what I had expected, and I took a sharp breath. He had reminded me yet again I was everything to him, that without me there was nothing for him. I felt so burdened and yet so privileged. I was overwhelmed. I leant forward and kissed him, once. I straightened up again. "What do we do when we know who has done this thing?"

"We may not find out. If we do, and if it's certain, we must meet with the principals and decide what to do together."

"What about Carier?" Carier was a full partner in Thompson's and entitled to a full say.

"I'll speak with him privately," Richard assured me, "and make sure his views are made known. My father wouldn't approve of the way we do things at the agency."

"No." I was unable to picture Lord Southwood in Alicia Thompson's little office in the City, with her mismatched china service and independent attitude. "But he has to be involved in this case, doesn't he?"

"He does indeed," Richard agreed. "This is his house; Sir Barnett is his heir, after me and Gervase. And I think we both suspect Sir Barnett of being involved in some way, don't we?"

"We certainly do."

I saw he'd begun to think analytically again, and I was pleased to see it. His despondent mood had passed and he was ready to do what was necessary to discover the murderer of the two unfortunate footmen. I thought of Hill, so strong and vital, filling his little room with his presence, and remembered him as I had seen him last. How small and insignificant he'd looked. Something had gone from him, and he had gone from a man to an inanimate object in an instant. I knew it would happen to me one day, and unlike my husband, I was afraid.

Chapter Eleven

The next day, when the ball was to be held, was spent in frantic preparation. With breakfast over, all the maids not involved in cleaning the bedrooms were commandeered for work in the state rooms. I foolishly offered to help with the flowers and wondered at Lady Southwood's incredulous stare. "My dear, that has been taken care of. You may, if you wish, view it when it is done, but the gardeners will see to most of it."

When I saw the acres of flowers brought in, I did feel foolish. I was thinking of the arrangements back at the manor in Devonshire, where a gathering of neighbours was a much more intimate affair. Here, it was all done on such a grand scale that it would have been impossible for one person to supervise the whole.

Still, this was ostensibly in honour of my child, so I wanted to involve myself in some way. The ball was to be preceded by a dinner, to which all the principal families of the county had been invited. The Duke of Devonshire's son and heir was to be present, but sadly the Duke himself was unwell and so couldn't attend. After tonight, our duties here were concluded, although there was the small matter of two murders to be resolved.

I toured the state rooms, making sure everything was done to make them as welcoming as possible. I was glad the day was warm but overcast, as the oppressive heat of recent days would be too tiring and the gown I planned to wear far too hot.

I went to see the housekeeper and insisted on viewing a

copy of the menu for dinner, and the supper to be provided later. The range of dishes staggered me. I looked in on the huge ice sculptures being fashioned in a separate room by the confectioners, and stayed there a little longer than I needed to. The work was fascinating and the room blessedly cool. The men didn't seem put out by my presence, and I enjoyed watching the creation of the birds. There was a pair of peacocks, a cockerel, several smaller doves and some exotic birds I was told were genuine copies of birds from the tropics. They showed me the book they were working from, and the pictures made me think the artist had used his imagination more than his powers of observation. I couldn't believe such creatures existed, but they looked very fine rendered in crystalline ice.

At two, I retired to my room for a brief rest. I wanted to look my best, but I knew I wouldn't sleep. After Nichols helped me off with my outer clothes and loosened my stays, I managed half an hour's rest on my bed before starting the arduous task of dressing.

Richard found me there. He sat on the bed and took my hand. "Are you quite well?"

"Of course," I assured him. "I just thought it might be best to rest for a little time."

He kissed my hand. "You're quite right. Shall I join you?"

The gleam in his eyes didn't betoken rest. "We would be late."

He sighed. "You're probably right." His gaze swept up my lightly clad body. "I came to tell you about the pistols."

I sat up. "Has Carier discovered who they belong to?"

Richard shook his head. "No. There's no sign of an empty case, and no one has come forward. Carier says he will search again tonight. Everyone will be busy downstairs, and in any case, no one thinks twice about the presence of a servant in their room." He glanced down at his hands, then he looked back at me. "We have, however, heard from Alicia Thompson."

"Have you read the dispatches?"

"No, I've deliberately left them until tomorrow. We'll read them together, if you like. We can do nothing tonight, and I'm determined not to spoil it for you." I hated waiting, but he was right. We could do nothing, and if the reports contained any disturbing news, it would only put a damper on the evening.

I smiled ruefully. "We've been waiting for them for absolute ages, and now they arrive."

"She also sent six men from the box. Four of them will leave after the festivities. I'll make them stay until this other thing is over, though. The other two will stay to replace Hill and Derring."

I spared a moment to think about the men and their families.

He helped me to my feet when I moved to get up, but kept his arms around me. "You are to enjoy tonight."

I smiled. "I'll try, but you know I dislike being the centre of attention."

"Not tonight." His mouth hovered over mine. "I'll see to it." He kissed me and went to his room to change before he could take our kisses further, as both of us wished.

I wore the dark blue gown I had first worn in Venice. I thought it would help me to stand out, since the prevailing fashion was for pastels. It was embroidered all over in a pattern of deep pink flowers, roses, in a conceit on my name. With it I wore the sapphire set Richard had bought me in Venice. He'd added to the original necklace and earrings, so it now amounted to a full parure, with brooches for my stomacher, a bracelet and hairpins. I powdered for this occasion. The provincial mind would have castigated me as an eccentric, had I not. Some people in fashionable society had called me a dowd for not powdering as much as most people did, but with Richard's help I had turned this around and was now considered an *avant-garde* fashion setter. It all depended on the way it was presented, he had told me, and he was right.

All I had to do was sit and stand as required and watch as

Nichols transformed me into the great lady of the portrait downstairs. I had a glass of wine brought to me, to give me some courage for the ordeal to come. Despite Richard's words, I still thought of it as an ordeal.

He came through as Nichols was putting the final touches to my hair. I was considering a patch, and I had it on the end of my finger ready to place on my face, but he came over and took it from me. He placed it for me, at the corner of my left eye, and stood back to look at the result, considering it as gravely as if I were a work of art.

I stood and spread my arms for him to see, and he looked me over with the close scrutiny of a connoisseur. He came forward and adjusted the set of one of the brooches, stood back and smiled in satisfaction. "Beautiful."

I smiled back at him and saw nothing in him to alter. He wore a coat of the deepest pink, embroidered down the front and over the pockets in blue, white and gold, with breeches in dark blue. The stiffened skirts of the coat flared away, accentuating the slim, firm body beneath. His waistcoat was white, but little could be seen of the base material under the beautiful embroidery that encrusted it. The diamond solitaire pin glittered at his throat, the buckles at his knees and on his shoes glittered in an echo of this. The black velvet tie from his wig was brought around to the front and tied over his stock in the style known as solitaire. Lace frothed at his wrists and below his neckcloth. He was magnificent.

"You don't need me to tell you how extravagant you look." I crossed the room and laid my hand gently on his sleeve. I was almost afraid to take it, in case I spoilt the set of the fabric.

He smiled in return. "And you look perfect. You always do." It was a typical male compliment. I'd made a great effort tonight, and by that comment he was equating this with every other appearance I made.

We went down to dinner.

The large dining room dazzled, even before the candles were

lit. The crystal set by every place glittered, reflected by the sparkling silverware, all set off by the crisp linen cloth, starched to the consistency of paper. The fireplace and the epergnes were aflame with flowers, culminating in the great silver centrepiece on the table, a waterfall of blossoms. The windows lay open, letting in what breeze was available.

We were seated formally today, so I could sit next to my husband. Lord Hartington, the heir of the Duke of Devonshire, had come over from Chatsworth, and I was delighted to see my friends the Flemings were in his party, since they were staying with the Devonshires for a few weeks. Lord Hartington was a pleasant man, and very welcoming, a great man in the land and likely to become greater, as his father was very ill and like to die.

I was thankful I wasn't married to him, or rather, that Richard and Lord Hartington weren't to change places. I liked him, he was intelligent and didn't condescend to me, but his wife would be expected to hold a great public position. The lady seemed to be more than adequate for the situation she was in, and I liked her. We had something in common. Theirs was a love match too.

Richard decided to flirt with me. I couldn't have coped with such gallantry a bare year ago, but tonight I didn't care. Whatever I did I would be closely watched, so I would be myself and devil take the hindmost.

So Richard flirted, and I enjoyed it. He was the most desirable man in the room and he wanted me, all his attention was on me. I wouldn't be human if I didn't enjoy that.

His parents didn't approve, but that only spurred him to more compliments. He toasted me, with his usual toast *sotto voce*. "To your beautiful brown eyes. May I drown in them forever." The people nearby heard, and some of them smiled, while others looked surprised. Richard wasn't usually demonstrative in public. His flirting tended to be of a more public nature, not revealing his inner feelings. It was one reason why some of society still believed our match was dynastic, arranged by our families.

Dinner consisted of four courses, each containing an enormous number of dishes and removes. I ate enough, helped by Richard to the dishes he knew I liked, but didn't overindulge as many people did. One gentleman, who I might describe as comfortably upholstered, never seemed to stop. His knife was constantly in action, his jaws likewise, working in perfect harmony. And yet he managed to maintain an amicable conversation with the lady by his side. I admired his coordination.

The talk was of local affairs and the fashionable world. No mention was made of the murders or of the necklace. That was too new, too fresh to be discussed outside the house, although I knew the news would be all over the neighbourhood by the morning. Scandal has a mind of its own, like an entity apart from its cause, and spreads by absorption. Although you never hear anyone discussing it, it is discussed and spreads like a puddle in the rain. With about as much accuracy and predictability.

Lady Kerre wore a pretty parure of pearls tonight. It was as though the diamond necklace had never existed. Her demeanour was absolutely normal. She had regained control over herself, and her behaviour tonight was for public consumption only.

After dinner, the covers were cleared and the toasts began. They celebrated the King, Helen, Richard and me, then to my surprise Richard got to his feet. "My wife." He looked at me and me only. "The woman who brought me a new life." A deliberate double meaning, and one which everyone took according to how well they knew us.

The sentiment took me by surprise, and I blinked away a tear before I could smile back at him. Across the table, Lizzie raised her glass and smiled fondly. She had always doubted the wisdom of my marriage to Richard, and I think she doubted it still, but tonight she recognised my triumph and accorded it its due. At that moment I felt the absence of Martha and James keenly, especially when I saw Ian, also raising his glass and smiling. My other sister, Ruth, had chosen to remain with Martha and James, to help care for the children, but we'd never been close, and she would, as the first Golightly to make her debut under the full spotlight of society, do very well for herself in the fullness of time.

Lizzie was sitting next to her Marquês. They looked wonderful together, and Lizzie had pulled out all the stops tonight. She was ravishing, dressed in celestial blue, the colour of her eyes, expensive lace frothing at her elbows and neck, only emphasising the creamy, perfect skin underneath. Her pointed, delicate face was alight with happiness. This was what she'd dreamed of when we were at home in Devonshire, what she had prepared for while despairing of achieving. Now it had happened and it was everything she wanted it to be. She'd created a sensation in society last year because of her beauty, was now accepted because of her charm, and had found a man to love. I saw by the way she turned to look at the Marquês that was true. I hoped Alicia Thompson's dispatches would contain no disturbing news about him, that he was what he claimed to be. I wanted to dance at her wedding.

Tonight was as much Helen's as it was mine, and when the ladies rose to leave the room, I sent to see how she was. I received the gratifying reply that she was well and ready to face her public.

The dinner had taken a long time, even longer than usual, so the county gentry not attending the dinner had begun to arrive. The more important arrivals were shown up to the drawing room, where they received tea or wine, and the others were made welcome downstairs, in the great hall and the rooms leading off it. I received the congratulations of the neighbourhood sitting next to my mother-in-law, in state. I still felt like a fraud, but they didn't see me as one so that had to be good enough.

The gentlemen didn't linger over their port. Word was sent to them of the arrivals, and they obediently joined us. Richard came straight to my side and chatted for a while before we excused ourselves to go upstairs to Helen.

I took advantage of the break by going to my room and having Nichols repair any damage to my appearance. It didn't take long. She was efficient and deft; my unruly hair was firmly put back into the elaborate style set for it earlier and the folds of my gown carefully smoothed into place. I stood and practised opening my fan for a few moments; it was new, and it had stuck over dinner, turning what should have been an elegant, casual gesture into a clumsy one.

Richard finished at about the same time I did and came through to the bedroom so we could go up together. I thought how frightening I would have found him if I'd met him for the first time like this. So ethereally perfect, so untouchable.

If I couldn't have remembered what he looked like without all the finery, I would have quaked. He came across the room to take my hands. "How anyone could have overlooked you for those years passes my understanding."

I smiled at the compliment, but didn't preen. I knew I could only look adequate next to his magnificence. He must have seen the doubt in my eyes, for he took me over to the dressing table and made me look at my reflection in the large mirror, standing behind me. "You are Rosalind Kerre, Lady Strang. Look."

I couldn't see it as he assured me he did. "You've learned the trick. You remember I told you once I was quite ordinary without all this." He waved a hand in a delicate gesture, indicating his apparel, and taking in mine as well. "Well, you must believe me now. Behave as though you are the most beautiful woman in the room, and you will be."

"You're never ordinary, Richard, you have something that draws people to you. Even naked—" I stopped, colouring up, and he laughed.

"Yes?" He kissed my bare shoulder, sending a shudder of desire through me.

"Even naked," I continued, gathering strength, "you move

like an athlete, you're somebody special."

He grimaced at my reflection and smiled again. "Only to you."

I shook my head. "No, or your reputation wouldn't be quite so fearsome. Women must have seen something in you they desired, or you wouldn't have made quite so many conquests."

He shrugged, still looking at me. He pulled out a piece of lace that had been caught inside the neckline of my gown at the back. "I was young and healthy. It was all most of them needed."

I turned to face him, forcing him to move away a little. "If you touch me much more, we'll have to start all over again."

This time he laughed, but offered me his arm. "Very well, my lady. Our guests await."

Whitehouse waited in the nursery with Helen in her arms, both of them dressed to the nines. Whitehouse wore her best clothes, her blonde hair neatly tucked beneath a lace and linen cap, standing straight and proud, holding Helen, gorgeously pink, and all in white silk and lace.

My dread today was of her catching something from one of the guests. When I mentioned it to Richard, he frowned in concern. "Yes, I've been thinking of that too. Perhaps if we show her to the populace, if you or Whitehouse hold her, we might reduce the risk a little."

"We don't have to show her for long, do we?"

"No," he agreed.

"Do you think she will stay this clean?" I asked the nursery maid, knowing how quickly babies could turn white into some other colour.

"I have more gowns ready, my lady, and I have a supply of clean cloths in my apron pocket."

I smiled my agreement. Whitehouse was proving an excellent choice as maid to head up our nursery.

"And, Whitehouse, if I say the baby looks tired, please think of some excuse and take her away. I don't want her too tired or exposed to too many people for too long."

We processed down the side stairway, Richard and me in front, and Whitehouse with the baby in her arms following behind us. I felt very proud, and very foolish. I had never expected to bear children, only look after other people's for them, and a few years ago, had I been told such a fuss would be made over my firstborn I'd have called them mad. I wondered if I had a succession of girls, would the gloss wear off, would the celebrations be that much smaller each time? I rather thought so, although I knew Richard would welcome them.

We went down to the great hall, where the people of the county waited for us. It was full of strangers, but people whose appearances were oddly familiar. I couldn't work it out at first. While they weren't completely identical, they were so similar to the people I had grown up with they might be able to change places with each other. They were dressed respectably but not extravagantly in clothes that were out of date or made over from another year to suit the current fashions, and they were made to last of good material and sober colours. I was now moving in circles where extravagance of dress was expected, and it had taken a moment to restore my vision as Miss Golightly, but I saw it now.

These people were important to my father-in-law, as important collectively to him as he was to them, and they were fully aware of it. They kept his Members of Parliament in place, the basis of his web of interests throughout the county, and the county was the power base of the nobility. It occurred to me that with so many grandees in such a relatively small area of Derbyshire, it might be possible for them to play one off against the other. Not the tenants, but the freeholders. Legal disputes at the highest level would filter through to the lowest very quickly, quicker than they would in Devonshire where there were fewer great nobles. I would have to talk to James about it when I saw him. He would understand.

A sea of faces lifted to watch us as we descended the great

staircase to the hall. In a way, I felt far more apprehensive about meeting what I still thought of as my own kind, knowing how they would talk about me later between themselves.

Still, one thing Richard had told me held true. I knew I looked as well as I could, in my blue gown and my sapphires, and if I did nothing, they would still take away an impression of me as a great lady. Only I would know how fraudulent that was.

I pushed the recent events of the necklace and the murders to the back of my mind as I descended the stairs, my hand disposed gracefully on Richard's arm. I didn't look at him, as I knew the guests in the hall would spot the hesitation in a moment. I heard the tap of my shoes on the great wooden staircase over the quiet murmur of the people below, but I couldn't hear what they were saying, strain my ears though I might.

When we reached the bottom of the staircase, Richard began to introduce me to the people there. I saw Croker, Lord Southwood's steward, stood by his elbow, just in case he needed a reminder of the names. Croker knew these people like no one else did. I hoped his successor was currently being trained, since it was likely Richard and I would have to deal with him one day.

Richard needed little help, or Croker was so discreet in passing on the information it seemed that way. I was greeted with a low bow or curtsey and the occasional curious stare from the bolder ones. The women took in all the details of my appearance, and most of them turned to the baby, to coo over her and tell me she was truly beautiful—as if I didn't know already. The younger ones took more interest in me than they did in my daughter, and some stared at Richard in frank admiration. His appearance was remarkable enough in London; here, with the other members of the family and the other houseguests only slowly entering in our wake, he was exotic.

When we were about halfway through, and I was running out of original things to say, the orchestra struck up, which was a great relief, and better still, Helen slept through it. It was a

171

quartet, playing quiet airs to provide background music, so it might have soothed her for all I knew.

I was asked a great many impertinent questions which I answered as best I could. "How long were you in labour?" *Long enough.* "Are you quite recovered now?" *Yes, thank you.* And one middle-aged lady asked me if I'd swaddled the baby. She seemed quite indignant at my quiet "No," so I waited to hear what she would say next.

"I fear, my lady, your daughter will grow up with crooked limbs." She lifted her head to stare at me, challenging me to contradict her. So I did.

"Many of this generation have been brought up without swaddling. And they all seem to have perfectly straight limbs."

"It's always been the way," the lady replied, unbendingly.

I'd got the smell of her by now; the gown she was wearing had been laid away in camphor for a very long time. This was probably the first time it had seen the light of day this year. It reminded me of the tenants on my brother's estate, that smell which pervaded the rooms for days after quarter-day, when they came to pay their rents. "Fewer children die in the first few years of life these days," I informed her, only too aware this was for my class only. The poor still died like flies under the swatter.

She was ready for that one. "I lost three," she told me, almost proud of her achievement. "It's a hard life, my lady, and it's best if the weaklings die young."

That sort of talk sickened me. I realised I would never persuade her to think in any other way, but I couldn't resist a parting shot. "Physical strength isn't everything," I said, smiling, and moved on.

Richard was at my elbow. "Mrs. Davenport," he told me, his mouth close to my ear. "Always terrified Gervase and me when we were children. You came out of that better than we ever did any of our altercations with her." We were on to the next person, and he couldn't say any more.

Everyone got to see the baby. I talked to all of the people

and tried to remember as many names as I could. I'd been studying the names of the tenants, their holdings and their complaints, and I was surprised to find how much of the information had stuck.

The people looked quite prosperous to me, for although the farming in this part of Derbyshire was poor, farther south lay fine animal pastures, and this area was also rich in minerals. My neighbours in Devonshire made their livings from fishing and free trading, often indiscriminately mixed. I wondered what sort of illegal activity these people indulged in, but mentally scolded myself for suspecting the worst. I had seen too much of that in too short a period recently, and it was making me cynical.

I watched Richard as he worked. He seemed to remember the business and location of everyone in the hall without effort. Later he told me he could link the businesses, as long as he knew the person's name. "It's the names I can't always remember. I can picture them in their rightful places, but if I don't have the name, I'm lost." That was why Croker was with us, to supply the names. Richard hadn't visited Eyton since February last year, when he'd left to come down to Devonshire for our wedding. He'd never seemed to take much interest in the estate, but he knew these people, and they certainly knew him.

I handed my baby to Whitehouse and nodded at the door. She started to thread her way through the crowd. They had more to entertain them now as the dancing was starting. These were real country-dances, not the *contre*-dances used in society, romping and jumping the order of the day. I remembered some of them, and others seemed to consist of the man seizing a partner around the waist and bouncing around the floor in a manner that would be considered indecorous in polite society. I wasn't sure I liked it, but it was required of me, so I chose a delicate young man to squire me around the floor a couple of times. Richard plunged right in and chose an extremely well-upholstered matron, but I saw the wisdom of his choice when his partner refused to go above a sedate trot, thus sparing him the breathtaking gallop affected by some of the others.

At one point Freddy Thwaite hared past me with a very well-endowed young lady whose looks of melting adoration seemed to augur well for his future prospects, her nearly unfettered bosom getting as much exercise as her feet.

My delicate young man proved to be much stronger than he looked, and I feared for the pleats at the back of my gown, so firm was his grip, but I managed, and was restored, breathless, to my husband at the end of the romp. His grin of mischief couldn't be interpreted by many, but I knew he had gained great amusement from it, and I feared his teasing later. He might even insist on a repeat performance.

After joining in with one or two more dances we excused ourselves and remounted the stairs. Our departure was hardly noticed now. The drink flowed freely and the music became wilder, several local musicians having joined in with the hired quartet. I paused to look back down at them all, safe in their own world, a microcosm of society at large, their politics and their concerns repeatable all over the country, but with so many variations each pattern was unique.

Upstairs the atmosphere was much the same, if more refined. This was where my sort belonged, the county gentry with real local influence. I had to put a guard on my tongue here until I knew and understood who I was talking to. Some of the names I knew already, but I must make a real effort to learn them all.

Lord Southwood met us at the door. "I thought you'd got lost," he said.

Richard replied, "They were most insistent downstairs that Rose be made welcome."

With his back to the other guests, my father-in-law let his eyes roll in an expression of exasperation. "It can get very robust."

"Indeed," Richard agreed smoothly, his suave exterior belying the gleam in his eyes. He led me farther into the room.

"Shall we make a start?"

Whitehouse had brought Helen here, and she'd woken up now, but didn't seem to be in need of anything, being content to stare about her. Her innocent eyes, wide and blue, seemed to take everything in. We were in the Painted Chamber, the huge drawing room that served as a ballroom on occasions like these. It had been painted in the last century, when such things were fashionable, but it was still fresh and impressive, one of the sights of the county. People travelled miles to see it. Now strangers packed it.

They were similar to the people in the great hall, but the quality of their dress was better and more up to date, and their manners more refined. And they smelled better, less pungently of camphor and sweat. These were my kind, the more substantial landowners, the MPs, the judges and professional men. And, perhaps more importantly, their wives.

The Hartingtons were doing very well here, and I watched them as an example of how to work through a room. His lordship got through the room in no time and remembered every person without effort. I could only admire and be thankful we had Croker to look after us.

Lord Hartington was thirty-six, not much older than my husband, but more substantially built and trailing parliamentary baggage. He duly admired Helen and turned to business with Lord Southwood.

"Bute has got 'em all by the ears," he told my father-in-law, while I was standing by. "He's got the Prince well and truly under his thumb, and until he gains his majority, looks fair to be an important part of any Regency that might be formed." He meant in the event of the old King's death. "Pitt and Fox are turning somersaults to attract his attention, and they can't decide yet if they want him or not. At least, Pitt would somersault if it wasn't for his gout, but Fox is fit enough."

"How is the King?" asked Lord Southwood.

"Well enough," Hartington answered him. "I've left Pitt and

Fox to it for a little while, but I have to get back soon or they'll tear each other's throats out. Hardwicke is acting as go-between, and I don't envy him that."

Gervase arrived to give his opinion. It was well known Pitt wanted to investigate the East India Company for corruption, and Gervase had considerable interests in that direction. Politics was presently going through one of its seismic changes, begun by the death of the Duke of Newcastle's brother, Henry Pelham, in March. Newcastle was stunned by his brother's unexpected death, and it looked like Henry Fox was in the ascendancy, but rumour had it Pitt had somewhat recovered from his severe attack of the gout and was coming back in force. Only the King's dislike of him told against him. To add to all this, there was the upcoming General Election. My father-in-law was a supporter of Fox, but Richard had not yet declared any interest. In fact, his interest was entirely in other directions, and if he became the Earl of Southwood, the politicians would be hard put to attract him to their cause. He was deeply interested in law and order, something that didn't occupy the heads of many politicians for long, only when a resurgence of disorder threatened to lose votes.

Gervase, on the other hand, took an active part in the conversation. His involvement with the East India Company had begun his concern and had formed the basis for his increasing involvement in current affairs. He had, earlier this year, expressed his desire to stand for Parliament, and while I would offer him every support in his enterprise, I was glad it was Gervase and not my husband who took an interest in such things. He had every hope of being returned to the House this autumn, in fact, it would be a miracle if he did not. Lord Southwood had been delighted to see one of his sons extending the family's influence in this way, and it had gone a long way to reconcile him to Gervase's earlier behaviour. I hoped peace would reign in this difficult family.

I had news of my own. "I've heard Mr. Pitt's interests are somewhat engaged at the moment," I said, and had the satisfaction of seeing Lord Hartington turn to me with renewed interest.

"It seems he's finally decided to tie the knot," I added.

That quietened them all. I was pretty sure of my facts, since a maid in the employ of the lady in question had confirmed it for me, through Thompson's. A little private enterprise of my own. "Would you happen to know the lady's name?" Lord Hartington enquired.

"Yes indeed. Lady Hester Grenville."

That created a small sensation. Only Richard knew how I could be sure, and I wasn't to be put off my opinion. "But he has known that family forever," Lord Southwood said. "How is it he should decide now?"

I smiled. "I heard that his recent bout of ill health concentrated his mind wonderfully, and he decided to act where he'd been circumspect before. I've also heard the lady seems willing, and we can expect an announcement in due course."

The maid had been definite in her observations. I usually kept such gossip to myself, but I wanted to create a good impression and show them a provincial nobody could also have some knowledge of events.

I was only worried about the reaction of one person, but when I glanced over at him, I saw Richard had a gleam of amusement in his eyes.

"I think I've been out of affairs a week or two too long," said Lord Hartington. "Thank you, my lady, I was totally unaware of this."

"My wife does not engage herself in general gossip," Richard informed him. "You may be sure of any information that comes her way." I was grateful for his support, but I didn't need it.

We left them to discuss the new event and continued on our way with Helen. I thought my daughter was looking a trifle fractious, and sure enough before too long she opened her mouth and exercised her lungs. It was impossible to soothe her, so I sent Whitehouse away with her. I could now take my time and not worry about the effect all this attention and heat would be having on my daughter. After such a quiet start to her life, the sight of so many strangers all at once might be frightening to her, and I was still concerned about any illnesses they might carry with them.

Richard was pleased with my interjection earlier. "He won't forget you now," he murmured, as he led me out onto the floor for the first minuet, "and he could be very useful to us, and Thompson's. I'm proud of you, my sweet."

I barely refrained from preening. "I thought it might be worth popping into the conversation." I carefully disposed myself for the start of the dance.

Although it wasn't forbidden for the guests downstairs to come upstairs, it was not encouraged. Each to his own, Lord Southwood often said, but some of them had come up to watch the dancing. Some of the upstairs guests, especially the local gentry, were pleased to see them. It gave them somebody to condescend to.

Richard was worth watching, although when he danced with me he was very careful of me, and made sure I was noticed. I wasn't nearly such a good dancer. His movements were grace personified, his natural elegance emphasised by the studied gestures he brought to bear. At least we weren't dancing on our own tonight. Lord and Lady Southwood had led off the minuet, and we were merely one of the followers. I was intrigued to see the large Lord Southwood held himself very well and was much more nimble on his feet than anyone could have supposed. Perhaps that was where Richard got it from.

I also saw Lizzie dancing with the Marquês de Aljubarrotta. They made a fine couple, she so fair, he so dark, and both fine dancers. Richard raised his eyebrow, and when we had done, I asked him why. "He has more than a partiality for your sister, I've seen the way he looks at her. This is no formal courtship."

Richard saw me to a chair and smiled reassuringly down to where I sat before leaving me for the first time that evening as

Gervase approached us to ask me for his dance. He wanted to know any developments about the murders. "We've had despatches from Thompson's, but we haven't looked at them yet. We'll look at them tomorrow."

"I don't want any scandal," he said anxiously.

"There won't be."

We parted in the movement of the dance and he caught my eye and grinned self-deprecatingly. He had been the one who'd brought the greatest scandal to the family. "I know what you're thinking, but I'm determined to make my new leaf as comprehensive as my brother's."

"Do they still talk about it?"

"Not before me. You've done a lot to smooth things over, you know."

I stared at him in surprise.

"Richard is now a respectably married man. They were looking for something outrageous in his wife when it was discovered he was marrying an unknown, but I've not heard anything against you from people I respect. You seem to be a hit. I knew you would be."

"Even when you saw me at Hareton Abbey?"

He smiled again. He'd seen me in outmoded, well-worn gowns, an affectation because I didn't want people to look at me, and in mourning, which didn't suit me half as well as it suited my sister. "Even then," he assured me gallantly. Gervase was a very good friend.

Freddy had brought his new, amply proportioned friend upstairs and was trying to teach her the niceties of the minuet in the corner of the room. Gervase took me over to him at the conclusion of our dance.

"Freddy teaches the dance very well," I said. "Do you remember?" I demonstrated the twist of the wrist Freddy had taught me in Venice, an elegant turn I had now made my own.

He laughed when he saw it. "I shall never forget."

Neither would I. The young lady watched us wonderingly. Freddy's reputation was shocking, worse than Richard's even, and I didn't wish any tenant of this parish to come under his spell. He was a very attractive man, but a careless one, with little thought for the consequences of his actions.

"Are your parents here, my dear?" I asked her, trying hard to think what her name was.

She bobbed a curtsey. "They are downstairs, my lady."

"Have you met my brother-in-law, Gervase Kerre?"

Gervase had realised what I was at, because he bowed low, and I asked her if she would like a glass of something. When she blushed and nodded, he held out his arm and led her away. She would be much safer with Gervase.

I frowned at Freddy. "Not here, Freddy. Not on our doorstep."

He had the grace to look shamefaced, but spoiled it with a grin that few women, including myself, could resist. "She seemed willing enough. You know I wouldn't have done anything she hadn't wanted me to do."

"Yes, of course," I agreed. Freddy was a seducer, not a rapist. "But her parents might not have been so desirous of the outcome. If you seduce one of these maidens, it gets all round her society in no time at all, and no one will have her. She'll be soiled goods."

"Pah!" He made a dismissive gesture. "Give her the right dowry, and anyone will have her. I should know, I've done it time out of mind myself."

"I don't doubt it." His eyebrows went up when he heard the chill in my voice. "I can't like this attitude, Freddy. What does it do to the poor girl? Seduced once and abandoned. She'd never look at her rightful swains properly again, and you would make her dreadfully unhappy."

His mouth quirked up at one corner. "You have a very kind heart, Rose. I pray life doesn't tear it out of you."

I couldn't think what he meant; I was merely trying to

prevent a possible scandal by nipping it in the bud. "There'll be plenty of others willing to accommodate you, but that was a respectable girl, and her parents would have been very upset had anything happened tonight."

He got to his feet. "And it's your night, isn't it?"

"And Richard's."

He shook his head. "No, it's yours. At least he thinks so. When I saw you in Venice I thought it was the effect of the honeymoon, but you still feel the same way, don't you?"

I nodded, smiling now, but Freddy sighed heavily. "Pity. I would have loved to have had a crack at you myself."

Despite my righteous indignation, his melancholic look made me laugh. "Really, Freddy. How could you?" His natural charm got him out of a lot of trouble, but, at the same age as Richard, it was time he was thinking more seriously. And more responsibly. I wondered what had caused that twist of cynicism I didn't see in him very often.

He laughed too, and bore me off to find some wine, promising to be good while he was here. I didn't believe him for a minute. "You should find a bride, Freddy. Your poor father must be desperate by now. You said you would find one when I met you for the first time, and you still haven't come up to scratch."

He sighed. "Truth is, I've not found anyone I could fancy, and unlike Richard before he met you, I can't settle on marriage without any affection. I thought I might make a play for your lovely sister, but it seems someone got there first."

This made me look to where Lizzie was sitting on a sofa at the far side of the room, carefully attended by the Marquês. They did indeed look very absorbed in each other.

"Don't give up," I encouraged him. I still wasn't certain about the Marquês. He was a charming man, and a perfect gentleman, but I wanted to be sure he could make my sister happy.

By mutual consent, we went over to where the *tête-à-tête*

was taking place. Lizzie smiled charmingly, making room for me on the sofa where she was sitting. Her new beau stood behind, leaning over her, to get the best view one supposed, and Freddy joined him there. When I glanced up at him, I thought I detected the merest flicker of a wink from his humorous brown eyes. I sipped the wine Freddy had given me, wondering if this was my lot in life—to break up things I saw as not proper. I decided not. I knew how much I used to hate designing people. I almost wished I had left Freddy's target to her fate.

"You seem to be a great success, Lizzie. I never hear your name without the word 'charming' somewhere in the vicinity."

"And I never hear yours without 'beautiful' somewhere," she retorted, and we looked at each other and burst into laughter. "I should like to import the whole of Exeter Assembly Rooms here wholesale. When you come to see us, shall we go back?"

"I think it's expected of us," I replied, not wishing for it as much as she did, but I remembered a time when I had. "Especially you. I belong here now."

She smiled while she watched the stately movements of the richly caparisoned dancers in front of us. "I'll say you do."

I stared at her in surprise. I never felt like it. It made me wonder how many of the people I was watching felt the same way I did.

"Should you like to dance, Miss Golightly?" Freddy asked her. She looked up at him with a dazzling smile, and he responded to her beauty. "Since Mr. Kerre seems to have forgotten his obligations, I'd love to take his place."

She went off on Freddy's arm just before Mr. Giles Kerre arrived to claim her. He looked suitably dismayed and asked me if I was engaged for this dance. I accepted his offer and stood with him. Conversation was necessarily restricted, even during the country-dances, but he managed to ask me a few questions about Lizzie that gave me pause. He wanted to know if her affections were engaged, and if I thought she would welcome an approach from him.

"She welcomes an approach from most personable men, but she has the government of her own affairs, and it is almost entirely her decision."

"Almost?" There was a pause while we threaded the needle.

"My brother James has to decide whether to bless the marriage or not, and of course," I added, keeping a good watch on him, "the disposition of her dowry."

Unfortunately, the dance took us apart at that point, so I couldn't see his reaction properly, but he looked sanguine enough when we came together again. "I shall have to court her properly."

I was surprised. "Are you serious, sir? I haven't noticed any partiality."

"I might have one," he answered lightly, but would say no more.

The gentlemen didn't ignore any of the eligible females in the company, and many other young ladies from the ranks of the local gentry were present tonight. I was intrigued to notice a small group of the younger element who stood by the fire together. They reminded me of the girls who had made my life a torment at home in Exeter. I knew I had the upper hand here, so after the dance with Mr. Kerre I decided to go over and talk to them. I was curious to see if they were the same.

They were very similar. There was a ringleader, one who considered herself prettier and wittier than the rest, who the others deferred to. She led the opinions of the others and tried to think ill of anyone who didn't openly admire her or defer to her. In this case, I was excused that duty. Since I'd never undertaken it at home, I'd been one of the people to suffer. Perhaps I *would* go back.

They curtseyed to me, and I acknowledged it with a stately inclination of my head and set myself to listen. Despite the initial reserve engendered by my approach they were soon gossiping again. I could still be quiet when I wanted to be. I discovered a lot from this group about which families were allied, which at loggerheads, and who had eligible young bachelors worth watching, and they were hardly aware of imparting any knowledge to me at all. It made sense of some of the patterns I had observed, and I saw it might be worth cultivating the acquaintance of one or two of the gossips in the district. It gave me an idea of how to go on in the local area.

My enquiries were interrupted by my husband, come to claim me, and a flutter went through the little group. He smiled, bowed, and remembered every name. When we were out of earshot, I quizzed him about it. "You had no problem with their names, my lord."

His smile was a wicked one. "I practised my skills on their older sisters, my love." He led me onto the floor. "Don't look at me like that, it was all perfectly aboveboard. My wicked reputation wasn't enough to drive them away, but I knew by then what my course in life was to be."

He had known when he was fourteen. "Now there's a new crop for you."

"Oh no." The dance was beginning.

"Not even a flirtation?"

He took his lower lip between his teeth. "That, my angel, is different. If you have no objection? Flirtation can be very useful at times. It puts women off their guard."

"Why should I?" In truth, I didn't object to him flirting with a pretty woman. It was all verbal these days, and it helped to bolster his image as an attractive man. I knew for sure nothing else would ever ensue. He couldn't hide something like that from me, because by his own choice he had decided to give me everything he was, without constraint, so I would notice when it appeared. It flattered me he had chosen me above all the other women he could have married, and it added an extra smokescreen to our relationship. Fidelity was considered unusual in our society, and to demonstrate affection in public would be seen as positively impolite, so I was as guilty of flirting as he was, when I felt like it.

My sister Lizzie was in her element. She flirted with and led on every eligible man who came her way, and received some very flattering offers, but had not yet made her final choice. There were several young men hanging on the strings she held in her pretty hands, but she had not yet met the one, she had told me before this, who had met every one of her exacting requirements. "I want wealth, a title, an amiable disposition and an indulgent nature." She'd counted the points off on her fingers. I was sure she would succeed, but now the Marquês had entered her life I thought her priorities had changed. She would run away with him if he proved to be penniless.

I woke in the night, and when I came back from my dressing room, Richard was awake too. I slipped back between the sheets and into his arms.

"What time did you come up?" I asked, for I had come away before him.

"About two. They keep early hours here." Many functions in London didn't break up until four or five in the morning.

"Did it go well, do you think?"

"Very well." He kissed my forehead, and I settled against him, loving his warmth. "You made an excellent impression."

"I hope so. I was afraid they wouldn't like me."

"Liking isn't important, but they must respect you. You even impressed Hartington with that bit of gossip about Pitt. How did you know?" The sheets rustled as he turned his head to meet my eyes. Dawn was breaking, filtering through a gap in the curtains, and I could just make out the fine drawn planes of his face.

"Thompson's. I heard the rumour from Lizzie, and I asked Nichols to find out if it was true. She wrote to a ladies' maid in the Pitt household and got a reply by return."

"Very clever." His hand moved up my back, and I lifted my head for a proper kiss, opening my mouth to allow his tongue to enter and explore. We took our time, but eventually he drew away. His breathing wasn't as steady as before.

"I pass, do I?"

"Even my mother was satisfied. Momentarily." The wry comment made me laugh. "I saw you approach the gaggle of females by the fire. It reminded me forcibly of another time. Is that why you did it?"

I smiled. I'd already guessed he must have recognised it. "Yes. I wanted to see how similar they were to Eustacia Terry and her cronies from my position of safety. In the past, whenever that sort saw me coming they would have been as likely to turn their backs on me. Now they have no choice, so I can approach them with impunity. Lizzie says we should go back to Exeter Assembly Rooms again."

"I had a very amusing evening there, with only one unfortunate incident. I'd have no objections, when we go to see your brother's new house."

"You spent most of the evening teasing Miss Terry," I reminded him.

He chuckled. "That was why it was so amusing. She had the impudence to assume she could take me away from you any time she wished, and she had obviously done it to other girls before. She was due a set down." His voice became more serious. "And she intruded where she wasn't wanted."

"By accident."

"I don't think so."

I stared. "What do you mean?"

"She knew there would be other people in the room where I'd arranged to meet her. She must have known she'd have more chance of a private meeting in the end room. I think she misunderstood deliberately and was taken off guard when I brought you with me." He kissed me again. "Are you tired?"

"Not really." And I'd remembered to make the small alteration to my bedtime routine that would mean no babies, at least for now. Tired, but hopeful, I thought it worth my while.

"Good." He raised himself on one elbow and leaned over to kiss me.

I smelled him now, the remains of his perfume and the maleness of him combining deliciously. "I love you, Richard. As much as the day we first made love."

"I love you more than that. You're beautiful...sensual...essential." He kissed me on each word, increasing the compliment and the growing warmth inside me.

"I had given up looking when I met you." I let my nails slide up his spine and felt his responsive quiver.

"And I was only just starting to look. I can't begin to describe my good fortune." He ran his hand up from my waist to my breast and delicately fingered my nipple between his thumb and forefinger, making me gasp in delight. He laughed softly when he heard my response.

"You were betrothed," I managed to remind him. I would be beyond coherence soon.

"She took advantage of my indifference." He let his tongue take over from his fingers.

I laughed at the comparison between his words and his actions, then sighed in pleasure. He moved slowly down my body, kissing and caressing, touching the places he knew I liked, following the touches with soft kisses. Familiarity had only given him more weapons. Now he knew what I enjoyed best he could play on me as well as I could play on the harpsichord, delicately, expertly building to a passion I could never deny, even if I'd tried to. He'd brought a great deal of skill and experience to me when we'd first made love, but now he knew me better his lovemaking was unsurpassable. He'd seemed so cold, so severe when we met, but nothing could have been further from the reality; the physical act of love was important to him, and he'd made it important to me. While it wasn't the most vital part of our relationship, as we had proved during and just after my pregnancy, it was a constant joy, a jewel to be treasured. We proceeded to treasure it as much as we could.

He reached the sensitive heart of my body and took a gentle taste. I arched up, reaching down to grasp his hair, as best I could because it was cropped close to his head, but enough for me to get hold. I released it, grasped it again when he sucked the knot of flesh into his mouth, the part known as the clitoris, or the *amor Veneris*. I liked the latter term, but right now I didn't care what it was called, only that Richard didn't stop.

He drove his tongue into me, licked and sucked, the sounds once embarrassing, now an invitation to enjoy, to share my body with his. I wished he'd turn around, because all I could reach was his hair and shoulders, if I leaned up against the pillows. Nothing else, and I wanted to hold him. But I didn't want him to stop. He loved doing this to me and I loved him doing it. Now, with brandy added to the mix, he seemed to enjoy it more.

When he growled against my skin, he sent me into a spiral of ecstasy and I screamed, careless of who might hear me.

It filled my mind with one thing only, and I grabbed his shoulders and dragged him back up the bed, fastening my mouth onto his as he pushed his way into me, his hot breath redolent of me, my body. The warmth and the release flowed through me, the rhythm of our bodies echoed our heartbeats. He made love gracefully, like the consummate dancer he was, but bolstered by a steely strength, reinforced and enhanced. His body slammed into mine, driving deep and hard, and I lifted my legs to hold him close.

Before I could curl my legs around his waist, he sat up. Whispering "Come here," he lifted me onto him so we were breast to breast. It gave me a chance to move more freely. I was almost past voluntary movement, but that insistent rhythm continued unbroken, and we danced together as if under the spell of the finest orchestra in the world, perfectly attuned to each other's needs and desires. His hands gripped my waist, his mouth caressed my breast and I cried out his name when I felt sudden white fire surge up inside me. I couldn't remember how often he'd made this happen, but each time was reborn, new to itself, and time meant nothing. At the same time as I called to him, I heard him cry and felt him thrust deep as he reached his own sublime moment of joy. He pulled my body hard onto his and held me tightly.

We stayed like that until he lowered me as gently as if I were made of porcelain until I came to rest on the rumpled sheets. I opened my eyes to his, his customary ice blue turned warm with love. "I love you." Superfluous, considering the circumstances, but well worth saying.

His smile told me all I wanted to know, but he said, "My sweet life," and came to lie down next to me and hold me close.

It was my turn to raise myself on one elbow, smiling, looking down at his adored face, clearer now in the growing daylight. I rested my hand lightly on his chest and leaned down to kiss him. "You're so clever."

He raised a fine-drawn eyebrow. "Clever? Not at all. You're here, I love you, it seems so easy. There's never anything else here when we're together like this. It's as though nothing else is real."

"I know it."

He touched my cheek. "I never knew it before I met you. And you've never taken advantage of it, either. Do you know how rare that is?"

His last remark puzzled me. "Why would I want to spoil that?"

He laughed. "Many women, if not most of them, would have taken the opportunity to ask for something. Jewellery, a carriage, something of that nature."

I smiled. "You've always given me everything I need. More than I need. It would be wasting the time we have together if I did that."

"Some women would think it a waste of time if they didn't."

"You're talking of courtesans?"

"Not at all. Some husbands purposely keep their wives

short of money so they're invited into their beds from time to time."

"That's sad."

"It's the way the world works," he told me.

"But not us."

"No, not us."

I was sleepy again. Lovemaking often did that to me. I settled against him and yawned, hearing his soft laugh. "Sleep now, my love. I'll be here."

"So will I."

"I missed your loving so much."

"Not as much as I missed yours."

Chapter Twelve

When Richard had finished his business with his father the following day, he returned to our sitting room where Carier and I waited for him with a large pot of coffee and some refreshments. Carier had put up a folding table, and we sat around it, the papers from Thompson's in a pile in front of Richard. His father would have been outraged to see us sitting at the same table as the valet, sharing coffee with him, but this was a meeting of the principals of Thompson's, and in that enterprise we had an equal say.

Richard picked up the first paper on the pile. "It's about the Marquês, the information we asked for." He passed the paper to me.

I examined it and looked up in relief. "He's genuine."

Richard smiled. "He is. Will you tell Lizzie later?"

"I don't think it will make much difference to her. But it will matter to James."

We passed on to the next item. Richard read out the relevant parts for us. "The footmen Alicia sent are the best available and have all taken on special duties for us in the past." He looked up. "I only have a skeleton staff in Oxfordshire. Shall we take them with us when we go?"

I knew the footmen would be expensive, but I also knew Richard needed to do this. He surrounded me with the best servants we could find, not only for the service they provided, but to care for me, and now our daughter, to act as bodyguards.

We had our enemies. At one time, I'd have cavilled at his tender care, preferring more personal freedom, but now I knew his needs better. I agreed.

Richard read the next paper more closely, studying it carefully. "This concerns our present situation. Giles Kerre is deeply in debt. He has gamed away everything he owns, and he owes money to some very unsavoury people." He passed the paper to Carier and I watched as the valet's mouth pursed in disapproval.

Richard turned to me. "We've seen these people before. They lend out money at exorbitant rates of interest, and use extreme measures to recover it. Giles has been borrowing on his expectations. Now we've produced a child, those expectations are severely reduced. These people will want their money back."

This was very worrying. These people wouldn't concern themselves with Giles's position and consequence. They would get their money or take their debt in another way. "It's so stupid."

Richard sighed. "I've watched him. He seems to need it like a man needs air. He's getting edgy now, because the company here don't game to excess, and he needs his own kind. I expected him to make a bolt for London before now, but this explains why he hasn't gone."

"They'll come here, my lord," Carier commented.

"We must stop them," Richard replied. "They have resources, but ours are better. I won't have them in this house."

"Absolutely not, my lord," Carier agreed, glancing at me. It seemed the desire to protect had emerged again. I sighed, knowing I could do nothing about it. They would do whatever was necessary to look after Helen and me, whether I agreed or not.

Carier cleared his throat. "May I suggest I make enquiries in the villages? If any strangers have been seen hereabouts, they would know."

"Excellent plan," Richard agreed.

"But Giles? Can we help him?" I asked.

Richard frowned. "We can protect him while he's here, but he's been very foolish, and short of paying these monsters, there's little we can do. I won't undertake to wean him from the tables. I don't think anyone could. He can't keep away."

"We may be able to stop him borrowing from the sharks in future, my lord," Carier said mildly. "We can warn them he is a bad risk and indicate that it wouldn't be worth their while to invest in him any further." He meant that we would present these people with a gentle threat and the promise of more to come. With influence, and with brute strength, a great deal could be achieved.

Richard nodded tersely. "I think we must try." He looked at me for confirmation. I also nodded. "It seems he has a very strong reason to steal the necklace, if he believed it was real. It wouldn't have paid all his debts, but it would have given him breathing space."

"Do you think he could have murdered for the money?" I had formed an opinion of him. I wanted to know what the others thought.

Richard sighed heavily. "He's certainly capable of it. He has a temper, but the person who killed Hill and Derring went prepared."

"He may not have intended to use the guns," I pointed out. "They could have been meant as a threat."

Carier nodded, and Richard agreed. "It's a possibility. I don't think whoever did it was planning to kill them both, because he only took two flintlocks, but a bullet would have stopped Derring long enough for him to kill Hill."

"Why would he want to do that?" I thought I knew, but I wanted to make sure we were in accord.

Richard confirmed what I thought. "To silence him. We had made it clear at dinner that Hill was going to begin naming names."

"Was it worth that kind of risk?" I reached for the coffee pot and stood to refill the cups. Carier would have taken it from me, but I forestalled him with a small shake of my head and a smile.

Richard leaned back in his chair. "Murderers don't always think clearly when they're committing the crime. Panic can account for a great deal, as can the feeling of power. Hill was helpless in bed; his killer had all the weapons. It can be intoxicating."

I didn't ask how he knew. I'd seen Richard kill, and although he suffered afterwards, he might have felt that intoxication at the time. It would help to explain his later reaction: guilt at the feeling of exhilaration in killing another human being.

"In this hypothesis, Giles paid or blackmailed Hill into stealing the necklace. Finding it was paste, he replaced it in Hill's room. When he found that Hill was about to name him, he went to his room to kill or threaten him, found Derring there, armed, and having killed Derring, killed Hill as well."

"Sadly, my lord, it makes sense," Carier said, "but we're not sure of any of it. We've not found a trace of an empty pistol case yet, and there's no evidence for any of the rest."

"He may have stolen and replaced the necklace," I said, "but we don't know he killed the footmen. He may have done one and not the other."

Richard shook his head. "Unless we have a confession we may never know for sure."

"Don't we owe the victims' families something?"

Richard sighed heavily. "Yes, we do. It's the main reason to discover who's done this, in my opinion. I don't think this murderer makes a habit of it or will ever do it again, but we owe the families some justice."

"What about Hampson?"

"He's being dealt with, my lady," Carier informed me. "We're sending him on a wild goose chase until the trail is cold."

"Hopefully," Richard put in. He picked up the next paper in the pile and perused it, casually at first, and with more attention. "Dear God."

"What?"

He looked up and met my look of surprise at his exclamation. "It seems Giles isn't the only Kerre in need of money."

I didn't think Lady Kerre or Sir Barnett were in need of money, and Amery was so engrossed in his books he wouldn't need any money. "Charlotte?" I suggested, puzzled.

Richard shook his head. "Amery."

Carier and I stared at him. Richard gazed back down at the paper in his hand and took a draught of coffee before he began to read out loud. "Amery Kerre has asked for the hand in marriage of one Gertrude Cassell. She is the daughter of a Cit, one Henry Cassell. He is a wealthy cloth merchant."

"I thought I knew the name." I had visited Cassell's in London, a most superior establishment. Richard glanced up and smiled at me by way of confirmation, then turned back to the paper in his hand. "She is his only daughter, the apple of his eye. He doesn't approve of the match, but his daughter is sincerely attached to Amery, and he has said he won't stand in her way if she is of the same mind after six month's separation. Sir Barnett Kerre has forbidden the match. He told Mr. Cassell he would publicly cast Amery off if he insisted on this connection." He looked up. "I always thought Sir Barnett was too superior for his own good. Good Lord, if Gervase had felt that trade was below him, he wouldn't be back here richer than anyone I know."

"It explains Amery's excessive shyness," I said. "He won't go near any of the young women. He may be afraid his father will make him come up to scratch with one of them. Do you think I should talk to him?"

"We both should," Richard replied. "He is naturally shy, he's always been so, but he's opened up to me in the past. If the attachment is sincere, we could try to help."

I thought of what I might have missed. "Is it Sir Barnett's

superior attitude that makes him refuse to consider the connection?"

"It's most likely," Richard said. "He always felt he was a cut above the world of commerce." He grinned. "Without it, where would we all be? Some people think everyone has their place in the world and should stick to it. That's a feudal throwback, to my way of thinking. Sir Barnett seems to believe some sort of superiority goes with his position, that he is in some way above other people. That, I believe, is crass stupidity." Although his father didn't share Sir Barnett's prejudices, he would have been most displeased to hear his son speaking in such a way in front of a servant. It was as well he wasn't here.

Richard put the paper about Amery aside. "There's something about the twins." He meant his children by Lucy Forder. We had set up the girl, Susan, as a Covent Garden lady of the night, a courtesan, at her request. She had a small establishment now, chose her own clients. It was what she'd been brought up to do, and although Richard disliked the idea, he hadn't stood in her way. The boy, his son, was missing after leaving home when he was thirteen years old. Richard's voice held heaviness in it. "Susan is making waves in her particular world." He consulted the paper on the table. "There's no sign yet of the boy."

I didn't know what to say. Richard hadn't spoken with any particular emphasis, but Carier and I knew how he felt about this terrible deception by his parents, spiriting the pregnant Lucy away before Richard had realised. It had been the start of the breach between the Southwoods and their son, and it was one that might never be healed.

Later when I went to my room to change for dinner, I found a letter waiting for me. I had been expecting it, and when I saw its address, I realised why it had taken so long to reach me. Tom had written to our house at Brook Street in London first, and it had been redirected from there to our Oxford house. This letter had followed us around the country.

Dear Rose, it read.

I hope you and your family are as well as when I saw you last. You seem to be settling down very well in your new life, quite the grande dame. Do you remember us as children watching the ladies parade about by the shops? I remember you telling me you would never do that, you would die first. You poured scorn on all the ladies, telling me how long it took them to dress, and what you could do with the time instead.

I smiled at the memory, although I thought it was most ungentlemanly of Tom to remind me. I read on.

We've both changed since then. You met your lord, and I— well I've met someone too. Well not exactly met her, I've known her for years and so have you, but I never really noticed her before. In short, Rose, I've offered for Barbara Sturman. She's a very good kind of girl, and my parents like her. I like her too, once she's away from that Terry girl, and I know we'll deal very well together. It might not be the love match of the century, but I don't look for that, and neither does she. It's time I married. Will you come? I know you'll be busy, but I'd love to see you there, and you did promise me once. I won't hold you to it, though, if you'd rather not come, or you're engaged elsewhere.

Yours etc,

Tom Skerrit

I sat at the dressing table and stared into space, letting Nichols busy herself about me. I had changed, it was true, but Tom was still the same. I hoped I hadn't hurt him too much, and I still thought they would do well, but I was sorry he didn't love her as much as I loved Richard.

When Richard came in to take me down to dinner, I showed him the letter. He read it in silence. "It seems Tom has made a clearheaded choice. I think you're right, they will suit." He saw me sigh and said gently, "Many people who marry out of liking make a love match of it. They have a good basis for marriage, something solid to work on."

I managed a smile. "I suppose so."

"And we have a more immediate concern," he reminded me. "We have to tell the guests something tonight. The ball gave us a rest from it all, but they'll want to know."

I had to agree.

During dinner, the only time in such a house party that the whole company were gathered together, Richard spoke about the discovery of the pistols. He announced it quietly, when the covers had been removed, and there was only wine and desserts left on the table. We were sitting together tonight, as for some reason Lady Southwood had insisted on precedence. I thought she looked well after her rest, and she was supremely in control.

"I would like to ask for your help." Silence fell and all eyes turned to him. "I'm sorry it came to this. You all know what happened before the ball." He gestured with one hand, and the footmen waiting on us silently filed out of the room.

Richard waited until they had all gone and gave the company a small, frosty smile. "I hope you don't mind if we serve ourselves for the next few minutes, but since it was two of their company who were killed, we thought it best to ensure some privacy."

I met Freddy's look across the table. His expression of lazy amusement hadn't changed, but I saw a spark of alertness in his eyes and from the way he lounged back in his chair he could see the faces of almost everyone sat at the table.

"We know what happened," Richard said when the company had fallen silent again. "It's unfortunate, but we have to deal with it. There's a constable on the premises, or at least he's been here ever since he heard about it. I think he's gone home now, but he'll be back."

The stillness was eerie. Freddy lifted his glass to his lips and the gleam of his polished glass against the candlelight caught my attention, but that was the only movement.

"When the rooms upstairs were being cleared," Richard continued, with a delicate turn of phrase, "they found something the constable is as yet unaware of." He stood and crossed to one of the sideboards with a graceful, smooth movement that was almost part of himself. He opened a small drawer and took out the pistols. "They found these." He held them so everyone could see them. "They must have been used in the...occurrence." His pause before the final word gave everyone the chance to fit in the word "murder" in their minds. He waited, let everyone take a good look at the weapons in his hands, and he came back to take his seat unhurriedly.

While he had been doing this I hadn't been watching him— like Freddy and Gervase I'd been watching the people sitting at the table. The reactions varied from indifference through interest right through to avid curiosity. I thought I knew who the pistols belonged to. I glanced at Gervase, not letting my gaze rest on his face, and I saw his slight nod, confirming what I had thought.

Richard was talking again. "These don't belong to the house. They're from King's in London, and a fine pair, so it's likely they belong to someone here. We would appreciate knowing the owner."

"You're not saying that whoever these pistols belong to is the murderer," Freddy pointed out.

"No, of course not." Richard gave Freddy an easy smile. "The person—or persons—could have stolen these. It would help if we knew where they had come from, and when they could have been stolen. I'll keep them here so you all see them if you wish."

"What if they were brought in by the killer?" demanded the Marquês.

Richard bowed his head in acknowledgement. "It's a possibility. We would also like to know that."

"Does the esteemed constable know any of this?" drawled Giles Kerre from his seat next to my sister farther up the table. "My feeling is, Strang, that you've kept the man in the dark."

"I wanted to look into it myself first," Richard replied. "If it does involve anyone here, we might have a chance of—calming things down first."

"You don't expect us to lie to the official?" I heard someone say anxiously. It was Lady Georgiana.

He smiled reassuringly at his sister. "Of course not. But he might not ask, and you don't have to volunteer the information."

"What if someone says something?" Freddy put in.

"If they do, they do," Richard replied, fatalistically. "We'll cope with it. This is just an attempt to prevent too much gossip and scandal, that's all."

Lord Sambrook, Freddy's father, spoke up. Usually his lordship was the epitome of joviality, but now, eyes narrowed in suspicion, his keen intelligence showed through. "You've done this before, haven't you? Stopped too much scandal getting out?"

Richard turned a limpid gaze onto him. "It has been known." He didn't elaborate. "This matter, however, involves my own family. I shall do my best to prevent any scandal on my own doorstep."

"More than you did before," said his lordship, and received a daggers look from Lord Southwood for his pains.

"Ah, but this one isn't of my making," Richard murmured. "It positively cannot be allowed."

"Well, I never thought I'd see Strang wanting to clear matters up," Lord Sambrook declared. "I only ever saw him stirring things up before. Marriage has changed you, my boy."

The look he received form Richard could have frozen him to an icicle where he sat, but all Richard said was, "Just so, sir."

With a rustle of skirts, Lady Southwood got to her feet. "Well, I don't think we will gain anything else by remaining here. Ladies, shall we leave the gentlemen to their discussions?"

For once, this was not a euphemism for drinking and carousals. We were glad to go, as the subsequent discussion looked as though it might become quite heated.

I could have done with more than tea, but I was stuck in my duties of brewing and distributing for some time. We were in the long gallery upstairs tonight. It was at the top of the house and caught what breezes there were on this sultry night.

As soon as I could I left the tea table and went to join Lizzie, Louisa and Georgiana who were sitting together engaged in deep conversation. "Am I butting in? Can I join you?"

They looked up and smiled in welcome. "Not at all," Lizzie said.

I sat next to Georgiana. Our sofas were set at right angles to each other. The maids had arranged them around the room while we were at dinner, and they would replace them against the wall afterwards.

"Your husband certainly has a flair for the dramatic," Lizzie commented.

I smiled ruefully. I knew what she meant, and I knew it came naturally to him. "It seemed the best way, to confront everybody after dinner. It saved having to explain the same thing over and over again. Has anybody said they want to leave?"

"Dear me, no," Louisa said. "We haven't had such excitement since your wedding. We wouldn't miss this for the world."

Georgiana looked troubled.

"I'm sorry, my dear, but you must admit it is exciting," Louisa protested. "I'm sure Lord Strang will do his best to stop anything getting out, but the right people will get to know something. Most of them have enough sense not to announce it to the general delectation of the public."

"Oh, I hope so." Georgiana was still single, and she couldn't bear any scandal at this delicate time of her life. Something occurred to me for the first time since we'd found the bodies. Lizzie knew me well enough to notice the serious expression that crossed my face, but although I saw her looking at me, she said nothing. She knew as well as I did what a gossip Louisa was.

I laid my hand over Georgiana's. "I'm sure it will be sorted out. If it wasn't for the necklace, it would be a sad occurrence, but very little to do with us. We must remember to forget it."

They found some amusement at the way I had phrased that last remark, but they understood what I meant. We must try to keep the two affairs separate, at least in the minds of people outside this house.

"What necklace?" asked Lizzie innocently, and smiled. "It seems to me what Lord Strang wants to happens, happens. I'm sure it won't get out."

It was my turn to smile. "We hope so, but we can cope if it does. By the way," I added, reminded of my purpose tonight, "does anyone know who those pistols belong to? They're very distinctive, engraved silver, but there's no monogram or coat of arms on them, so we don't know where they came from."

They all shook their heads. "I wouldn't know one pistol from another," Louisa confessed.

"Oh, Louisa, you must know," I protested.

"Rose is a very good shot," Lizzie informed her.

They looked at me with new eyes. "I'm a country girl. And when I found I had a flair for it, I continued. I don't have very many social accomplishments—"

Lizzie interrupted me. "With your skill on keyboards? Rose, you are joking!"

"I don't sew very well," I said. "And I don't dance at all well."

"I've seen you dance with Strang," Louisa said. "I can't say I thought your dancing was poor."

I laughed. "That's him. He dances so well he does it for both of us. When you see us dance next, watch how he makes sure I know what I'm doing."

"I've seen that too," said Louisa. "You astounded the whole

of Venice that night."

Lizzie was agog. "Why? What did they do?" She turned to me. "Why didn't you tell me?"

I didn't know what to say, but Louisa did. "First of all there was a couple in Venice who were calling themselves Lord and Lady Strang, but who weren't, so when that was discovered it was assumed the real ones were elsewhere. Then Richard and Rose turned up at the Contessa Marini's smelling of April and May, and she made them lead out the minuet, as they had missed doing it at their wedding. The whole room watched them." She paused, remembering, and an unusually tender smile curved her lips. "It was obvious Richard Kerre had been well and truly caught."

I couldn't protest, but I flushed when the others looked at me. It hadn't been deliberate, but in Venice we had begun to explore what we had together. I tried to change the subject, and Lizzie, seeing my confusion, allowed me to, although had we been alone she would have pursued it. She seemed to be looking to me for an example, as she had not done since we were little. I thought she might be feeling confused. My sister Lizzie confused! It indicated she was feeling more than she had expected to. She'd always said she would marry for position, money and friendship, and not look for what I'd found, but what if she had found it, was going through the same things I had gone through?

Lizzie favoured Louisa with a bright smile. "And how about you and Sir Willoughby? Do you suit?"

She met my look with her cool grey gaze and smiled. "I think he'll do. I don't wish to stay single for much longer. Girls seem to be coming on the marriage market much younger these days, and it's about time I settled. I've known him for a long time, but I can't say I really noticed him before."

"Is his fortune what you were looking for?" Louisa had always said she would marry wealth, so she knew the suitor wasn't marrying her for her money.

"It's adequate," she said carelessly with an elegant shrug that nearly pushed her gown off her shoulders.

I was surprised by her response. "And you like him?"

"Well enough." She busied herself picking up her tea dish and sipped at her tea delicately so we couldn't see her face.

I'd been so busy watching my sister I hadn't noticed that Louisa, in her attempts to fix someone's affections, had been fixed herself. Clever Louisa, always so cool in her search for a suitable match, so aware that a woman can never call herself her own property unless she was a widow or penniless—in which case nobody cared.

Chapter Thirteen

Now I could watch the growing attraction between Lizzie and the Marquês with more complacency. He was undoubtedly the person he claimed to be, and the owner of estates and vineyards in his native Portugal that could keep Lizzie in luxury for the rest of her life.

Richard had asked me if I would like to watch Freddy practice swordplay with him. It was something they did regularly together, but I hadn't seen it before. We went to the ballroom, where the gentlemen stripped to shirt and breeches and had the sleeves of their shirts tied close to their arms with black ribbons. They looked very romantic, with the full sleeves held out of the way, wigs gone, to reveal the short hair both preferred to wear underneath. The contrast between Freddy's dark locks and Richard's golden waves was piquant and striking, something an artist would appreciate. Gervase joined us, and when he saw what was happening, prepared himself to fight the victor, acting as referee in the meantime.

There was a great deal of laughter about today. At first Richard and Freddy played, circling the thin, flexible blades around each other with no attempt at real attack, while they warmed up. Then they took up the formal stance, presented their buttoned blades to each other and whipped them down to the floor in salute.

They engaged with a sharp ring of blade against blade. They were still smiling, but absently, as though they had forgotten to change the expression on their faces. They were well matched, both still young and athletic, both well trained by masters, but with styles completely their own. Richard's style was of the dancer, quick footwork, fast attacks and defences, while Freddy had the lithe movements of an animal, one of the great cats perhaps, and the brute strength such an animal can show when it chooses.

It was hard to see which one would triumph, but the first hit went to Richard. He laughed as he disengaged. "In love, Freddy? You would have seen that coming last year. What can be on your mind?"

Freddy laughed. "I'm not the one who's in love." He glanced at me, smiled, and checked the tip of his weapon to make sure the button was securely fixed.

Richard laughed easily; his feelings towards me were well known in this company. "Shall we make it three hits or five?"

"First to three," Freddy said, and presented his rapier.

Richard presented his in turn and they were away again. After a few deft passes Richard tried to overreach himself and was rewarded by a light touch on his chest from Freddy's sword. They drew back immediately, and Richard acknowledged the hit. "That was stupid of me."

"Trying too hard," Freddy commented with a smile.

Gervase walked over to sit next to me. "They don't need a referee. They know when they've lost a point."

We watched as the third bout commenced. With one each, they seemed to be more engrossed in the sport—after all it was a little more than just the accomplishment of a gentleman.

The level of concentration in the room increased, and Gervase leaned forward in his chair as the fighting became more intense.

Richard's blue stare never left his opponent, as though he and Freddy were alone in the great, echoing chamber. Their feet slid on the polished floor, but they were never out of control.

The only sounds were the clash of blade on blade and the

movement of their feet on the polished wooden floor. With all this space to themselves they used it to advantage, but not a movement was wasted. There was no flamboyance here. The blades circled around each other, flashing when the sun caught them. Richard saw an opening and quick as a kingfisher darting down for its prey, he passed Freddy's guard and touched home. If this fight had been for real, he would have killed Freddy with that one accurate thrust.

The tension relaxed, and Freddy smiled ruefully, acknowledging the hit. They paused, and looked over to where Gervase and I sat watching in silent appreciation. "You're both very good."

"We practise," Richard said briefly, and engaged again. This time Freddy took Richard completely by surprise. In a sweeping gesture he spun around once, knocked Richard's sword aside and went straight for the breast, finding his mark almost immediately. Laughing, Richard acknowledged the hit, throwing up his hands in a gesture of submission.

"Of course, if you'd done it for real..." He suddenly dropped to one knee. His hand went to his waist, and in a movement so fast the onlooker couldn't follow it, he produced a knife, one of the thin, lethal stilettos he always carried.

"I wouldn't take you on in a knife-throwing contest," Freddy remarked. Richard laughed and stood, and with a seemingly careless gesture, threw the knife towards us. It pierced the floor at Gervase's feet, and we watched it quivering with the impact of its landing.

Neither of us moved. We had seen the glance Richard cast us to take his sights before he threw his weapon, and we trusted his aim. Still, it was impressive.

Gervase bent and pulled the knife out from its sheath in the floor. He threw it into the air and caught it by its hilt as it fell. "Nicely balanced," he commented, and with only one glance at his brother, he threw it at him.

Without that look it would have been a stupid gesture, but

Richard, balanced on the balls of his feet, was able to move aside as the knife passed. This time it landed across the room, in one of the window seats. Right through the upholstery.

Richard glanced at Gervase, smiling easily, but I became aware of the tension always present between the brothers. There was no rivalry, no outward antagonism, but Gervase was aware he had done Richard an injustice in the past by leaving him to face the consequences of his actions, and Richard resented the freedom which being the younger brother had given to Gervase. Gervase knew what he was doing, may even have deliberately cast the knife wide, and Richard was easily able to move aside.

They regarded each other for a brief moment. Then they both smiled, and the moment passed.

Richard turned to Freddy and presented his sword, but as the rapiers met once more, the door to the ballroom opened and Carier entered with Sir Barnett. Sir Barnett was carrying a box. A box which could only hold one thing. Or rather, two.

Richard was facing the door, and Freddy had his back to it, but he must have heard it open, because he immediately disengaged. Sir Barnett smiled expansively. "Please continue. I did not know you were busy. May I watch?"

Richard and Freddy bowed, and Sir Barnett went over to the little sofa by the window. Startled, he saw the knife and withdrew it.

"A little horseplay," said Richard by way of explanation. Carier took the knife from Sir Barnett and stood holding it carefully by the hilt until Richard could take it back from him.

Richard and Freddy turned to face each other, and reengaged. At first, all was accuracy, each waiting for the other to make a mistake, the blades clicking in the concentrated silence, but Freddy took a chance and lunged under Richard's blade. Richard moved out of the way of the lunge, but in doing so lost his balance and swayed. He moved quickly to regain his footing, but it gave Freddy the opportunity he was looking for, and his rapier flashed sideways in an accurate swipe.

It met steel. Richard, anticipating the move, had swung his sword around just in time, but it meant he had no time to regain his balance, and he dropped to one knee on the floor. As Freddy swept his weapon round to take advantage of the situation, Richard brought his sword up and knocked Freddy's weapon aside with one strong, potentially lethal flick of his wrist. The rapier spun into the air and landed behind the opponents, skidding to a halt along the floor.

They stared at each other in silence, the only sound their panting breaths. Freddy laughed and offered Richard his hand. "Clever."

Richard took his hand and stood. "You thought you'd won, so I used your arrogance. When you thought you had me you thought any old thrust would do. You should always keep fighting to the end, Freddy, don't ever assume you've won until he's bleeding at your feet."

Freddy gave Richard a mock bow. "I'm obliged to you, cousin."

Richard grinned. "And I had a lot of luck."

"Oh no, I cannot allow that. It was a fine example of the swordsman's art." Sir Barnett came to join us. Richard and Freddy smiled and bowed, acknowledging the compliment.

"I still think I was lucky," my husband said.

"I should like to see you in a bout with my son," said Sir Barnett. "Giles is a fine swordsman, but I think he might meet his match in you two gentlemen."

"It would be a pleasure," Freddy said politely, although I thought it might be less amusing for him to take on the volatile Giles.

Sir Barnett looked at us and bowed to me. I inclined my head, smiling, and Gervase stood and bowed to him. He didn't resume his seat but went over to join the other two. "My turn."

"Do you fight, my lady?" Sir Barnett asked me. I looked at him, surprised. "It's becoming quite the thing for young ladies to take fencing lessons."

"It's yet another opportunity for them to show their fine figures to advantage," Richard said with a smile. "No, my wife doesn't fence. But she's a fine shot."

"Really?" Sir Barnett asked.

"I found I had a natural aptitude, and I practised," I told him.

"I should like to see that," the older man said.

It was on the tip of my tongue to ask him if I could use the guns in the case he was carrying, but I desisted. I caught Richard looking at me, and I knew he was thinking much the same as me. I smiled at him and saw his answering gleam.

He turned back to his erstwhile opponent. "I'm afraid you must excuse us, Freddy. Can you make do with Gervase for a while?"

"It will be interesting," Freddy replied, turning to study Gervase. "You look so like Strang, but I have a feeling your style is very different to his."

"I'm afraid so," Gervase said with a self-deprecating smile. "Where Richard has finesse, I tend to use brute strength. It was always the way when we were children. While he was content to dissect something to see what was inside, I would smash it in my impatience."

The brothers exchanged a look and Richard smiled, recognising his brother's description.

"I'm sorry, but you'll have to manage without a referee." He turned to let Carier undo the black bands holding up his sleeves and help him back into his waistcoat. "I rather think Sir Barnett wishes for a private word or two." He raised a questioning eyebrow and Sir Barnett nodded solemnly.

Carier held up Richard's coat for him. He was wearing a light coat today, not the heavy, stiff coat which he used on more formal occasions.

Instead of putting my hand on his arm in the approved

manner, I walked over to him and linked my arm with his, smiling at Freddy and Gervase. Carier paused to tie up Gervase's sleeves for him, so we waited until he was ready, bowed to the swordsmen and left. Gervase was getting the feel for his rapier, swishing it through the air before taking his stance. I wished I could stay to see the difference in style for myself, but I needed to be with Richard.

Sir Barnett was not so sure. As Carier quietly closed the door of the ballroom behind us, he looked at me with his eyebrow raised. "I hope we're not keeping you from anything, my lady."

I would have taken this as a dismissal, but Richard felt me begin to withdraw my arm and gripped it tightly with his. "My wife shares my concerns, and she has my complete trust."

Sir Barnett said nothing more. Carier opened the door to one of the little rooms near the ballroom and found it empty except for a couple of housemaids, who exited after dropping hasty curtseys. Richard and I sat on a sofa, and Sir Barnett sat on a chair opposite us. Carier remained standing just by Sir Barnett where we could see him and Sir Barnett couldn't.

Sir Barnett sat clutching the box on his knees. With a sigh, he reached for the clasps and opened it.

It was fitted out for a pair of pistols. The equipment was there, the ramrods, the bullet moulds, the powder flask, but the point of all this paraphernalia, the pistols themselves, were gone. I would have bet my sapphire necklace that the label on the box read King's even though I wasn't close enough to read it.

"When did you miss them, sir?" Richard asked him.

Sir Barnett sighed heavily. "This morning. I remembered I had brought a pair with me and asked my servant to fetch them. They were gone."

"Could you tell me when you saw them last?"

"When we arrived," said Sir Barnett instantly. "I handed them over to my servant to clean and forgot I had them until this morning. They could have been taken at any time since then."

"That is unfortunate." Richard leaned forward, resting his elbows on his knees. "Do you know where they were kept in that time?"

"I questioned my man most thoroughly," Sir Barnett assured us. "He told me he gave the case to one of the servants here, who said he would clean them. He cannot remember the man's name, but he described him to me." He paused. "It occurred to me that this may well be the man who disappeared after the murder." He closed the case and held it up in the air with one hand without looking. Carier took it. I hated that kind of arrogance, but it came naturally to some people. They weren't aware they were doing it. I'd seen much more of it since I had come back to England.

"What man would that be, sir?" Richard asked.

Sir Barnett waved a hand in an expansive gesture. "I've been talking to that Hampson fellow, and he says there seems to have been an intruder on the night those two men were killed. Someone who pretended to be a servant, but had no right to be here. Has he not spoken to you about it?"

Since we had spent some time avoiding the constable, we could say with truth he had not spoken to us. We let Sir Barnett tell us. "None of the servants here know who this man could be. No one has seen him since, so it seems likely he is the murderer."

"Do we know what he looked like?" Richard leaned back, watching Sir Barnett closely. As Richard must have known he would, Sir Barnett preened. "By all accounts he was tall and dark complexioned, with a scar on his right cheek."

"Rather villainous for a servant," Richard commented lazily.

"I'm assured it was a small scar."

"Pity, I had imagined a large, sweeping line from eyebrow to mouth," Richard said with regret.

Sir Barnett gave him a disapproving look. "You should not

be flippant, Strang. This could be a murderer we're discussing." Chastened, Richard begged his pardon and was condescendingly forgiven. "I've seen this levity in you before, Strang. It doesn't become your position. Several servants, who assumed he was one of the extra staff hired for the ball, saw this man, but it seems your butler hasn't seen him or heard of him. His presence here is suspicious, to say the least, and Hampson has set up an immediate search for him. He suspects this man of the crimes, and he says once he has found him, he will make him confess."

"If he has any sense, he's long gone," Richard commented.

Sir Barnett sighed. "I'm afraid I have to agree with you. However there may be some trace of him. He must have used public transport or had a horse."

"Indeed," agreed Richard. "Unless he flew."

"Strang." Said as if he were still a child being admonished for some minor misdemeanour.

"I'm sorry. I suppose I must take it more seriously."

"I'm surprised you don't, considering how badly the scene affected your wife."

I hastened to reassure him. "It was a slight weakness, no more."

"You're too good." Richard bestowed one of his angelic smiles on me. I smiled back and he turned to Sir Barnett. "Do you think Hampson will need any help? I told him to come to us if he needed any manpower." Not quite mendacious, but bordering on untruth.

"I believe he is seeking an interview with your father to those ends," Sir Barnett informed him.

"Have you told him about the pistols?" Although he seemed to be taking his ease, I saw the gleam under Richard's heavy eyelids. He was watching his relative, very closely.

"Yes, naturally," came the reply.

"I shall have to see him. Explain why I didn't tell him about them earlier."

This made Sir Barnett's expression turn grave. It was coming too close to his family now.

Richard pursued his quarry. "Did anyone else know you had the pistols with you?"

"I suppose so." Sir Barnett's eyes narrowed. "I tend to carry some with me. The roads aren't safe these days, you know."

"So they were loaded?"

"They might have been."

Richard glanced up at Carier, who stood unmoving, still holding the case. "So whoever stole them stole loaded weapons? Careless."

"What good is an unloaded pistol?" There was a distinct edge to his voice now.

Richard tried to mollify Sir Barnett. "No use at all. Thank you for telling me. Have you told my father, or should I tell him myself?"

"I was on my way to tell him, but your manservant informed me he was engaged and offered to bring me to you instead."

"I see. I'll tell him if you wish."

Sir Barnett inclined his head graciously. "I would be obliged."

"I'll send Carier to you later with the flintlocks," Richard told him.

Sir Barnett inclined his head again and heaved himself out of his chair. "I'm doubly in your debt, sir." He bowed to me.

Richard stopped him as he reached the door. "Sir Barnett."

He slowly turned back to face us. Richard stared at him. "Why didn't you tell us before? You must have recognised the pistols when I produced them at dinner."

"One doesn't wash one's dirty linen in public," the man replied ponderously. "I wanted to be sure."

Richard smiled and nodded, and Sir Barnett left the room.

As soon as he had gone, Richard turned to me. "What do you think, my love?"

"You don't clean loaded guns," I said bluntly.

"Carier?"

"May I be frank, my lord?"

"Be who you like."

Carier didn't smile. "He's lying, my lord."

"Evidently. But why?"

I joined in again. "Because he knows who did it, and it touches him closely."

Richard smiled, but there was no humour in it this time. "I agree. So it was a Kerre. I don't think he did it himself, do you?"

"He knew the necklace was paste, so he wouldn't have stolen it, and therefore he would have no motive for killing Hill and Derring."

"Unless he was trying to cover for whoever did it, my lady," Carier pointed out.

"I don't think Sir Barnett would have panicked like the murderer did," Richard said. "It's a possibility, but an outside one." After a pause, he spoke again. "He jumped on the story of the servant like a dog on a bone. I would have believed it if I hadn't started that one running myself."

"With the scar?" I asked, amused.

He smiled. "No, my love, I think an imaginative footman must have started that one." He paused once more. "But he was looking for a smokescreen. He thinks we won't betray him if it involves the family, but I won't see a murderer go unpunished, family or not." He turned to face me. "Hill's and Derring's families arrived today. My mother is with them now, and I intend to see them too. Will you come?"

"Of course." I'd be ashamed if I avoided such a meeting.

Lady Southwood had given them guest rooms to use while they were here. Not the best rooms, but she had made them comfortable and had spent some time with them, assuring them of her sympathy, or so the servant who came to escort us told us.

We found them in a small parlour on the first floor. We asked them to sit after we had greeted them, and I helped them to some tea. Richard had changed into a more formal coat, feeling they deserved some respect, but had been careful not to don anything which might have emphasised his social position, and so denigrated theirs.

They were evidently respectable women, their eyes red from weeping. Mrs. Hill was accompanied by another tall, broad man who turned out to be Hill's older brother. He ran the farm now his father was dead. Mrs. Derring had her daughter with her. Derring's work kept him at home. Not every employer was enlightened enough to allow his people time off for funerals and mourning.

Richard gave them an account of what happened, leaving out the most distressing details. "They died instantly, so they would have known little." Mrs. Hill made a small sound and held her handkerchief up to her face. "They would have felt no pain," he told them. It was something I'd wish to know, if anything happened to one of my loved ones.

Mrs. Derring was made of sterner stuff. She stared at Richard, dry eyed now, but the lines etched into her face showed her distress just as clearly. "I was told you saw them soon after, my lord."

"I did," Richard replied. "There was nothing that could have been done at that stage."

I heard the tension in his voice at the remembrance, so I said something. "We are all so sorry this should have happened. We'll do everything we can to help you."

Mrs. Hill looked up, straight at me, and I saw the tragedy in her pale grey eyes. It occurred to me that motherhood was a very vulnerable state and I was afraid. "Will you catch them?" An edge of anger tinged the sadness.

"Yes," Richard said. "We will catch whoever did this thing,

and we will keep you informed. Please feel free to remain here as long as you like."

Mrs. Derring nodded. "We're going tomorrow. We'll take our boys home and bury them decently." She emphasised the last word, reminding me of how indecent their deaths had been.

"If you wish it, I'll attend one or both of the ceremonies," Richard said gently. "I don't want to intrude, but if you feel you would like it, I'll be there."

Both ladies stared at him in surprise. Neither seemed to have expected this. "They'll be quiet services," Mrs. Derring told him. "And they're in different parts of the country. Thank you very much, my lord, but I think my relatives might be overwhelmed enough."

Richard nodded, and received a similar reply from Mrs. Hill. He spoke to Mrs. Derring. "You know your son worked for Thompson's?"

"Yes, my lord, though he never spoke of it much."

"He has a bonus coming to him. I'll make sure it's paid as soon as possible." I knew Richard would ensure the bonus was more than the usual one. "Have you been told the circumstances of your son's death, Mrs. Hill?" Richard asked.

"Her ladyship said he was under house guard at the time. Had there been a problem?"

Lady Southwood had obviously been reticent to the point of obfuscation. Richard glanced at Mrs. Hill and at her other son, standing grim and silent behind her chair. He was the only person standing in the room, as tall as his dead brother and even burlier. He dwarfed a normal-sized person like my husband, but his vitality of character made Richard the centre of attention. He held them all effortlessly, almost without knowing it. "Hill was found in possession of a necklace belonging to one of the guests."

Mrs. Hill's hand flew to her mouth and her eyes widened in horror. Her son leaned forward to put one great hand gently on her shoulder, but he said nothing.

"We think he was paid to do it by someone in the household, if he did it at all," Richard said gently. "And that someone killed him. We will find out who it was, and we'll keep your son's hand in the affair as quiet as we can. I promise you both those things."

"Will the man hang?" the older Mr. Hill asked, with a voice that came from the depths of the earth.

Richard shook his head. "I don't know yet. He will pay."

Mr. Hill nodded. "If you would let me know, my lord, I can tell my mother."

Her hand went up to cover his, still protectively resting on her shoulder. "Thank you, Jack."

Richard continued, his soft, low voice filling the room as effectively as Jack Hill's had done but without the volume. "The constable is making enquiries. He knows about Hill's involvement, but he wants to find the murderers. The affair of the necklace isn't important to him, except in the way it affects his investigations, so we will ensure it doesn't."

Hill nodded in understanding.

Richard spoke to Mrs. Derring and her daughter. "You should know Derring was guarding Hill when he was shot, acting under my orders. He was a good employee; I had used him in the past. Thompson's will miss him, but not, I know, as much as you will. Did you rely much on his earnings?"

"My daughter is a housemaid at Blenheim," the lady replied, "and she helps me all she can, but my son did send home something for me every quarter."

Richard frowned. "Has my mother mentioned a pension of any kind?"

"No, my lord."

"I think something could be arranged from Thompson's." I knew something would be arranged, and not only because Richard felt some guilt about the murders. His sense of justice would see to it. "He has worked for them for a long time now."

"Thank you, my lord."

"Think nothing of it." Richard made no attempt to stand up, although the interview was drawing to a close. He was as near his natural self as he ever allowed in public, outside our own private chambers. When I had first met him, his society manners seemed a part of him, but he was capable of jettisoning them when they weren't appropriate.

I offered more tea, but they refused it, and finally, Richard stood. "I promise to let you know about the outcome. And if you need anything, please let me know."

"You have all been very kind," Mrs. Derring said quietly.

We left them to their grief. It was all too easy to imagine how I would feel if I were ever in such a situation. Outside, careless of who might be about, Richard drew me to him and held me. I felt his emotion, his muscles tense through his clothes. "Now I know why you took it to heart so much."

"Every mother's son. Everyone has a mother, though some are no longer here to mourn. They deserve justice, and they have a right to the truth. Even if Gervase were the murderer, I would tell them."

He released me, but kept his arms about my waist. His eyes were brighter than usual. I put my hand up to his cheek. "If I lost you, I would die."

"So would I, but I think mine might be more literal than yours."

"No, Richard."

"So you'd better not die, had you?"

He kept one arm around my waist as we walked slowly away from the room that held two grieving mothers.

Chapter Fourteen

At about midday the next day Lizzie and I managed some time to ourselves. We had tea served in the room where we entertained the Sturmans that afternoon, and settled down for a good gossip. And I had something to tell her, something I was delighted to be able to communicate.

She looked so delectable today, I wondered how any man could resist her. I had seen my sister in love once before, a sad business which had ended when the man had jettisoned her for someone with more prospects. I hoped he was sorry now.

She was dressed in pale yellow and white, light fabrics that took account of the hot weather and set her golden loveliness off to perfection. Lizzie was very clever with her clothes. The wrong shade of yellow would have been a disastrous mistake on a blonde, but this was ideal. Although she was fully aware of how good she looked, she wasn't too carried away by her own looks and this seeming unawareness added to her attraction.

I glanced in the mirror and grimaced before I sat. Lizzie gave me a scold, as she always did when she saw me denigrating myself. "You should know better by now, Rose. You've married one of the leaders of fashion, indeed you're one yourself, and you've found yourself."

"What do you mean, found myself?" I began to make the tea.

"Well, before, you didn't hold your head up in society. I can understand it then, but not now."

"I'm probably scorned by more people now than I was then."

She frowned. "But not to your face, and no one laughs at you anymore. What you're talking about is natural to someone in your position, you know that."

I put down the teapot. "I suppose so. But the thought is difficult to shift. Richard has helped me find a mask, something I can hide behind when I need to, but I've not changed, not really."

"Oh yes you have. You're far more confident now. You walk into a room like I always wanted you to do, as though you own it."

I laughed. "Do I? I don't mean to."

"If it's not deliberate, that's even better."

"They all look at you when you go into a room." I was anxious to get the conversation away from me. Although I had come far, I was still uncomfortable talking about myself. "You've been a sensation."

Lizzie sat back in her chair and smiled like a cat, full of self-satisfaction. "I know, but I've never been dazzled by it. You know why?"

"I think so."

"Because if we had gone as the Misses Golightly, dressed as we used to dress, the daughters of a country squire, no one would have looked twice at us." She was quite right, it was why I had never let my new position go to my head.

"You could have done it, Lizzie."

She accepted her tea with a smile. "I used to think so, but now I'm not so sure. They're very aware of who they are, most of them, even your husband. They pay to look their best, the clothes are wonderful, the ladies' maids can make the plainest girl presentable. Our dowdy provincial clothes would have marked us out from the outset. We would have had to have been very clever to vie with all that."

"They marry for money," I commented. "Our dowries were nowhere near adequate."

She nodded in agreement. "But you would have had your Tom, and I would have found someone. I would have married well."

I was reminded of the purpose of this meeting. "It looks as though you'll marry very well, Lizzie."

She looked at me with a sharper expression now. "Have you heard something?"

"Oh yes. The new footmen brought some dispatches with them." I waited, sipping my tea. I saw she was in a fever of anticipation, and I wanted to savour my moment. I watched her silently as she fidgeted. Even that was delectable. I would wager the Marquês couldn't wait to get his hands on her, but knowing my sister, the ring would have to be well and truly on her finger before she let herself go. She knew her worth, and she wouldn't sell herself cheaply.

"Well?" she demanded eventually, unable to wait any longer. "What did they say?"

I put down my tea dish and looked at her, deliberately blanking my expression, making her wait. "He's a catch. If anything, he's been modest. He owns vineyards and estates in Spain and Portugal that compare favourably with the Southwood inheritance." I watched as she absorbed the information. She couldn't hide her elation, didn't even try to, clapping her hands and throwing her head back in her joy. "Oh, Rose. Oh, I'm so relieved! It will make things so much easier with James and Martha."

"He's everything he purports to be, and more. He has lands, interests, and his people like him. I think you'll do well there. Has he proposed?"

"Yes," she admitted. "On the night of the ball. He must know how I feel about him, I don't seem to be able to hide it when I'm with him, but I couldn't say yes, could I, Rose?"

"I could," I reminded her.

"But we knew about your Richard. We read all about him."

"And even that didn't put me off."

She smiled. "I tried hard enough. I wasn't sure he was for you, Rose, and I still find it amazing when I see you together. I don't know what you did, but he's loyal to you, changed completely by all accounts."

"You've been talking about me?" I imagined she would, but I had to make the protest, for form's sake.

Lizzie took her time selecting a cake from the stand. "It's hard to avoid it. They're still waiting for him to fall, you know."

"Do you think he will?"

"No. He's happy."

"As you will be, my love."

Her expression softened, her heavenly eyes took on a dreamy aspect. "Yes. I will be, won't I?"

"Where will you live?"

She shrugged. "I don't care, but Portugal, I think. I'll have to learn the language, won't I?"

"We'll come to see you." It must be daunting, however much in love she was, to go to a land where she couldn't even speak the language, where she knew no one except her new husband.

"We will still visit England frequently. His mother came back to England when his father died, and she lives here still. We can't abandon her, can we?"

I smiled. "No." Although living in another country to your mother-in-law sounded like heaven to me.

We were interrupted when Louisa burst into the room, rushing in like a whirlwind but pausing to catch her breath and closing the door carefully behind her. "There you are. I must tell you—the most astonishing thing has happened."

That effectively stopped the conversation, and we watched her in silence as she settled herself on the chair next to me, happily anticipatory. Louisa didn't look upset, only mischievously excited. Her cheeks were glowing, her blue eyes sparkling. She sat and looked at us both. "Guess who just proposed to me."

"Sir Willoughby."

Louisa cast me a look of disdain. "No, but I don't despair."

"Gervase," I suggested facetiously.

She laughed. "No, same initials though. Giles Kerre."

"What?" Lizzie's exclamation came loud and strong, and I glanced in some surprise over to where she was sitting. "Did you accept him?"

"Of course not. You know I have interests elsewhere, and anyway—" She broke off and cast a glance at me. I was a Kerre now.

I smiled and lifted my hands for her to go on. "You should hear what they call him in private."

Louisa smiled back at me. "He's a gambler. And, let's face it, even if he wanted me, he wouldn't refuse my fortune. And it wouldn't last a twelvemonth in his hands."

"But he's very handsome," Lizzie demurred.

"And you'd accept a man because of his looks?" Louisa demanded. She turned to me. "Why did you accept Lord Strang?"

"Because I loved him." I couldn't equivocate in this company, they both knew too much. "And because I trusted him."

"You see?" Louisa cried, but she paused. "You *trusted* Richard Kerre?"

"I didn't know him as you did," I reminded her. "I met him in such a situation that I had to judge him for myself. We'd read the gossip rags, but they are often as wrong as they are right. I saw the man first, the fashionable gentleman second." I leaned forward to feel the teapot, and, deciding it was hot enough, poured out some more tea, more for the opportunity to busy myself than anything else.

Louisa, chasing other game, decided to let it be. "But if he had been a gambler, what then?"

"It would have made me pause, I probably would have taken him anyway, but I might have lived to regret it. Something else would always have come first."

"Exactly my point. Everyone knows what Giles Kerre lives for, and so no one will take him. I don't know why he offered for me now, he must be in more of a bind than usual. He must know I would never take him."

"He offered for me too," Lizzie confessed.

"What?" we both cried, totally astonished. I leaned forward in my chair. As a spectator sport, this was getting very interesting.

"Yesterday, before dinner," my sister explained. "He came to my room and asked me to dismiss my maid, cool as you please. I wasn't about to do that. Well, I wasn't quite ready, so I was a bit put out, and told him to wait, pretty cool." She looked at us to make sure we were agog. We were. "I dismissed her when I was ready and went with him downstairs, to walk in the garden. He said I had been the object of his regard since he first met me, and he would greatly appreciate it if I would do the honour of becoming his wife." She looked questioningly at Louisa.

"That's pretty much what he said to me," Louisa confirmed. "But he's known me for years, and when I asked him how it was he had only just noticed, he got a bit tongue-tied and said he had been too unsure of himself. Giles Kerre, unsure!" She laughed. "He was one of the most arrogant men I have ever met. It seems to run in the family—" She clapped a hand to her mouth and looked at me guiltily. "Oh, Rose, I'm sorry. I didn't mean..."

It was my turn to laugh. "Yes you did. Richard can be the most arrogant man in the world, when he wants to be." They both smiled, recognising the trait. "I might be in love, but I'm not blind."

"Have you both refused him?"

"Of course," Lizzie replied, at the same time as Louisa said, "Oh no." They looked at each other and laughed. "I never refuse them straight off," Louisa explained. "I like to keep them waiting."

"Rather cruel."

"Oh, that's nothing. I once encouraged Lord Trente so much he thought I meant it when I said I'd elope with him, and he waited for me at Ranelagh for hours. What made it worse was he was a convicted Jacobite, and he was risking his life. He was so romantic."

"Why didn't you take him?" I wondered.

"I didn't love him. And he had nothing. He lives abroad, on the charity of his relatives. It would have been impossible, and even if I had loved him, I would have done my best to overcome it." She smiled. "That's why I was in Venice when you were, Rose. My mother took me there when Lord Trente was nearly taken by the authorities, and the whole thing became public. It wasn't a great scandal, most people laughed and forgot it."

She gave us a bright smile, a little brittle, and we couldn't help but smile with her, but I reflected that it might be as well if Louisa accepted someone before her reputation became too tarnished. A man could live down a scandal, but a woman could be ruined by one.

"Does Giles think he has a chance?"

"Oh yes," she answered. "But I promise to tell him tomorrow. I have other things I want to do, so this game won't be a long one."

Giles was volatile enough without any extra pressures. I would watch him carefully, I promised myself.

I had an opportunity to keep an eye on Giles sooner than I'd thought. I went up to my bedroom, hoping to find out where Richard was so I could tell him about Giles, and I noticed the door to his dressing room was ajar. This was unusual, so I crossed the room to close it and found that Carier was inside. I smiled at him and made to leave him to it, but he raised one finger to his lips to motion silence and put his hand to his ear. I couldn't think what he meant at first, but I heard the sound of voices coming from the sitting room beyond. I was surprised Carier should stand at doors and listen, but recognising my husband's voice, I stopped.

"Uxorious?" I heard him say, "Yes, maybe. I cannot see the point of seeking out something that is bound to be inferior to what I have at present."

I smiled.

"But the variety. Don't you miss it?" It was Giles.

"No."

"Is she that good?"

"In what way, pray?" I heard the icy chill in his voice. Richard never welcomed intrusions on his privacy.

"In the physical department? She must be something special, to keep you to herself for so long." Giles sounded jocular, at his ease.

"She is what I want," Richard said. I thought he was keeping his temper remarkably well, and I realised he was after more than a casual conversation.

"When I think what you used to be..." Giles's voice trailed off, but he spoke again. "Do you remember Lady Romine?"

"Vividly," Richard said dryly, but the chill had left his voice. These exploits had meant little to him, had never touched his inner self. Giles was on safer ground here.

"She was the talk of the town for that season. She was so blatant in her pursuit, everyone was convinced it was true love. Did you...?"

"Oh yes." Richard got to his feet in a rustle of fabric. I heard the chink of the decanter and the glug as he poured wine.

Carier took the opportunity to lean over to me and put his mouth next to my ear. "He knows I'm here," he breathed. He didn't use the title, or any other superfluous information, and took care moving back. *Ah*, I thought, *but he doesn't know about me.*

"I got more than I bargained for with La Romine," Richard said, his voice travelling with him as he crossed the room. "Her husband came with her."

"What?" Giles paused, perhaps to sip his wine. "What do you mean?"

"That's why he stood by and watched his wife making such a cake of herself," Richard replied. "I was expected to—share."

"With him as well?"

"Yes. I did my best, made my excuses, and left."

"Well, well," Giles said, his voice brimful of amusement. "I never guessed. Why were you so discreet about that aspect of the affair?"

"I try to be discreet. It wasn't to my taste, but *chacun à son goût*," Richard said.

"I'm sure," said Giles. "What about the other way?"

"What other way?"

"*Deux femmes, un homme?*" Why were sexual matters often referred to in French?

"A better mix," admitted my husband. I tried to imagine him in bed with two women, but I didn't like the image and dismissed it hastily. I preferred to think of him as a different person now, and in many ways he was.

"At least it kept you away from the gaming tables," Giles said with a sigh.

"Yes. Is that why you're here? Rustication?"

"Something like that."

I could imagine Richard sitting at his ease, letting Giles talk. I had seen him do it with other people before.

"I owe money all over London," Giles said. "Strang—I owe the loan sharks."

"Fool." Scorn etched Richard's voice.

"I know, I know, but if I don't pay them soon, they'll—well, they'll not wait for me."

"What on earth makes you do it?"

"What made you try to run through every woman in London?"

"I enjoyed it, and I had some scores to pay," came the calm reply. So cold, so emotionless. He once told me he couldn't remember how many women he'd had or what some of them looked like. He merely assured himself they couldn't entrap him into marriage. Most of the women were married, or professionals. He avoided young debutantes and claimed they were not to his taste, too prone to demand something he wasn't prepared to give.

"I enjoy gaming," he replied. "But I need to recoup my losses now. It's a matter of having to."

"If I were you, Giles, I would stop now and try to pay off your debts. Are you in so deep?"

"Deep enough." The reply was gloomy, but the tone changed to a slightly higher one, as hope entered his thoughts. "Strang, could you...?"

"No."

"This may cause great scandal to the family."

"No," Richard repeated. "The scandal can be contained, and in any case, it will only be one more thing the Kerres do. Society is waiting for the next one. You're not dragging me into your problems, Giles, any more than I dragged you into mine."

Giles sighed heavily, and I heard the click as he put his glass down on the side table, presumably empty. "It's not so much, you could afford it."

"No. I'm not as wealthy as you seem to imagine. Why come to me and not to Gervase? He has more money than he can count."

Giles sighed again. "I did. Yesterday." There was no need for him to tell Richard what Gervase had said in reply.

"So what will you do? In fact, what have you done?"

"What do you mean?" Giles said, sharper now, the words more clipped. I carefully shifted to my other foot, not too much or my skirts would rustle and give my presence away.

"Have you done anything drastic?"

There was a pause while Giles thought this over. "My mother gave me some of her jewels."

"What about the diamond necklace? Did you know it was paste?"

"No—yes—well, not at first, not until—you told us."

"You hadn't noticed before?"

"No." The voice was firmer as Giles became more sure of his story, but Richard had undeniably caught him off balance. I exchanged a speaking glance with Carier.

"What about your father's guns? Did you know they were missing?"

"No, why should I?" The second part of his statement gave Richard an opening.

"Because they're a fine pair and your father takes them everywhere with him. Didn't you want to borrow them, check they were there when you knew the servants had been shot?"

"Well..." another hesitation, "...the thought did cross my mind, but..." the voice came quicker now, as the story came to him, "...they're not my weapons, they're my father's. Why should it have been them?"

"The first thing we did after the deaths," Richard said slowly and quietly, but without any undue heat, "was to check every firearm in the house. Didn't you recognise them at dinner when I showed them to everyone?"

"I—I wasn't sure."

"It would have helped if you had told me about the existence of the pistols."

"I'm sorry," came the reluctant reply.

"Don't mention it. We're not sure how the pistols came to

be at the scene, who would have used them. Anything you can help us with there would be useful."

"Yes." Giles got to his feet. "I should go now—my mother asked me to visit her."

He took his leave, and with a great deal of relief I pushed open the connecting door and went inside.

Richard took a quick breath when he saw I was with Carier. "How long have you been there?"

I thought about telling him I had only been there to hear Giles's stories about the pistols, but I decided against it. I had never lied to him yet, not even about the outrageous price I had paid for some of my gowns. It would be foolish to start now. "Long enough."

He clicked his tongue.

"Well you never hear any good if you listen at doors, so I suppose I deserve it. But you were putting him at his ease, weren't you?"

He smiled in acknowledgement. "Was it so obvious?"

"Not to Giles I would think." I sat, so Richard sat in the chair he had vacated when he saw me come in. Carier remained standing. "Never mind all that. I think Giles was lying." The other two agreed with me.

Carier bowed his head slightly in silent agreement and Richard said, "He knew his father had the pistols, and he knew them when I showed them that night." He paused and looked straight at me. "So why did he lie? Is he protecting himself or somebody else?"

"Lady Kerre believed the jewels were genuine," Carier said, "so we may assume her son did too. It seems Sir Barnett had a particular reason for not letting Mr. Kerre know he had substituted the stones for paste."

"But Amery might have stolen the necklace," I put in. "He could elope with Miss Cassell then."

"Yes," Richard agreed. "Or Sir Barnett may have wished to

replace the false necklace with the real one. He may have noticed how worn it was becoming and needed to replace it."

"Devious," I remarked. "Why would he kill those poor men?"

Richard crossed his legs and leaned back. "To silence them, or perhaps they tried to blackmail him, or make away with the jewels. We know Sir Barnett has the Kerre temper."

"So has Giles," I added. "And Amery, for all we know."

He smiled at me, his initial uneasiness when he saw me beginning to dissipate. "You are so right, my love. And they are only our principals. We must remember anyone else might have had a reason."

"But not the mystery servant," I added as a reminder of the man he had invented.

"No. I feel somewhat guilty, sending Hampson on such a wild goose chase, but there's little else I can do."

Carier saw the discussion was at an end, bowed and left us. I looked at my husband steadily for a minute. "Two men and a woman?"

He put his hand to his forehead. "Giles likes to hear about all that. He thinks it signifies some kind of kindred spirit, that we were both rebels against our destinies. But in my case, it was uncaring and cynical. Not in his." He looked at me anxiously. "Do you mind? Does it make any difference?"

I was forced to admit it didn't though I would have liked to tease him about it. I hadn't the heart, he looked so worried. I wasn't wearing a hoop that day so I was able to go over to him, sit on his lap and give him a kiss. "It would only make a difference if you did it now."

"I didn't want to do it." He held me tightly for a brief moment. "If you ever wanted to do that, I'd feel as though I'd failed you."

"Failed me?"

"Not given you what you needed. I could never do what he

did." I could feel his shudder through the thin silk of my gown. "I think someone said to me once 'why go elsewhere when I have all I need here?'"

To stop him saying any more, I kissed him again. "No doubts."

He smiled at me. "No doubts."

Chapter Fifteen

The next day was another hot one, but more oppressive than before; the heat seemed to bear down on us. Although Lady Southwood ordered every window opened, the pleasant breezes of the past few days were less apparent and we found little relief indoors. Richard proposed to take me to the summerhouse he had told me about before. I would have liked to take Helen with us, but the day was far too hot to risk a small baby, so we left her to her attendants and set off on our own.

We saw Louisa by the formal gardens near the house, but she declined our invitation to join us. "I want to sit quietly here and see if a total lack of action will make me feel better." She sat back in her chair, pulled her hat over her forehead to shade her face and closed her eyes.

We laughed and carried on. We walked very slowly because it was not a day for enthusiastic exercise, and we were walking uphill for most of the way. The slope was gentle, and we had the prospect of the summerhouse ahead to encourage us, so we got there before too long.

I'd had time to study the building as we slowly approached it, and when I could see it more clearly, I turned to Richard with a smile. "*This* is your idea of a summerhouse? We had one in the Manor, but ours was a little wooden one we rotated to face the sun. You couldn't rotate this."

"That is why it has six sides, my love," he replied. "And I

think this time we should face away from the sun."

We walked around the building. It was indeed six-sided, and all but one side was open to the air, fitted out with seats and small folding tables. The closed side seemed to be a storage area, with the door firmly locked.

When we reached a section of the pavilion away from the sun, we sat. There was a bench here where we could sit side by side, but we didn't hold each other. The day was far too hot for that. We faced away from the main house, overlooking the gardens and park, a pleasant prospect. The far distance swam in the heat vapour. It was still green from recent showers which had done nothing to dissipate the sultry weather.

I was surprised to see how steeply the ground fell away on the other side. The view was lovely, over the green of the park and the planted woods to the natural beauty of the Pennines in the distance. "If I hadn't seen the Alps I would have thought these hills mountains."

"They're the nearest we have," he answered. "May I take my coat off?"

"Of course. I wish I could take something off."

"So do I," he said with a grin. So he took off his light frock coat and his hat, I removed my broad-brimmed straw hat, and we were more comfortable. I stared out at the hills, which were craggy and lonely but just as hot as the rest of the country.

He put his arm along the back of the seat and I settled my head on his shoulder, not able to resist touching him. My sister had said we couldn't keep our hands off each other when we first met, and it wasn't very different now.

"Which niche did you use when you were Robin Hood?"

"This one or the one next to it. They face away from the house, and we couldn't be seen as easily. Every moment of every day was laid out for us, but enterprising boys can sometimes find their way around restrictions."

"What about Georgiana?"

"She had a better time of it. We were ten when she was

born. And she is a girl. She could never inherit, so she wasn't put under the same restrictions."

"Have they found a husband for her yet?"

"Father says he presented several hopefuls for her inspection, but she hasn't chosen anyone yet."

I smiled. I had a lot to smile about these days. "I'm glad. I waited and look what I got."

"A poor bargain. I got much more."

I lifted my hand to touch his where it lay on the back of the seat and let it fall back into my lap again.

"Georgiana is running rings around her suitors," Richard told me. "She is encouraging, then dropping young men so they don't know if she's serious or not. She told me she's waiting until she's your age, unless she meets someone special."

"There's no reason why she shouldn't." But something was wrong with that vision. "In my case, I didn't choose it. As a single well-born young female she's at the heart of society, the centre of attention."

"She says she's a commodity, paraded for inspection every season."

"So she is, but wrapped up so prettily you can hardly notice it."

He turned his head from the prospect ahead of us to watch me. "Would you have enjoyed it?"

"No. To go from the rejected older sister to the centre of society would have unnerved me. At least Lizzie was a success in Exeter society before she came to London, so she was used to it. And you would have been married to Julia by then. Locked out and frozen."

"Most likely." At the bleak note in his voice I turned away from the view to him. He was watching me, a warmth in his expression that Julia had never seen. Despite the heat, we kissed, long and lovingly, and that was how Lizzie and her Marquês found us.

Richard wouldn't let me break away when we heard the rustle of silk that heralded someone's approach, but held me tighter and only let me go when he was ready.

Unruffled, he turned to see who it was and smiled to greet Lizzie. He would have risen, but she made a hasty gesture to stop him.

"Pardon, but we intrude," said the Marquês in his perfect English.

Richard lifted his hand and indicated the seat on my other side. "Not at all. Come and sit down." If it had been anyone else, he might have agreed with the comment, but not Lizzie.

I noticed what he had already seen. Lizzie was hand in hand with the Marquês de Aljubarrotta.

Lizzie saw my look and smiled. "I have just accepted more than his hand."

Richard got to his feet immediately and held out his own hand to the Marquês. "Every congratulation. If this sister is anything like the one I married, you have a bargain indeed."

I got up too and embraced my sister, truly happy for her now we knew her Marquês was worthy of her. I loved her so much, I would have been heartbroken if she had married someone who wouldn't make her happy.

She was glowing with joy, almost radiating more heat than the day. I'd have embraced the Marquês too, but he seemed a little reticent, so I contented myself with giving him my hand to kiss. "I'm so pleased."

"I know you have had me investigated," he said. I was appalled. I glanced at Richard, but he was smiling. "I'm glad of it," the man continued, and I looked aback at him again. "I want Elizabeth to be sure she is to marry someone who can look after her properly."

I sighed in relief.

"I will take care of her," he told me, and from the look on his face, he didn't mean merely financially.

We sat again. Richard and I resumed our seats. Richard put his arm along the back of the seat again, but I didn't settle against his shoulder as I had before. The pose was careless, but not clumsy, and informal enough to help Lizzie and her intended relax. Richard was still in his shirtsleeves, but he didn't attempt to put his coat back on.

The Marquês was carefully dressed for the country and looked very fine, if a little formal. There was a small table between our seat and the one Lizzie and he took, but due to the shape of the building in which we sat, it was at a slight angle, so we could look at each other and converse without missing the view.

"Where will you live?" Richard asked. "Will you spirit your bride away and make us visit you?"

"I would be delighted if you would honour us with a visit," the other answered, "but I cannot allow Elizabeth to miss her own people. We will come back frequently."

"Your mother lives here, does she not?"

"She lives in London and Bath for the most part. She never liked the country, she says."

"Your father died some time ago?"

He gave a small shrug. "Alas, yes. When I was quite small. We always spent much time in this country, but Mama didn't retire to England permanently until she was sure I could manage the estates at home in Portugal on my own." I noticed the use of the word "Mama", indicating a relationship closer than the one Richard shared with his own parents. He never called his parents by any familiar name.

"I've never been to Portugal." I had only been abroad once, on my wedding trip, but we had travelled around Italy and France. I felt like a seasoned traveller next to my sister.

"I'm sure I'll love it." Lizzie turned to exchange glances with her Joaquin. It made me so very happy to see the warmth of their regard for each other. With Martha absent, I felt responsible for her, in a way. I was three years older, married, and in possession of the means to discover far more than most people knew. Thompson's tentacles were spread wide and deep, even abroad.

"We must write to James and Martha."

"Oh yes," Lizzie said. "I'll write to them today." Although she was over the age of majority and James couldn't dictate who she should and should not marry, even if he had wanted to, he had control of her fortune. Women were never free. The best they could hope for was an understanding guardian. Even as widows, their grown-up sons had official jurisdiction over them. However, what the law said and what in practice happened was, as usual, worlds apart.

"May I give you an enclosure?" I asked her.

She grinned at me. "To tell James how eligible Joaquin is? I wish you would. I don't want them to worry, I want them to be as happy as we are." She exchanged another look with the Marquês.

Strangely, I didn't feel intrusive or unwanted. They were happy to sit together and talk to us, unlike Richard and I, who had used every contrivance to be alone while we were courting. Lizzie and her Marquês seemed happy just to be with each other. I sensed no tension, none of that frantic lust that had so consumed me in that six months between meeting Richard and marrying him. It had made the people around us uncomfortable, but we hadn't noticed at the time.

"James and Martha will be delighted. I've gone, you're going and Ian lives in Oxford as much as he does at home these days. There's only Ruth, and once she's settled they can have their new house to themselves and their own family. Have you decided where you'll marry, and when?"

"He's only just proposed to her," Richard pointed out. "Give them a chance."

Lizzie smiled at that, but answered me. "I'd like to marry in Exeter Cathedral, as you did, but Joaquin is a Roman Catholic." She turned to him. "Will I have to convert?"

"Would you?"

"Yes," she said simply. "It's the same God."

He smiled at her. "I do not think you have to do that, but our children must be brought up as Catholics."

She blushed at the mention of children but met his gaze steadily. "I'll be guided by you."

Richard sighed heavily. "If only that were always the case." He gazed out at the park, then back at me. He was smiling, daring me to respond. So I did.

"You mean I don't let myself be guided by you in all things?"

He dropped a kiss on my forehead. "Only if you agree with it."

"I'm not mindless—my lord."

"I never said you were. Nor would I want you to be."

We fell into a comfortable silence. It was then that we heard someone else approaching. Whoever it was couldn't see us because they were approaching from the house side, but we heard someone panting. It sounded like a man to me, although I couldn't be sure. He must have been in a hurry, because he sounded quite out of breath, but the heat of the day could have contributed to that.

Richard lifted his finger to his lips. We heard the man sigh and move again. We heard some scraping, like metal on metal, and a curse. It was obvious from the language the man thought he was on his own up here.

We saw a backside as the man bent down, and Richard cleared his throat. The backside abruptly disappeared. After a short pause, the whole man came into view.

"Taylor!" exclaimed the Marquês.

The man looked equally surprised to see him. He was a servant, but a superior one; he was well dressed and not in livery. I assumed he was the Marquês's valet, and it seemed I was right.

"Am I needed?" Joaquin asked him.

"I— That is—" stammered the man and, remembering his manners, he bowed to us. It gave him a moment to think. "My lord, I was not aware of your presence here."

The Marquês smiled. "You have an assignation?"

Taylor smiled, and his features relaxed. "I beg your pardon, my lord. I thought I would be alone here and you dismissed me for an hour."

"But you are not," said his master. "You must explain to your lady."

"At once, my lord."

Taylor bowed again and as quickly as was decently possible he left, moving with some haste down the hill.

Richard turned to the Marquês. "Does he always go about at such a pace?"

"I've never known him to run before," came the reply. "He must have been keen on the girl."

Richard took his arm away from the backrest and sat up. "I don't think there was any girl. Shall we see what he dropped?"

He went outside and in a moment returned with something in his hand. He held it out so we could all see. It was a key.

I stood and went to him, and the other two weren't far behind me. "Do you know where it fits?" I asked.

"I've a fair idea," Richard answered and went outside. I knew where he was going.

The key fitted the lock of the small store with no trouble at all, since the lock had been oiled recently. We peered inside.

The small space was windowless and crammed with gardening implements. With the door open wide it was easy to see inside, but I had no desire to soil my gown so I let Richard investigate. The Marquês followed him in, and Lizzie and I exchanged speaking glances. While they had their backs to us I seized Lizzie's hands and pressed them warmly. "Who would have thought it?" I whispered.

"Who indeed?" she whispered back, and she was once more the mischievous centre of Exeter society, not the languid young lady of fashion. We smiled at each other, two children afraid some grownup would catch them in mischief.

The Marquês turned and came out of the store, followed by Richard, who was carrying another of those infernal laundry bags. We went back to our shady shelter.

We all sat except my husband, who loosened the strings at the neck of the bag and shook out what it contained.

Snuffboxes, jewelled and enamelled, engraved and painted fans, pins set with precious stones, an amethyst bracelet and several brooches, none of them matching, met our eyes. It was the beginnings of a pirate's treasure chest, none of it breakable, all of it small and precious. Lizzie got up and swooped down on one of the brooches. "I wondered where that had got to."

"Well," said Richard. "That's one mystery solved."

We looked at the hoard, and the Marquês sighed heavily. "This is terrible. How can I look the Countess in the eyes again?"

"She'll be delighted," said Richard. "Especially when she finds out you discovered it and can return everything to its rightful owner."

"I cannot take the credit for this," said the Marquês.

"Why not?" said my husband. "It was good luck we were here, nothing more, or he might have got away with it. It mitigates the sin of it being your body servant, the fact that you discovered it and restored the items to their owners. The most unfortunate part is you will be left without a valet for a while. May I offer you the services of mine?"

The Marquês smiled and shook his head. "If I can't get myself dressed, I would think myself a poor specimen. There is no doubt he stole the jewels."

"But not Lady Kerre's necklace," I put in.

"No," said Richard regretfully. That would have been too easy.

"I'll dismiss him as soon as we return to the house," the Marquês continued.

"I'll send a footman to you," Richard said. "He can escort your man off the premises. If you wish it, he can act as your valet too, on a temporary basis. You may not know but my wife and I are part owners of a staff registry in London. I can obtain someone for you there who I promise you will be more reliable than your last employee."

The Marquês opened his dark eyes wide. "An unusual enterprise."

Richard shrugged. "Perhaps. It keeps some of the young people constantly flooding into London every day out of trouble, and it provides me with a source of thoroughly reliable servants. There are one or two other functions they perform on my behalf from time to time."

The Marquês looked at him shrewdly. "I shall not ask, but your philanthropy is commendable." He looked at me and inclined his head. "Yours too, Lady Rose."

I smiled and acknowledged the compliment, and the fond nickname bestowed on me by my family since my marriage. "Rose" was too familiar for some, and "Lady Strang" too formal for my taste, so the name was a good compromise.

"I would be very grateful if you could help me obtain a more reliable servant," the Marquês went on.

"It would be my pleasure," said Richard. "I'll write a dispatch before dinner."

Richard returned the treasure to its bag and came to sit by me again. I felt a bead of sweat trickle down my back, and I moved a little to disperse it, but other than that, nobody moved. There we sat like an oil painting: Lizzie in striped green lustring, still wearing her hat, me in pale blue, bare-headed except for the wisp of lace that passed for a cap. The gentlemen sat at their ease, one in shirtsleeves and a fairly plain waistcoat, the other in a drab brown frock coat. All of us sat quietly in a pretty pavilion enjoying the view. If we were painted like that, I wondered, what would the spectator make of the old linen bag lying carelessly on the floor? It would make a nice mystery.

The heat haze made the trees in the distance swim, and I felt a little dizzy so I looked back at Richard. He met my gaze and smiled, but sighed and stood, offering his hand to help me up. "We must go. We have to make sure the man leaves without replenishing his stock."

The idyll was over, but it was a tableau I would never forget.

The servant was duly sent on his way without a character. I wondered what would happen to him now he had no way of obtaining another position, but Richard assured me he would probably forge a reference. There was a thriving trade in such things. "He won't get anything through Thompson's. I've written as good a description as I can and I've warned him off. He could have been hanged for what he did."

"Perhaps he should have been," I said.

"Maybe we should have handed him over to Hampson," Richard replied with a smile. "That gentleman is feeling decidedly spiteful at the moment, and I don't think he would have been merciful. We will inform him when the man has a clear start. It's the least we can do. Maybe he'll get himself hanged yet, if he continues in his larcenous ways."

With the next day came bad news, for us at least. Hotfoot from London. Richard and I were both in the house when he arrived, and Carier sent to tell us. I was with Lady Southwood and Georgiana at the time, but as soon as I read the note I excused myself and left, after I had explained briefly what had occurred.

By the time I got to the Yellow Drawing Room, Richard was already there. He sat in his accustomed easy posture facing our unexpected guest. Smith's natty red waistcoat proclaimed his profession, although his jovial appearance didn't deceive me to his real worth. We couldn't fool one of Mr. Fielding's special

Bow Street men like we could hoodwink the local officials. They both stood when I came in.

"Mr. Smith, how nice to see you," I said mendaciously, offering my hand. He bowed over it but didn't kiss it. Mr. Smith was not one for social accomplishments. "How are Mr. Fielding and his brother?"

"Mr. Henry Fielding continues in ill health," Mr. Smith told me. I was genuinely sorry to hear that. I had only met him once, but I liked him very much. "He will be leaving for Lisbon next month." I exchanged a glance with Richard. It seemed Lisbon was becoming very popular. Mr. Smith saw the look but didn't comment. "He has been told it will be kind to his health, and one more winter here might be his last." He sounded regretful too.

"We must hope he improves," Richard said. He led me to a seat and resumed his own, as did Mr. Smith. "You will of course convey our best wishes to both Mr. Fieldings and their families?"

"Yes of course, but I don't think I'll be returning immediately."

Richard sighed gently. "I suppose John Fielding sent you?"

"He has the authority to send us anywhere we are needed, my lord," Mr. Smith replied. "The constable here, Hampson, wrote to him. He hasn't much experience with murder, and he felt out of his depth."

"I thought he was," said Richard thoughtfully, "but I didn't know he would have heard of Mr. Fielding and Bow Street."

"Mr. Fielding sent word to all magistrates and justices in the country when he set up the runners. He made sure they all knew."

Richard nodded. "Of course he would." He glanced across at me and smiled, wryly. "So how can we help you, Mr. Smith?" I could see Richard was thinking the same thing as me—Smith had seen our names and hot-footed it to Derbyshire.

Mr. Smith was not an obsequious man, which was to his

credit. "I would appreciate it if you could tell me the occurrences, my lord. I can't think of anyone I would rather have tell me."

Richard obliged, and while he brought Smith up to date, I listened quietly and thought about what we could do now. Mr. Smith was a clever man, one of the twelve chosen by the Fieldings to help the authorities with their more difficult cases. I suspected the Fieldings of charging Mr. Smith to watch us. They knew more about Thompson's and its activities than almost anyone else, and they had found out by enquiry and deduction. We tried to be discreet, but it was all there for the asking, if one knew where to ask, and it seemed the Fieldings did know.

Mr. Smith asked more questions than Hampson, and more to the point. He dismissed our story of the stranger in the house with hardly a second thought. "There must have been many strange servants around in the house. We will take that into consideration, but I don't listen to unconfirmed rumours. I understand that more than the necklace was stolen? Perhaps he had something to do with that."

"Perhaps," Richard agreed blandly, but Smith watched him carefully. Richard sighed. "Very well, you'd better know. A manservant stole the other things, and he fled when he realised we knew. Everything has been recovered, and there's no link that we can discover between that and the theft of the necklace."

After studying his face, Mr. Smith nodded curtly and thanked him. "If you can supply us with a description of the man, we can put out bills for his recovery, but I should warn you that it's unlikely he'll ever be caught."

"I'll see it is done," Richard promised him. He seemed to make a decision. "What will you want to do here, Smith?"

"I'm to catch the murderer and bring him to justice. First and foremost I'm the Fieldings' man, and I believe in the justice of the law."

"How can you, when it's so full of inaccuracies?"

"It's all we have, my lord," Mr. Smith said. It seemed to be a continuation of the conversation I'd had with my husband a few days ago. I saw both sides of the argument now, but I was still no nearer making up my own mind on the matter. With the lack of an effective national policing authority, justice was piecemeal. "The magistrates will try to change what they perceive as wrong, with the support of Parliament, and I will carry out the law to the best of my ability."

"Commendable," Richard commented. "You know what may be at stake here."

Mr. Smith nodded. "Nevertheless, I must do as the law tells me."

They couldn't have made it much clearer. Smith would do his job, no matter what the consequences, and we must work around him. I knew Richard wouldn't allow family matters to become public knowledge, so we must find the murderer out before Smith did.

Mr. Smith was despatched with one of our servants to inspect the murder scene, although there was little to see now. It was just another anonymous servants' room, and would be occupied in a day or two by one of the new footmen Alicia Thompson had sent us.

Carier was also present. "He has rooms at the inn in the village, so he'll be asking questions there."

"There's nothing for him there," Richard commented. "If he had stayed here, we would have had our work cut out."

"We have to work faster now," I said. "He's no Hampson. He'll be on to the real facts very quickly, one way or the other."

Richard grimaced. "I know. We're agreed that it's most likely one of the Kerres?" We concurred. "We have no time to consider other possibilities, and anyway, if it isn't a Kerre, we can work with Smith instead of against him because it won't involve one of the family. We must find out which one, and quickly."

There was no time for subtlety now. We decided to tell them.

Chapter Sixteen

Sir Barnett had asked me if he could see my prowess with a firearm, so we obliged him. Gervase accompanied us, as the day was so fine, leaving Ian to inhabit the library on his own. The other guests went about pursuits of their own, since at my request we didn't advertise our contest.

I wore my blue riding habit and was pleased to receive Richard's approval, not as my husband, but as an arbiter of fashion. "That shade of blue suits you delightfully," he commented as I put my hand in his. "And the jacket fits you like the one you had before never did."

"You mean the brown one?"

He grimaced. "The brown one."

I had been particularly proud of my new brown riding habit, but Lizzie always told me brown didn't suit me, and Richard concurred when he had seen it. Also, it seemed to fit in all the wrong places and had never been comfortable, although I'd never have admitted it at the time. It was only when I had my new one I realised how wrong the old one was.

He touched my waist. "Your figure is just as lovely as it ever was," he said softly and kissed me. I was happy with the reassurance as I had become a little self-conscious about my figure since Helen was born.

I found my hat and we left, accompanied by Nichols and Carier, who bore the boxes with the guns inside. We met the Kerres in the hall, and to my surprise, Lady Kerre and her daughter had decided to come with us. Amery looked uncomfortable in his outdoor frock coat, as though open air might harm him. Perhaps he just felt uncomfortable with his father, with matters as they stood. Nichols helped me don the cocked hat at a becoming angle and carried a parasol for me, in case I needed more protection from the sun on this relentlessly hot day. I pulled on my gloves and we went out into the bright sunshine.

It could have been a day like any other except for the knot of tension I felt inside. Richard was his usual self, seemingly unaware of any latent hostility, but the air was alive with it. Amery tried not to walk too close to his father. Every now and then his mother would cast a brief look at her eldest son, insouciantly walking by my other side, and their daughter kept her eyes down. I wondered how much she knew, and whose side she was on. It would be time for her to find a husband soon, and any scandal must diminish her chances.

We walked some distance from the house, to a field that had been set up for us with targets. Servants waited with the boxes that held the firearms we were to use, and there was a small table set with the inevitable refreshments. As we stopped to take some cordial, we heard a voice behind us. "I should like to see how well you shoot, my dear."

It was Lord Southwood. Richard had managed to see him privately that morning and tell him what we planned, and it was clear he didn't want us to do this on our own. Lady Southwood was notable by her absence. She had informed us that she never ventured out in such weather. "So bad for the skin." I could be thankful for her care for her complexion, at least.

"I have seen her shoot," Gervase told his father, "and I can vouch for her prowess."

Richard laughed when I blushed, for that time had been on my honeymoon in Venice, and I had forgotten all propriety. Gervase had seen more than my prowess with a gun that night.

He touched my hand. "You're a fine shot, and that painting was a daub, not worth keeping."

I dropped my head but lifted it again to meet his gaze, knowing the brothers would tease me if I didn't respond.

"It was good to see the position of the arm without any encumbrance," Richard said, as calmly as if he was discussing a technical point. Since I'd been half naked at the time, it was far from technical.

"I don't think I can oblige you today," I said as steadily as I could, still looking at Gervase. "I can't think what came over me."

"I can." The soft voice came from behind me, mischief in every syllable.

Gervase smiled, so like Richard it pulled at me slightly in a faint echo of the emotion I felt every time I saw him.

"Another time," I said firmly.

"Oh yes," came the response.

I put my hand on Gervase's arm. "Will you take me to see the weapons we've been provided with?"

"Surely," Gervase replied as I heard a light chuckle. I would make him pay.

Richard was keyed up—now a conclusion to this sad affair was in sight, I think he felt lighter and knew this little scene depended on him. He loved to be the centre of attention, enjoyed being in control. Despite the tragedy that had struck two families, he would still get some enjoyment out of this. I just wanted it over with.

Gervase took me to the table where several cases were open, displaying the pistols. I picked one up and hefted. It was a fine weapon, beautifully balanced, so in action when the bullet had been discharged it could be swung round the other way and the butt used as a club in an instant. Not that I planned to do that today. It wasn't loaded, so I tried the action. Smooth and well oiled. The hilt was inlaid with ivory in an intricate design that looked strange to me.

"I brought that pair back from India," Gervase told me. "The workmanship there is very fine." I had to agree with him. "If you like them, they're yours."

I turned my head to look at him and saw him smile. "You are so kind. You shouldn't do this."

"Why not?" He moved closer so he could speak privately to me. "You've returned my brother to me. You brought him back from the dead."

I shook my head, but I couldn't say anything further as people were now too close. So I thanked him and moved away to sight on the targets.

The others were also selecting weapons, and there was much interplay, some of it not so pleasant. Giles sighted on Amery, who looked genuinely startled and ducked, which made his brother laugh out loud. "You should spend less time mooning about the City." Too jovial, too superior.

Amery threw him a look of pure hatred and returned to the table, seizing a pistol at random. "I can shoot well enough when I need to."

His mother came between them, deliberately walking across the sight lines. "I wish my sons would behave in a more civilised manner." She shot her eldest son a warning glare. "You should try to conform more, Amery."

"Why?" her younger son demanded. "Giles conforms so well that you hardly ever see him out of Whites' when we're in town."

Richard took a hand. "I don't care much for the place myself. Too insular, too respectable and far too dangerous. You could waste the whole of your life in there."

He busied himself with his flintlock, the pair to the one I held, so he didn't have to look at the Kerres. He came over to me. "These should suit you very well."

"Gervase is very generous."

"He is indeed." The soft note in his voice disappeared when he turned back to the others. "What are you doing in the City, Amery?"

Amery flushed, his pale skin sporting red flags on both cheeks, but before he could speak his father replied. "He has an interest there." The look he gave his son was openly contemptuous. "A female interest."

"A respectable one?" Richard pursued.

"Not in my opinion," said his father.

This time Amery did reply, stung into protest. "She is a most respectable young lady, and her father is well thought of in the City. It's most unfair to infer she isn't proper."

Richard exchanged a glance with his father, standing only a little distance away. "You have a lady friend, Amery? Is it serious?"

Sir Barnett sighed heavily and looked at his wife and back to my father-in-law. "I have forbidden it."

"Why?" asked Lord Southwood.

"It would not be suitable. The girl is the daughter of a Cit."

"Rich?" asked Lord Southwood.

"What has that to do with the matter?" Sir Barnett didn't hide his irritation. "She is a vulgar girl who could not possibly fit into society."

"What makes you think that?" I wouldn't have spoken, but I hated to hear anyone spoken of so disparagingly. "Do you know where I came from? But for that unfortunate accident in Yorkshire, I would have been the daughter of a country squire. Not even the squire," I corrected myself. "That was Sir George Skerrit."

Richard put up his chin. "Have you noticed any vulgarity in my wife?"

"No of course not," Sir Barnett replied. "The cases are different. This is a girl brought up with commerce."

I decided what I would do. "If Amery will give me her direction, I would like to visit her when I visit London next."

"I'd like to come with you," my husband said. He fixed his gaze on Sir Barnett, who looked stunned.

"I might take her up," I continued. "If she shows promise." I met Sir Barnett's gaze, only slightly aware of Amery's stumbled thanks. The older man said nothing. "Do you think, sir, that I will be considered vulgar, for taking up with such a girl?"

"No, vulgarity comes from elsewhere." So Lord Southwood was on our side. That made a pleasant change.

"You've never met her," Lady Kerre protested.

"I shall make sure I do." I felt stronger now I knew my family supported me.

I turned away and broke the scene to punctuate it. That should ensure something was stirred, but I hoped Amery wasn't the man we were looking for. I sighted on the targets again, not because I needed to but because I didn't want to look at the others. I had perhaps spoken too hastily, but I had no patience with that kind of narrow-minded attitude, and suddenly I felt uncomfortable.

I felt Richard's hand on my shoulder, ostensibly to guide my aim, but really to give reassurance. I smiled at him and gave the weapon to the servant standing waiting by me, so he could load it.

The servants were loading other pistols, and the knot in my stomach tightened. Richard now stood in front of me, his hands free. "It could be the answer to some of your problems. The family is wealthy, I take it?" With another person, he wouldn't have had to be quite so direct, but we had already assessed Sir Barnett's density.

Sir Barnett exchanged a glance with his wife. How this hadn't occurred to them before I wasn't sure, but perhaps it was that very narrow mindedness that had blinded them to this aspect of the situation.

It was Amery's turn to surprise us. "If I should be fortunate enough to win the lady's hand in marriage, the disposal of her fortune would be mine. Not my family's, and certainly not Giles." He turned away and took a gun from a servant. "I would shoot him first rather than bring ruin on her."

We all stared at him. "Well that would certainly guarantee her ruin," said Richard dryly after a moment. "How do you know you're capable of it?"

Amery met his gaze unflinchingly. "I don't. Could you kill for Lady Rose?"

"Yes."

"How do you know?"

He knew, but that was our secret. Richard and Amery stared at each other until eventually Richard broke the impasse. "I believe you. You didn't need to steal the necklace, did you?"

"No, of course not," Amery replied. "My lady has enough for us both, should we need it, though I'm determined not to depend on it."

"How do her parents feel?" Lord Southwood asked him.

"They welcome the match. Now, though at first there were some doubts."

"I'll wager they do," his father said gloomily.

Lord Southwood turned to him. "It seems, Barnett, you may be forced to bow to the inevitable. Learn some sense at long last. When Strang came to me and told me he was to marry Rose, I may say I wasn't best pleased, but I have to admit I couldn't have chosen better for him myself."

I stared at him in surprise. I hadn't been aware he'd done anything but tolerate me. He smiled at me, so like his son in that moment that I smiled back, as I would have done to Richard.

"Perhaps, Barnett, you will find the same thing. We will receive her and judge her on her own merits. It wouldn't be the first Cit we had in the family."

He glanced at Gervase who bowed, acknowledging the fortune he had made in trade, albeit in another country. "Not a Cit, sir, but a lowlier version of merchant."

Sir Barnett glanced at his wife and sighed. "I cannot say

the prospect overwhelms us with joy." Lady Kerre didn't look at all pleased, but said nothing. Her cerise gown lifted slightly in the wake of a passing breeze, but other than that, all was still. Sir Barnett spoke to his youngest son. "You may ask her to visit, if you wish."

The mulish look Amery had worn ever since I met him seemed to lift. He looked at his father and smiled. "Thank you, sir."

To cover the pause that followed, I glanced around to make sure everyone was aware I was about to fire, took aim at the target and shot.

I was reasonably pleased with the result. Taking their cue from me, the twins also stepped forward and took aim, both shooting at about the same time. We stepped back to murmurs of "Well done" and the like, and waited for the others to take their turn. I handed my weapon to a waiting servant, who took it away and reloaded it. It was usual to wait until everyone had discharged their weapons before collecting the used targets and reloading, so there would be no accidents. I took the pistol back without a word when the servant gave it to me.

Everyone took their turn at the targets and the attendants went down the field and collected them. They gave us our own to study.

I was quite pleased with mine, and I received some flattering comments. What pleased me most was that I had done better than Richard, himself considered a very fair shot. He used the excuse of examining my prowess to slip his arm about my waist. We were *en famille,* I supposed, so a measure of informality was allowable. These small gestures of affection showed how far he'd come since we first met. He would have found it much more difficult before.

"I love these," I said to Gervase. "Thank you."

He smiled and bowed his head in response. The servants took the pistols away and began to reload them all, but Richard, Gervase and I held ours, freshly loaded. Richard released me and moved away a little. I was instantly alert, and I watched him for a cue.

"I think we should discuss the unfortunate matter of the murders."

Lady Kerre shuddered. "Oh don't call it that. It sounds so dreadful."

"It was dreadful," Richard said. "It needs no embellishment."

He used his trick of remaining perfectly still, only the breeze whipping up the tails of his light country coat until he had everyone's total attention. "We need to discover the murderer and deal with it. A man arrived from Bow Street yesterday. He is very astute, it won't be possible to pull the wool over his eyes as we did with the constable." People exchanged glances as they understood the increased urgency of the situation, but nobody said anything.

"We know that the pistols belong to Sir Barnett. They were taken—maybe—" He paused and looked at his cousin, to make sure he understood his meaning. I felt the breeze on my cheek and moved my face to take advantage of it. Someone coughed.

"They were used to kill Derring, and dropped. The murderer took Derring's guns, went into the room and killed Hill before he had time to respond to the noise outside. He fled. I don't think he'd killed before, not like that, in cold blood." He let his gaze drift round the company, taking his own sweet time. Now, I thought.

"Hadn't you?" He looked directly at Giles Kerre.

I heard Amery's sharp intake of breath, Lady Kerre's "No!" of protest, and I knew Richard was taking a chance. All along we had suspected Giles, but we had no proof, could find nothing to definitively link him to the murders.

Lady Kerre held her hands to both cheeks, her mouth wide with horror. "How could you, Giles?"

"I—I—" Giles protested, before he got his wits back. "You can't know that for sure, there's nothing you can do."

"True enough," Richard replied calmly, "but we do know it." He moved a little closer to Giles. "You have gambled your expectations away—and more. You're in debt to some of the worst, most villainous people in London. You were desperate, you still are, aren't you?"

Giles put up his chin. "So how would killing two penniless servants benefit me?"

"They wouldn't, not materially. But you paid Hill to take your mother's necklace. You knew things were going missing, and you wanted to make it seem all of a piece, as though it was the work of the same thief."

"Giles, how could you!" His mother was in tears now, holding a large white handkerchief to her face. I felt so sorry for her, but we'd agreed this was the only way to force the issue. "I would have given it to you if you had asked, you must know that."

Richard turned his head, his expression softening a little when he recognised Lady Kerre's distress. "That's why Sir Barnett had the necklace copied, so it wouldn't sink into the bottomless pit of Giles's debts. Giles never realised that, did you?" He turned back to his prey. "Not until you had it in your hands, when you visited Hill. What had you on Hill that you could make him do that?"

Giles glanced around from beneath lowered lids. "I needed—need—the money. They'll kill me if I don't find it soon, and   you"
—he turned to his father, his look so cold, so hard I could scarcely bear it—"you said I couldn't have any more. Hill left us after he'd made one too many maids pregnant." He glanced at Richard. "I threatened to make Lady Southwood aware of it, and he agreed to help."

Lord Southwood spoke. "We were fully aware of Hill's proclivities. We considered letting him go."

"And so," Richard said, "you contacted Hill, threatened him with exposure about his womanising, knowing my mother would not accept it, and made him help you steal the necklace."

Giles's expression amounted to a contemptuous sneer. "It was easy. Who can tell the difference between one footman in livery and another?" I don't think he realised how much trouble he was in. The son of a privileged family, used to obsequiousness and getting what he wanted if he demanded it, he couldn't quite believe that it all stopped here. I cradled my weapon in my arms. I doubted we'd need it.

I glanced at his mother. She seemed smitten by horror, and I saw her daughter move a little closer to her and put her hand on her arm. Lady Kerre shook her daughter off, continued to stare at her eldest son. She must feel so betrayed, but there was no need to do that to her other child.

Giles didn't look away, and neither did Richard, the tall, dark burly man confronting the delicate, elegant fineness. "It doesn't mean I had anything to do with the killing."

"Killings," Richard corrected him softly. "Two men with families who loved them. Two men with lives of their own, killed for nothing."

"Nothing?"

"Pieces of glass. Panic and spite."

The breeze dropped and everything became still. A bead of sweat trickled between my breasts, bringing a welcome, if temporary coolness. Two people would never feel that everyday relief anymore.

Giles Kerre said the one thing bound to incense my husband. "They were only servants. What does it matter?"

I was close enough to Richard to hear him take a few breaths and let them out slowly. He was so carefully in control I knew he was deeply angry. "They were men. They had families, people who cared for them. There is such a thing as natural justice, Giles. It matters."

Giles gave him such a look of contempt I thought Richard might have struck him for it. I gripped the hilt of the flintlock in my hand, feeling the tension increase. I glanced at Lord

Southwood who stood close to me, and he looked at me for one brief moment. We were in accord.

"Servants." Giles almost spat the word. "They're ours, we can do what we want with them."

"I never thought of myself as a Roman emperor before," said Richard quietly. "We have no slaves in this country, Giles, although we still send them elsewhere."

"Even the Romans considered their slaves," Gervase added, unable to let this reference to the classical world he loved pass. He stood close to my left shoulder. He and Richard were determined to protect me, and the thought vaguely irritated me, while their concern warmed me. But I'd just proved I could shoot straight, after all, and I had a loaded pistol at my disposal.

Lord Southwood came to the point. "Did you kill them?"

Giles looked away, looked at us, and finally sighed. "Yes. The first one was insolent and wouldn't let me pass. I had no choice. Hill's life was over anyway, as far as I could see. Once you handed him over to that constable, he'd have been hanged."

There was a pause while we took in the confession. So simply put, conveying such an ocean of misunderstanding and selfishness, it fair took my breath away.

"Not necessarily," Richard said. "Miscreants aren't always hanged. He could have been transported, if the judge's quota of hangings was reached. He might yet have had something useful to offer society."

Giles's lip curled in a sneer. "He wasn't even a good thief."

"He got you what you wanted."

"No he didn't. I wanted diamonds, not bits of glass." He glared bitterly at his mother, who met him with a tragic stare. "How could you, Mother?"

"I didn't know!" she cried, tears in her voice.

"How could you not have known? I saw as soon as I had them in my hand that they weren't what I needed. Good God,

Mama, they were *chipped.*"

"I knew I should have replaced them," his father murmured.

"Well, it doesn't matter now, does it?" his son demanded bitterly. "If I don't throw something their way, the sharks will kill me anyway. Do you think they have any consideration for rank or consequence? Gold is all they care for, and I have none." He threw up his head to stare at the cloudless sky. "None!" he cried to the unheeding canopy above.

Tears filled his eyes. Not for anyone else, just for himself. "I'm dead now so what does it matter?" He turned to Richard. "If you hadn't proved your fertility, perhaps they might have waited longer. You and your promises. You told me once you would never marry, remember? Then when you spread yourself about so much and still didn't produce, I was sure you wouldn't produce children." His voice turned quieter, sly. "Are you sure it's yours?"

Gervase's hand pressed on my shoulder. Richard must have kept an iron control on his temper, because all he said, in a voice that would freeze ice was, "Perfectly sure."

Oh God, I thought. *He's trying to provoke someone to kill him. He wants to die.*

Gervase took his hand away. I held my pistol a little tighter, but I wasn't looking at Giles. I looked around and tried to see who might take the bait so I could prevent them taking my weapon, the one of three within reach that was loaded.

His father. Sir Barnett stepped forward one pace. "I was so proud of you once." Quickly for such a large man, he pushed Richard and, taking advantage of my husband's temporary loss of balance, snatched his flintlock.

Richard dropped to the ground as Sir Barnett lifted the pistol and took deliberate aim at his son. I heard Gervase's movement behind me, and I lifted my own weapon, more in reaction than thought, but before either of us could fire, Richard cried out a warning.

He had been given a small device in Venice, originally designed for cheating at cards, which he had pressed into a very different service. Instead of a playing card, he had fixed a small, razor-thin knife to the device, and when he moved a muscle in his wrist, the knife flew out. He had practised this until his aim was true, and the effect was quicker than if he had to withdraw the knife from his pocket. It was not something he habitually wore, for there were great dangers of him slicing his own hand as the knife burst free, but he must have suspected he might need it today.

His aim was perfect. It landed in Sir Barnett's shoulder, forcing him to drop the pistol, but not before he fired. Sir Barnett fell, the knife deep in his shoulder.

Richard quickly regained his feet, but it was too late. It was done.

They didn't touch him. A red stain crept over the pristine grass. Like a felled oak, Giles lay still on the ground, his face torn away by the impact of the bullet fired at such close quarters. Gervase ripped off his coat and tossed it over Giles's upper body.

There was an agonised cry, "Barnett!" and his wife moved to kneel by her husband, but I was nearer so I got there first. The first thing I did was pick up the pistol and throw it away from me. I turned to see to the wound of the man I could help. Giles was beyond it now.

The knife prevented us removing Sir Barnett's loose frock coat, so I undid his neckcloth and withdrew the knife, holding my breath, wishing Carier was here to help me.

The resulting spurt of blood was alarming, but not life threatening. The artery had not been hit, there was no fountaining of bright red blood such as I had seen elsewhere.

Above my head, where there had been quiet, now there was shouting and seeming chaos, but I did my best to block this out as I attended to my patient.

Sir Barnett was conscious and groaning. I tried to assure

him. "It's all right, you'll live. Lie still and I'll do what I can before they take you back to the house." He stared at me, confusion in his face, but he was sentient, for he nodded and did as he was told.

I slipped the pad I had made from his neckcloth under his coat and pressed down hard, moving to put my weight behind it. I glanced up to see Lady Kerre dry eyed, blessedly free of panic, so I took her hand and drew her down, put it on the pad. "Press hard and I'll try to get his coat off." Silently, she obeyed.

It wasn't too hard to get his coat off, and I saw Richard's handiwork more closely. He was by me now, and as I eased the sleeve down the injured arm, he slipped the other one off for me. I left the ruined garment to lie under him and took over from Lady Kerre, now kneeling at her husband's head.

I looked up at Richard. "It's not too bad," I told him.

He smiled wryly. "It was all I could do. It was either that or stand by and watch."

"I wish I'd done it years ago," Sir Barnett said, just as quietly as Richard. His wife cried out, and the tears came now, trickling unheeded down her carefully powdered cheeks, leaving tracks behind them. "There's no way out."

"This was an accident," Richard said firmly. "Remember that. A light-hearted family contest that ended in tragedy."

Sir Barnett gazed at Richard as though my husband was his saviour. "An accident?"

"Why not? I have no wish to see my family dragged through the mire. If you hadn't done it, I feel sure someone else would have. He wouldn't have come to trial, he would have been dead long before that."

Sir Barnett sighed and nodded, tears misting his eyes but sense still paramount. "It seems the only option. But what if someone talks?"

"They won't," Richard assured him. All the servants with us today were from Thompson's.

Because they had spoken so quietly, none of their

conversation had penetrated the cacophony going on above our heads. Even the heretofore quiet Amery was shouting.

I ignored them and got on with my task. The wound was deep, but small. It wouldn't need stitching. The main problem would be infection. I looked up at Gervase who knew what I wanted and silently handed me his small brandy flask.

I unscrewed the top and glanced at Richard who moved to hold Sir Barnett's shoulder down for me, and then I splashed the fiery spirit onto the wound.

Sir Barnett's cry of pain lacerated the other shouts and stopped everybody as they looked down at us. The man's shoulder jerked up in an instinctive reaction, but Richard's restraint helped, and I was ready for it, moving out of the way.

I gave what brandy was left to Richard to let Sir Barnett take some in the usual way, and set to binding the wound tightly. I sat back on my heels when I had done, and Richard, flask in hand, studied the result. "A beautiful job, my love."

"It should heal well. You didn't hit anything important."

"I'm relieved to hear it." He got to his feet and held his hand out to help me up. "Perhaps you should join the army, as a surgeon."

"A female surgeon? Do you think they would accept me? And would you let me go?"

"I'd follow you." He kissed my hand before he let it go and looked down at where Sir Barnett lay. "Fetch something from the house to carry him indoors, please."

One of the servants ran off.

I had no doubt the sharks would continue to dun the Kerres, but they would find no satisfaction. Their principal was dead, and his debts with him. If they had any trouble, Richard could contain it through Thompson's.

The remaining servants collected the pistols and put them away in the cases. Gervase picked up Richard's weapon and proceeded to empty the loaded ones before he handed them to someone to take away. The other guests were still confused by what had just happened. Richard and his father looked at each other. "We have to tell Smith."

"Smith," his father agreed. Richard turned to me and offered the support of his arm.

We left the Kerres to discuss the fate of the heir, the two burly footmen still standing by him, in case he should try anything foolish.

We walked towards the house to face the Bow Street man.

Chapter Seventeen

We told Lady Southwood. She listened to us as if sitting in the audience of a play, as detached as a critic. She gave Richard and me a brief nod before picking up her handbell and ringing for tea. A small matter satisfactorily resolved. She was satisfied. Richard had contained the scandal.

She received Amery's news with complete indifference. "I'm sure I wish them happy, but it is fortunate we no longer have to rely on the Kerres for an heir to the title."

Smith arrived hotfoot from the village inn. His spies were almost as good as ours. Sir Barnett, considerably shaken by events, had been put to bed, and Giles had been taken to the chapel. Amery and Gervase went to the library, no doubt to tell Ian what he had missed and discuss events in a rational way.

We saw Mr. Smith in one of the smaller drawing rooms. I was armed with the teapot, and while I served Richard, my father-in-law, Mr. Smith and myself, they discussed trivialities like the weather and the approaching hunting season. The twelfth of August had passed, and Lord Southwood had planned a new house party, this time at his lodge in Leicestershire. And it would be exclusively male.

"Are you coming, Strang?" He addressed Richard as if we were still *en famille,* his arrogance strong enough to disregard the Bow Street man as if he were a servant. But the conversation had an ulterior motive.

Richard smiled at me. "I think not, thank you, sir. I'd like to take Rose and Helen to Oxfordshire. I want her to rest."

"An excellent notion." Was it my imagination or was his lordship's voice warmer when he spoke to me? I couldn't be sure. "Make sure you don't do anything too strenuous, my dear. I'm glad you like the house."

"She disliked the Hampstead house," Richard told him. "I've sold that. And the Paris house. I may just hire something when we go there."

"Are you planning to go to Paris?"

"Rose should be presented at Versailles," Richard replied. I frowned. I had found my London presentation an ordeal, and Versailles might be worse. I still hated being stared at.

"Take good care of her," Lord Southwood warned his son. "There's a great many men in Versailles with little to do but dance, fornicate and play cards."

The tea served, I nodded to the footman and he left. We could speak more freely now. "Has Giles been to Versailles?"

"No," Richard told me. "Thank God. His debts would've been tripled if he ever set foot there."

Mr. Smith looked interested, as he was meant to. Richard addressed him now. "The unfortunate accident aside, we have things to discuss before I can take my wife away. Now, shall we discuss the murders of the servants?"

The sudden transition made Mr. Smith blink. Richard had not raised his voice or changed his tone, but he had effectively linked Giles with the murders, and they both knew it. "It's what I'm here for, my lord. Was the sad death of your cousin an accident?" Mr. Smith's thin mouth turned down. His great hand, clutching the base of his tea dish, was out of place, swamping the poor little piece of china. He took a draught of tea as though it were beer, finishing it in one gulp.

"You'll hear no different from anyone in this household," Richard said gently.

Mr. Smith frowned and nodded. "I know it." But he also knew what had really happened, even though he would find no witnesses to swear to it. "I hope, my lord, that you don't forget what happened to these men, what was done to them."

Lord Southwood had been silent up to this point, but now he spoke. "We can hardly forget that. We were all deeply affected by it. I hope the reparation we can give to their families will help them in some way."

Mr. Smith looked at him sharply. Payment meant bribes in his world.

In fact Lord Southwood didn't mean payment alone. He would give the families some compensation for the loss of their wage-earning sons, but at Richard's prompting in a swift conversation on our walk to the house, he intended to tell the mothers of the unfortunate victims the identity of the murderer. The argument had been short, but to the point. Richard made it clear that he'd tell them, come what may, that in his opinion they had the right. Lord Southwood had reluctantly agreed to it. Either he saw the justice of it, or he realised his son would do it anyway, with or without his agreement.

Mr. Smith gave Richard a cynical glare. He must know Richard was outmanoeuvring him. As one of the elite, one of Mr. Fielding's precious runners, he wouldn't be used to this, although he might be used to people closing ranks before him. "Would you let the murderer go unpunished if he wasn't a member of your—society?" John Smith made it clear the word he would have preferred to use would have been "family".

Richard looked at him steadily. "I think justice was done."

The two men stared at each other for a full minute. Smith was the first to look away and continued staring into space. When Lord Southwood cleared his throat, he came to with a start that made me smile, so reminiscent was it of my attitude in the past. I served more tea to fill some time.

"I'll never find out who did this thing, will I?" He smiled his thanks as I poured some tea into his dish, now resting lopsidedly in the saucer on the table at his side.

"No," I told him. "There's no proof one way or the other."

Having filled the other dishes, I sat down again.

"I want a promise before I go away," Smith said. He had forgotten the courtesies entirely. I liked him for it. "I want your assurance that justice has truly been served."

Richard caught his gaze once more. "You have it. I don't want to make an enemy of you, Mr. Smith. In return, I would like us to work together in the future. If there's anything I can do for you, please come to me and let me know."

Lord Southwood grunted, looking doubtful, a frown furrowing his brow. Richard took no notice.

Mr. Smith remembered the proprieties at last. "My lord, I would like to think I could do so."

Richard was offering him help from Thompson's, in return for his silence in this matter. Mr. Smith must know enough about our organisation to know it would be useful to him if he could ask for its help. Our information must rival the files held at Bow Street.

He left shortly after that and said he'd travel back to London the next day. His colleagues there would probably not get to hear about his agreement with Richard. He had his career to think of, and any advantage he had would not be shared with others, even if it led to a better service.

I rested my hand on Richard's arm when we had seen Smith leave the premises, and he turned a grave face to me. "I'm glad that's over," I said.

"It won't be over," he replied. "It will never be over. Giles's mother loved him. Did you see her face when he confessed?"

"No, I was looking at his father."

"She looked at him as though she was looking for the first time and she didn't like what she saw," he answered. "She always preferred Giles, was always ready to excuse him."

"What of his father?"

"It would have broken him, I'm sure." Richard sighed. "Only the strongest and the weakest can take a life and live with it."

"Which are you?"

He looked at me and smiled, recognising what I was saying. "I don't know, my sweet, and I don't pretend to. But you're right, this part is over. The only good thing to come of it is Amery's news. They will have to accept his bride now my father and I have made clear we will accept her."

"And me."

He covered my hand with his own. "And you. Shall we go home, my love? Soon?"

It was a proposition to which I readily agreed.

About the Author

Lynne Connolly has been in love with the Georgian age since the age of nine, when she did a project about coffee and tea at school. One look at the engraving of the Georgian coffeehouse, and she was a goner. It's the longest love affair of her life.

She stopped looking around old houses and visiting museums long enough to go to work, fall in love for a second time, marry and have a family, but they have to share her with her obsession, which they do with good grace and much humor.

To learn more about Lynne Connolly, please visit www.lynneconnolly.com. Send an email to lynneconnollyuk@yahoo.co.uk or join her Yahoo! group to join in the fun with other readers!

http://groups.yahoo.com/group/lynneconnolly. She can also be found at MySpace, Facebook and the Samhain Café.

GREAT cheap fun

Discover eBooks!
THE FASTEST WAY TO GET THE HOTTEST NAMES

Get your favorite authors on your favorite reader, long before they're
out in print! Ebooks from Samhain go wherever you go, and work with
whatever you carry—Palm, PDF, Mobi, and more.

LaVergne, TN USA
31 October 2010
202926LV00003B/1/P